GRAY GENESIS

by

ALAN MCDERMOTT

Books by Alan McDermott

Gray Justice

Gray Resurrection

Gray Redemption

Gray Retribution

Gray Vengeance

Gray Salvation

Gray Genesis

Trojan

Run and Hide

Seek and Destroy

Fight to Survive

Motive

Dedicated to our essential workers

AUTHOR'S NOTE

This is a work of fiction. Some of the locations you might recognise (Afghanistan, for one) but the people mentioned are all figments of my imagination (a few well-known heads of state excluded). As far as I have been able to determine, there is no 2nd Battalion, 187th Airborne Infantry Regiment, 101st Airborne Division. I also fabricated the 654th, 667th and the 698th infantry regiments.

I'd like to thank Liam Saville, Bram Connolly and Alex Shaw, three fantastic authors who helped sculpt the outline. This book was supposed to be a collaboration between the four of us, but as other commitments got in the way, it was agreed that I would take it on and turn it into a Tom Gray story. If it hadn't been for my wonderful friends, this tale would never have been written.

Prologue

Miriam Dagher had never had a fear of flying. But as she stood at the gates waiting to board the British Airways flight to Kabul, she felt ready to throw up. Her hands trembled as she gripped her boarding pass, and the sweat accumulating in her armpits was growing increasingly uncomfortable.

Am I doing the right thing?

She'd asked herself the question a hundred times that day, and she still didn't have the answer. Only time would tell. It was too late to back out now, anyway. The decision had been made, plans put in place, promises made and bridges burnt.

Her old life was over.

A cheerful steward motioned her forward and held out her hand. Miriam gave her the sweat-stained card.

"Are you okay? You don't look so good."

"I'm a nervous flyer," Miriam lied with an apologetic smile. "I've done it hundreds of times, but it never gets any easier."

"Well, don't you worry. You're in good hands. This is one of the safest planes in the sky."

Miriam tried to smile graciously but it came out as a grimace. She hurried through the gate and down the tunnel that led to the door of the Boeing 777, where a stewardess checked her seat number and pointed Miriam towards the first class section. As this was going to be her last flight for some time—perhaps forever—she'd splashed out on an expensive upgrade.

She took her seat by the window, buckled herself in and clasped her hands together, her eyes closed tight.

Why am I doing this?

She wanted nothing more than to leap from her seat and run from the plane, go back to her home and undo everything she'd done. But that was impossible. She'd made a deal to protect her country, to take lives in order to save lives.

That was the hardest part; knowing she'd be responsible for countless deaths. It flew in the face of the Hippocratic oath she'd taken as a medical student, as well as the years spent looking for ways to improve healthcare outcomes.

A stewardess cleared her throat to get Miriam's attention, and when she opened her eyes she was offered a hot towel. She took it and wiped her hands and face, knowing that little luxuries like this would soon be a thing of the past. Where she was going, all she had to look forward to was baking heat and basic sanitation at best.

The itch under her breast was annoying in the extreme, exacerbated by the sweat accumulating under her ample bosom. She turned to face the small window and massaged the area gently, the sensation clawing at her like the never-ending doubts that flitted around inside her head.

She declined the offer of a pre-flight drink, preferring instead to try to sleep. But her vision was immediately filled with images of the dead, men young and old torn from families, their agonising death throes ringing loud in her ears.

And it was all her fault.

Chapter 1

'Contact, south wall.'

The moment the call came over the radio, Master Sergeant John Balmer jumped up from his bunk and picked up his Heckler & Koch HK416 rifle and ANVIS-9 night vision glasses. He pulled the NVGs on as he ran out into the courtyard. Behind him was the accommodation block and armoury, and the other three walls separated the old fort from the vast void of the desert beyond. Only now, it wasn't empty.

He sprinted up the stairs on his left, to the parapet where the huge bulk of sergeant Hank Lomax stood alongside one of the troopers.

'What have we got?'

'Two o'clock, six hundred yards,' Lomax said, looking out into the darkness. Like the team leader, he too was wearing the vision enhancement gear.

Balmer checked the area and saw what Lomax had spotted. It was a man wearing the traditional Afghan *perahan tunban*—a form of shalwar kameez. He was hard to spot against the desert floor, but when he moved he gave himself away. His actions were clumsy, almost inviting attention. Balmer watched him inch closer to the fort, and in his peripheral vision he saw a second figure off to the first one's right.

3

'They're early.'

'At least they showed,' Lomax shrugged.

'We've got two visitors on the south wall,' Balmer said over comms. 'Check your zones.'

'Clear east.'

'Nothing to the west.'

'I've got movement to the north. Two... wait, three contacts.'

Lieutenant Joel Harding trotted up the stairs and stood looking out over the parapet. 'What have we got, sergeant?'

Harding was the leader of 2nd Platoon, Company B, 2nd Battalion, 187th Airborne Infantry Regiment, the current occupants of forward operating base Tork. Balmer and his team had been sent to reinforce the camp following intel that the fort was due to be attacked, much to Harding's annoyance. He'd told Balmer that his men could handle any assault, and clearly didn't like Delta Force stepping on his toes.

'Contacts to the north and south, sir.'

Balmer tried to hide his contempt, but calling a product of OCS 'sir' just stuck in his throat. Balmer had been in more firefights than this puke could ever imagine. Harding looked like he was just weeks out of officer candidate school, or perhaps he'd been one of the fortunate ones whose daddy got him a place at West Point. He was five ten—an inch shorter than Balmer, and not as heavily built.

'How many?' Harding's voice was steady, but Balmer could sense his trepidation.

'Five so far.'

The size of the opposing force seemed to settle the lieutenant. 'Okay sergeant, stand your men down. We'll take it from here.'

Balmer wasn't about to take a back seat if there was action to be had. He was sure the thirty men under Harding's command could handle five insurgents, but there was no way he was going to stand back while the bullets flew. Besides, he knew the Taliban wouldn't send just five men to attack a heavily-defended fort. This had to be either a scouting party, or a distraction.

'Maybe I should deploy my men to the east and west walls,' Balmer suggested. 'We'll be out of your way there.'

'You do that, sergeant.'

Harding began issuing orders, positioning his men to cover the north and south.

Balmer gripped Lomax's elbow and led him around to the west wall, scanning the open desert. He got on closed comms so that he was only communicating with his own team.

'I want Rees, Hubble and Johnson on the east wall, now. Jacobs, with me on the west.'

The fort was relatively small. The north and south aspects were just a hundred feet long, while the other walls were close to a hundred and fifty. Below them in the courtyard sat Balmer's vehicles; two GMVs with turret-mounted Browning M2 .50 calibre machine guns, as well as two Cougar H 4x4s that the infantry used to scout the local area. There was also a fuel dump. The consumables, such as food and ammunition, were stored inside the buildings built into the east wall. The DFAC, known as the mess hall, was on the ground floor with an office and stores, while the upper floor was the accommodation block. In all, there wasn't a lot to be gained from attacking it, especially with such a small force that wouldn't be able to hold on to it.

Jacobs ran up the stone stairs just as Balmer reached the middle of the west wall.

'Something's going down,' Balmer told them, 'and the LT is underplaying it. Not even the Taliban are stupid enough to try and take the fort with five men. There are more out there. Find them.'

Balmer relayed similar orders to the team on the opposite side of the base, then looked out over the wall. He didn't detect any movement, but his pulse had quickened, just as it did before every skirmish.

'Anything?' he asked over the comms.

'Nada,' Hubble replied.

Perhaps the Taliban *were* that desperate, though it seemed a waste of men. They had to have some idea of how many men were manning the base.

His thoughts were interrupted as a bright flash stung his eyes. Balmer whipped off his NVGs and saw a flare descending over the desert to his left and right.

'What the fuck is the LT playing at?'

'They haven't got night vision,' Lomax pointed out.

The night erupted as dozens of rifles opened up on the handful of targets. Balmer snapped his glasses back on and checked his zone, just as several figures rose from the ground a couple of hundred yards away.

'Contact west!'

He sent three-round bursts at the targets, dropping the first and quickly seeking the next. Rounds pinged off the concrete all around him as Hubble reported ten more Taliban at the other side of the camp.

'That's more like it!' Balmer felled another, and two more went down under the onslaught from Lomax and Jacobs.

'RPG!'

Balmer saw it just as Lomax shouted the warning. They both targeted the man as he raised it to his shoulder before he collapsed backwards, blood spurting from half a dozen wounds. Another figure appeared as if from nowhere, rising out of the sandy floor and running to his fallen comrade's side. Any thoughts of picking up the grenade launcher and finishing the job were quickly dispelled thanks to a barrage from the fort.

'Alpha Three, how you doing?' Balmer asked Hubble.

'One to go.'

It was the same for Balmer. The last of his targets had crawled behind a rock, shielded from fire.

'Alpha Two, finish it.'

Jacobs sent a round from his underslung M203 hurtling towards the boulder. It exploded just behind and to the side of the stone, and shrapnel tore the last of the aggressors apart.

The shooting had also stopped on the far side of the camp.

'Alpha Three, anyone hurt?'

'Negative,' Hubble replied.

It was unsurprising. The fire directed at the base had been erratic, undisciplined—as if the dead Taliban had never held a rifle before.

Balmer and Lomax walked over to Harding who looked pumped. Balmer knew it was the adrenaline from the fight.

'You need to requisition some night gear, sir. You could have lost men if they'd made it in closer.'

'Already tried, Sergeant,' Harding said. 'Billions of dollars spent on this campaign so far, and they can't throw a few thousand bucks our way. I'll add it to my report, though. In the meantime, I need to get the area cleared.' He turned to one of his men. 'Send a squad out to collect their weapons and call in transport to pick up the bodies.'

The corpses would be transferred to a mortuary next to Kandahar airfield, where they would be printed, photographed and checked for unexploded ordnance. The Red Cross would then take the dead insurgents to Mirwais Hospital in Kandahar city, where family members would collect the dead so they could be granted a martyr's funeral.

'Remind them to check for booby traps,' Balmer said. 'I've seen these guys go into battle wired up. When they get killed, there's someone nearby ready to detonate their bomb vests remotely.'

Balmer hadn't actually witnessed it, but the lieutenant's action this evening seemed a little gung-ho, and he needed to exercise caution if he and his men were going to survive their time in Afghanistan.

His words didn't seem to hit home, though.

'Thank you, Sergeant, but my men know what to do.'

That's master *sergeant, you dumb sonofabitch!*

'Yes, sir.' Balmer whipped off a salute and walked away, with Lomax in close attendance. 'Tell the men to get their heads down, we're moving out early.'

'Will do,' Lomax said as he swapped out his magazine for a fresh one. 'What did you make of that?'

'The LT or the attack?'

Lomax laughed. 'Both.'

'People that poorly trained and ill-disciplined have no right picking up a rifle,' Balmer said.

Lomax nodded sagely. 'And the Taliban?'

Balmer chuckled and slapped Lomax on the back. In truth, they had little time for the common foot soldier. Balmer and Lomax were Delta Force—the best of the best.

They had few rivals in the game of warfare, and the only fighting unit they had any grudging respect for was the British SAS—and that was only because Delta Force had been built on the Special Air Service model. Twenty-five years earlier, Colonel Charles Beckwith had spent a year with the boys from Hereford with the aim of creating a tactical team to respond quickly to international terrorist threats. Delta Force and the SAS still operated side-by-side and often exchanged members in their cross-training program. In fact, Balmer's first mission was a joint effort alongside the SAS to rescue a Japanese ambassador held hostage in Peru. His British counterparts had performed well, executing the job with consummate professionalism, but that didn't mean Balmer had to like them. Respect, perhaps, but they'd never be friends. There was an SAS contingent at Kandahar, but he'd never been able to get on with them.

The British might have the history, but Delta Force was the future.

'Seriously, John, what were they thinking? One RPG and a few rifles?'

'I reckon it was a test of the defences,' Balmer said. 'They should have seen enough to convince them to find another target.'

'Maybe… unless they're willing to throw hundreds of men at it. Can't see the point, though. This place has no strategic value, and there's not much worth taking.'

'Who knows what they're thinking,' Balmer said. 'I'll write it up and let the Captain deal with it. In the meantime, if you're still having trouble sleeping, get the vehicles loaded up. I want to be out of here at first light.'

Chapter 2

When the crew chief signalled five minutes to the drop point, sergeant Tom Gray nodded his acknowledgement and checked his gear one more time. The other three men in the back of the Boeing CH-47 Chinook mirrored him, ensuring magazines were locked and loaded.

'Game time, big man,' Corporal Simon 'Sonny' Baines grinned at Len Smart, the other sergeant in the four-man patrol. 'Cast aside all thoughts of Melanie from the DFAC and get your killing head on.'

Smart glared at him. 'She's more your type. Loose morals and low IQ.'

'Wouldn't have them any other way.'

'Stop it!' Carl Levine shouted. 'I can't get that image out of my head. It's like an ant riding a hippo.'

'She's not that big,' Sonny laughed.

'Not that big? I dreamt about her last night and woke up with a lard on!'

Gray wasn't one for banter just before a mission, but he couldn't help but chuckle. Some men, like Gray and Smart, blotted out everything to ensure they were focused on the job ahead of them. With Sonny and Carl, it was humour. It was an odd mix, but had seen the eclectic team bond so well over the last two years.

Gray considered them the family he'd never had. He'd been placed in foster care at an early age, moving from home to home, school to school. He hadn't really had much of an opportunity to form ties with anyone during his youth, but he more than made up for it when he joined the junior leaders at sixteen. It had been his careers officer at high school who had suggested the army. On reflection, Gray assumed it was because he didn't tend to take crap from anyone—especially fellow students—and he'd been up before the headmaster on many an occasion for looking after himself. If they'd hoped a stint in green would help him channel his aggression, they'd been proven right years ago. Gray had dovetailed with army life from the very start. He loved the discipline and the physical activities, but most of all the camaraderie.

Sonny was the youngest of the quartet at twenty-four, though he looked like he'd just left school, hence the nickname he'd been given after passing SAS selection. He was also the smallest at five-nine, with blond hair and boyish good looks. Levine had a couple of years—and inches—on him. Next in the height charts was Gray, while Smart was the tallest of the group at six-three. His hair was already receding even though he was only twenty-six, and the bushy black moustache made him look more like a company executive rather than a man of action.

'Okay, knock it off guys.'

When Gray got the two-minute warning, he ordered his team onto their motorcycles and the crew chief removed the fastenings. With fifteen seconds to go, the rear door of the chopper slowly descended, revealing darkness. Gray started his engine, and the moment the ramp hit the desert floor, he popped the clutch and rode out, stopping thirty yards from the bird. As soon as the last rider was on the ground, the Chinook took off, heading back to base.

Gray led the way, keeping his lights off and using the passive NVGs to illuminate the landscape. The four men rode in single file, with Smart behind Gray and Levine next. Sonny brought up the rear. Their target was ten kilometres from the drop zone, a small village near the border with Pakistan, a hundred and eighty kilometres—or klicks as they called them—south of Kandahar airfield.

It was two in the morning by the time they reached the first marker point. They hid the bikes at the base of a mountain, pushing them between huge rocks and covering them with grey tarpaulin, then set off on foot to cover the last two klicks.

It was uphill all the way. Their proximity to the target meant they had to be as quiet as possible, making progress painfully slow.

It was almost four by the time they reached the outskirts of the village. It sat on a plateau, with the north side overlooked by a towering mountain. The satellite images they'd studied before leaving the base showed a cluster of twenty-three dwellings, and the one they wanted was right in the middle.

'Sonny, check it out from the east,' Gray said. 'Carl, you take the west.'

The two men split off to recce the target, while Gray and Smart observed the south aspect.

'A tenner says he's not here,' Smart whispered.

It wasn't a bet Gray was willing to take. This was their third attempt to capture Taliban commander Abdul al-Hussain, and the other two had been busts. It was all down to poor intelligence, or rather, the way it was gathered. The locals were promised more money than they could ever dream of in return for information on Taliban leaders, but most of the time the details they gave were either highly inaccurate or deliberately misleading. With seemingly infinite funds, the green slime—a derogatory name for the army intelligence corps—persisted with the exercise safe in their comfy barracks, while Gray and his men battled it out at the sharp end.

'Whether he's here or not, I'm more concerned about walking into a trap.'

From what he could see, the village was occupied; a couple of goats were tethered to the nearest house which, like the rest, was a one-storey building.

Gray asked the other two if they'd spotted anything.

'Clear,' Levine replied.

'All quiet here,' Sonny said.

'Roger that, we're moving up.'

Gray instructed Smart to join up with Sonny, then ran in a crouch to Levine's position.

'We've got half an hour until sunrise,' Gray said over comms. 'I want to be out of here by then.'

He got three clicks in his ear as acknowledgement.

'Okay... time to dance, gentlemen.'

There was no need for any other orders. They'd been over the entire plan many times, and everyone knew their role, the rules of engagement, and what to do if everything went to shit.

Gray and Levine closed in on the village, aware Sonny and Smart would be doing the same from the other direction.

Cover ran out thirty yards from the nearest building, and if this was an ambush, the bullets would start flying the moment they were exposed. Gray took a deep breath, then raced towards the house while Levine covered him.

It seemed the longest sprint of his life, but seconds later Gray was pressed up against the side of the house. He stuck his head around the wall and signalled for Levine to move up, all the while training his rifle down the alleyway. When he felt his mate hit the wall next to him, Gray pushed on, sticking close to the building as he made for the next corner. After checking his angles, he moved forward once more, until he could see the target house. It was the largest of them all, a fitting place for someone like Abdul al-Hussain to reside in.

Gray waited until Smart and Sonny came into view twenty yards away. As planned, Sonny broke off and ran to the house at the same time as Gray, with the other two ready to offer covering fire if needed.

Gray had chosen to storm the house with Sonny because he was one of the best in the regiment at close quarter battle. He had few equals in the killing house, the building in Stirling Lines near Hereford where CQB training took place. In fact, though short on years, he was already tipped to be a future instructor.

Gray readied an M84 stun grenade and nodded to Sonny. They'd discussed what to do if they got this far without incident, and it had been a toss-up between a quiet entry to avoid waking the entire hamlet and full-on assault. The latter had been agreed upon, in case the ambush had been restricted to al-Hussain's residence.

Sonny kicked in the front door and Gray tossed the grenade inside. The moment it exploded, they piled in, weapons raised. The living room was empty, so Sonny peeled off to the left while Gray checked the room to the right.

Gray kicked the door open to see a man in his twenties scrambling out of his bed. Gray's instinct was to put a couple of rounds in his head, but he could see that the young man had lost his left leg below the knee, and there were no weapons in sight.

'Down!' Gray shouted. 'Down on the floor!' He motioned with his rifle to emphasise his order, and the man fell forward onto his stomach, his arms out by his side. After swivelling his head to check there was no-one else in the room, Gray produced a set of plasticuffs and secured the man's hands behind his back, then ran out to help Sonny find the man they'd come for.

Sonny was already in the living room. 'Clear. There's no sign of him. A woman and two kids in the back bedroom, that's it.'

'We've got movement out here,' Smart said over the comms. 'No sign of any hostiles, but you woke the whole fucking village.'

'We're coming out,' Gray said, and gestured for Sonny to follow him.

A dozen people were now forming in the streets, and though none were armed, the ambience was tense—and growing.

'Let's get out of here,' Gray said.

'You don't want to ask these people if al-Hussain was here?' Levine asked.

'If he was, it's too late, and there's no way they'd tell us. We haven't got time to force it out of them.'

Gray set off at a jog, signalling an end to the discussion. Smart and Levine followed, while Sonny watched the rear. Once the other three were back in cover, Sonny turned and sprinted towards their position. When he reached them, they set off as fast as they could towards the bikes. It was all downhill and there was no need for stealth, so they made good time.

When they reached the machines, Gray called in the support helicopter to pick them up at the pre-arranged point. It was ten klicks west of the original drop-off point, just in case that location was now compromised.

'Do you have the package?'

'Negative,' Gray replied.

'Roger that. Yankee five-two will be at the RV in four-zero.'

Gray acknowledged the transmission and let the team know they had forty minutes to meet the chopper, otherwise it would be a long ride home.

'One day this dodgy intel is going to get us killed,' Levine said as he folded up his tarpaulin.

'I'm with him there,' Sonny said. 'If we keep checking out every sighting, how long before they have a brigade waiting for us? I'm just surprised we haven't come a cropper already.'

'Agreed,' Smart added. 'The head shed needs to get its arse in gear and find us some real targets.'

'Careful what you wish for,' Gray warned him. While he, too, was frustrated at the lack of action, returning to base unscathed was far better than being vulture food. The SAS were trained to fight, to kill, but had no problem walking away from a mission rather than push a bad position. If that meant chasing shadows and getting back to camp in time for breakfast, Gray wasn't going to complain. Better to live to fight another day.

With their camouflage stowed, Gray checked his handheld GPS device, got a bearing, and told Sonny to take point.

Chapter 3

It was the dust. That was what Ben Cooper hated most about Afghanistan. It got everywhere; his eyes, his hair, his throat. Riding through the desert in convoy was the worst part, breathing in the cloud kicked up by the vehicle in front. Even now, in the confines of the air-conditioned Nissan SUV driving through the centre of Kabul, it somehow seemed to find him.

Just four more weeks.

The money he made as a private contractor was good—seven hundred bucks a day—and in his three tours he hadn't had to discharge his weapon once. That still wasn't enough to make up for having to live in such a god-forsaken shithole.

The funny thing was, when he was here as an enlisted soldier it hadn't seemed so bad. He'd done his tour, rotated back to the world, finished up his seven years and got his DD214. He'd followed his dream of starting his own business, pumping his fifteen grand of savings and forty thousand borrowed from the bank into a coffee shop in the heart of his hometown of Tuscaloosa, Alabama.

It fell into trouble almost immediately. His sales projections were way off, and his income never exceeded his outgoings. The house he'd put up as collateral was soon in danger of being seized by the bank and so he felt obliged to return to the dustbowl to pay off the lender. His biggest mistake had been to leave the shop open. His sister now ran it, but every day it accumulated more debt, and finding a buyer had been impossible. His only option was to pay off the lease and walk away—and in four weeks he would have enough to do just that.

He had no firm plans for when he got stateside, but he'd never look at a cup of Joe the same way.

Cooper glanced over at his principal. Usually he acted as bodyguard for company executives and the like, but this one was different. Miriam Dagher was some kind of scientist from what he could gather. She was a heavy-set woman who appeared to be in her mid-to-late fifties. She had an American accent, but she'd told him she'd spent the last two years in London. Their destination was the Kabul Medical Institute where she would give a series of lectures on something or other to do with childbirth. As usual, Cooper had paid little attention. His job was to deliver them from point A to point B, period. If he got involved in a conversation he couldn't do his job properly—which was to scan for threats along the route.

'Traffic's stopped up ahead,' Joel Johnson said from behind the wheel. He, along with Sam Parker, made up the rest of the close protection team hired by the American pharmaceutical company.

'Okay, guys, stay frosty,' Parker said, checking his mirrors and looking for threats in the passing crowd.

Cooper unholstered his Glock 17 and checked their six while a knot developed in his stomach. It was unusual to be attacked in the middle of the city, but there was a first time for everything. 'What's going on up there?'

'Looks like a police checkpoint,' Johnson said.

'Is there a problem?' Dagher asked Cooper.

'Nah,' he said, holding the pistol by the side of his leg, out of sight. 'Checkpoints are thrown up all the time. We should be through it in a few minutes.'

The vehicle edged forward, and Cooper relaxed a little. No-one was paying them any particular attention, and there were just three cars ahead of them now. They'd be through and be at the institute in about ten minutes. He could then clock off and tick another day off the calendar.

Through the front windscreen, Cooper could see that the local Afghan police were giving each car a cursory inspection—as if they were looking for somebody specific.

When the SUV reached the front of the line, Johnson wound his window down as directed. He spoke Pashto fluently and asked the nearest policeman what they were looking for.

The officer glanced into the back of the SUV. 'Step out.'

Johnson turned his head slightly towards Parker in the front passenger seat. 'Heads up.'

Cooper heard him too, and immediately tensed. From the corner of his eye, he saw one of the police officers to his right remove a pistol from his belt, while another had brought his AK-47 up to a firing position.

'Out!' The policeman shouted this time.

'We've got papers,' Johnson said, removing their travel documents from inside his jacket. He held them out the window, but the Afghan officer slapped them out of his hands.

Ben Cooper had trained hard for moments like this, and when the first round flew through the open side window and punched a hole in Sam Parker's head, he pushed his client into the footwell and fired back, hitting one of the attackers in the chest with two rounds. A bullet flew past his head, missing by millimetres and embedding itself in the coachwork. The attackers opened up with their automatic weapons, but the bullets bounced harmlessly off the SUVs armour-plated bodywork.

Johnson had fired in reply and was now stamping on the gas, trying to reverse out of the trap. But the line of vehicles behind him made it impossible. He spun the wheel and selected first, hitting the accelerator as he tried to duck down an alleyway to the right.

For a moment, Cooper thought they would make it, until a puff of blood erupted from Johnson's head and he fell forward, his foot still flat to the floor. The vehicle shot forward for a few yards, then smashed into the corner of a building. Cooper saw it coming but couldn't prevent himself being thrown into the back of the front passenger seat. His head hit hard, and blood immediately began pouring from a deep gash in his temple.

Time seemed to slow down. He could see Dagher was screaming, and that a police officer was shouting, but no sounds reached his ears. There was a blast of heat as the door was pulled open and Cooper was dragged from the car, landing heavily on the ground. Two of the Afghans stood over him, the muzzles of their rifles inches from his face.

This was it. He was going to die, helpless on his back, in a country he hated. All he could hope for was a quick death, a bullet in the head that he wouldn't see or feel. The strange thing was, he didn't fear it. If somehow he managed to get out of this, what then? Another month in Afghanistan to pay off his debts followed by a lifetime working for minimum wage to make someone else rich? His poor business skills meant he would never make a success of running his own company, so his future looked bleak. He would spend the next fifty years existing, not living. Imminent death suddenly didn't seem that bad.

'Do it,' he heard himself say.

The end didn't come. Instead, he watched as Dagher stepped out of the vehicle and walked away, flanked by two of the Afghan police officers. They weren't holding her or forcing her towards their vehicle. She seemed to be going willingly.

One of the attackers opened the rear door of a Toyota Hilux and Dagher climbed in. Cooper watched as she pulled at her seat belt without a glance back in his direction, then pushed a niqab forward over her face. Her bags were taken from the Nissan and carried over to the Toyota.

One of the Afghans shouted something before getting in beside Dagher. Ben Cooper understood maybe a couple of dozen words of Pashto—and this was one of them.

Before his brain had a chance to process the barked order, everything went black.

Chapter 4

Tom Gray and his team rode their bikes down the ramp that led towards the motor pool used by the British forces. They signed the Hondas back in and carried their equipment back to the barracks in anticipation of a shower, food and sleep. Gray, though, had other matters to attend to. After dropping his gear next to his bunk, he walked to the CO's office.

It was one of few permanent structures on the base, though more were springing up all the time. The airport had been captured and secured just six months earlier, and the coalition forces were obviously keen to show they were there for the long haul. Engineers from several countries were engaged in the building process, and Gray often dreamed of the day he could swap his tent for an air-conditioned hut. He knew it would never happen; such luxuries were not afforded the front line men.

Captain Paul Russell's adjutant told Gray to knock and go in. The CO looked up from his paperwork when he entered.

'Before you say anything, I'm as frustrated as you are, Tom.'

Gray had served under a few senior officers, most of whom had seen the SAS as a career step; doing their couple of years before moving on to greater things. Those were the people who would accept the impossible missions and expect them to be carried out so that they could sit back and claim the glory. Russell wasn't like that. He would discuss the mission with the boys, and if it seemed too risky he would kick it back upstairs with his recommendations. His approach had earned him the respect of his subordinates, if not his superiors.

Russell was thirty-three, former 2 Para, and a couple of inches shorter than Gray. His black hair and black moustache reminded Gray of eighties TV shows. He'd been in charge of B Squadron's 8—Mobility—troop for just over a year.

'It's not frustration, sir. I'm worried for the safety of my team. If we respond to every sighting, how long before they realise they can walk us into an ambush?'

'My thoughts exactly,' Russell said, 'which is why I raised the issue with Lance Durden. We need more reliable intel if we're to avoid that situation.'

Durden was the CIA liaison to the Combined Joint Special Operations Task Force (CJSOTF)—also known as Task Force Sword—headed by the Joint Special Operations Command (JSOC). He had been in country before Operation Enduring Freedom had even kicked off, and was supposed to be the expert on the region. So far, though, his efforts at pinpointing the men on the Joint Prioritized Effects List had proven fruitless. The JPEL was the Taliban most wanted list, and at the top was Osama Bin Laden. The target of that morning's raid, Abdul al-Hussain, was third.

'What was his reaction?'

'Durden said he's working on someone,' Russell said. 'His mole is well placed within al-Hussain's network and above suspicion, but not high enough that he knows all of his movements. It's a waiting game.'

'Is he the one who gave us the latest intel?' Gray asked.

'No, that was a walk-in.'

The rewards offered for information leading to the capture or death of the players on the JPEL had meant a steady stream of Afghans heading to the gates of the camp in search of easy pickings. But the outcome was almost always the same; in exchange for a wad of dollars, they gave Durden and his small team locations of the Taliban leadership. Ninety-five per cent of the tips proved to be worthless, and the others only led to the death or capture of minor figures.

Gray wanted to rant, but it wasn't the CO's fault. Russell was under orders from CJSOTF to investigate all sightings, no matter how minor the likelihood of success. What pissed Gray off was that the US teams got to see real action while he and his mates were traipsing the mountains looking for ghosts.

Gray and his team had been in the country for a little over two months, and they had yet to loose off a round in anger. All of their missions had led to nothing, though on a couple of occasions they'd arrived just too late to capture their targets. Bad intelligence and poor timing had conspired to deny them the action they craved.

'Go get some rest,' Russell said. 'I've got a meeting with Durden later this morning, and I'm guessing he'll offer us another opportunity to waste our time.'

Gray offered a wry smile and left, knowing well that the CO was right. He decided to head for the mess tent, and on his way bumped into Sonny, Smart and Levine.

'What's the plan for tonight?' Sonny asked Gray. 'Martinis and Jacuzzi with the Spice Girls—or another night in the hills with our dicks in our hands?'

'Sporty couldn't make it.'

'Even better,' Levine chipped in. 'No fighting over who gets two of them.'

'It just isn't a Jacuzzi party without Sporty,' Gray said. 'We're going out again tonight.'

'Better intel this time?' Smart asked.

'Probably not. JSOC is an American venture, so we should just think ourselves lucky we got invited and be grateful for any scraps they throw our way.'

'Speaking of our colonial friends,' Smart said, tapping Gray's arm, 'here comes Delta Farce.'

Gray looked to his right to see John Balmer and his cohorts approaching.

'Khaíre!' the American smiled.

'Do what now?' Sonny said.

'Khaíre. It's Greek. From the ninth century BC. Thought you'd recognize it, what with you guys being ancient history and all that.'

Gray looked at his men, confused.

'Ah!' Sonny exclaimed. 'I think it's meant to be a joke about us being around for so long, while Delta Farce are the new kids on the block.'

'That's right.' Hank Lomax grinned.

'New kids on the block?' Levine said, his brow still furrowed. 'Wasn't one of them gay?'

'At least one,' Sonny said, looking at Balmer's men. 'Hard to tell which.'

'Aw, the little one's cranky.' Balmer laughed. 'Just got off a hard night of traffic control, have you?'

'We spent the night in the mountains looking for Taliban,' Smart told him. 'What about you? An evening in your tent eating cheeseburgers and watching I Love Lucy re-runs?'

'We were in a real firefight,' Lomax said, 'saving the 187th from an ass-kicking.'

'An old man on a donkey stray too close, did he?'

'Guys, knock it off,' Gray said. 'You'll never win a pissing contest against huge dicks like these. Let's go eat. I'm famished.'

'Yeah, run along,' Balmer said. 'Tiny needs his nap.'

'How about I shove this tiny fist down your fucking throat,' Sonny snarled, but Smart grabbed him by the collar and pulled him away.

'You have to learn to pick your moments,' Smart said as he pushed him in the direction of the DFAC.

'He's right,' Gray added. 'Wait until there's ten of them, then it'll be a fair fight.'

Sonny shrugged off Smart's grip. 'I'm sorry, but he just winds me up so much.'

'Yeah—because you let him,' Gray said. The problem was they had no release for the tension. Day after day they were wound up like springs, only for the mission to end in disappointment. What they needed was an outlet, a way to vent all the pent-up frustration. They had the makeshift gym and the rifle range, but nothing came close to actual combat.

An idea sprang into Gray's head, one that would relieve the tension and settle things once and for all between the two groups. He'd suggest it to Balmer the next time they met, but right now he needed chow and sleep.

Chapter 5

A small boy chased a young goat through a vast orchard that was just about ready to give up its crop of apricots. Abdul al-Hussain watched him with envy.

When he'd been a nine-year-old—almost half a century ago—Abdul could never have imagined the decades of conflict that lay ahead. Back then, life had been so simple: the morning spent tending the crops and ensuring the irrigation system was well maintained, followed by lunch and free time to enjoy with his twin brother, Muhammed.

They'd played soccer with a ball made from goat skin, and Abdul day-dreamed of one day representing his country as the national team's goalkeeper. He would spend hours diving to his left and right, pretending to save a last-minute penalty that earned his nation the World Cup. But that dream, like so many others, had faded with time. Once he reached his teenage years, the football was long forgotten as his attention turned to Buzkashi.

The game starts out with a headless goat carcass in the middle of the arena, and the objective is for players on horseback to get it to the scoring area. It had seemed such a simple concept when his father had first explained it to him, but after watching his first competition Abdul had recognised it for the brutal sport that it was.

The next decade saw him become one of the youngest champions in history, but the sport took a back seat as he approached his thirtieth birthday. His bravery was required elsewhere; the Soviet Union had arrived in Afghanistan.

Abdul was recruited by the Mujahideen, swapping his leather Buzkashi whip for a Kalashnikov AK-47. And over the next ten years Abdul had taken part in dozens of confrontations with the Soviet aggressors. At first, he and his compatriots had been heavily outnumbered and outgunned, until the US decided to intervene on the logistics front. The Mil MI-24 helicopter gunships that once gave the Soviets total air domination were no match for the Stinger missiles the Americans were shipping into the country, and what had once looked a one-sided affair on paper soon ground to a stalemate. The Soviets, having suffered many losses, started bombing from higher altitudes. This made accuracy more difficult but kept them out of range of the American-built surface-to-air missiles.

The communists had been invited into the country by the new communist president, Babrak Karmal, but they never managed to occupy more than twenty per cent of it. Their troops numbered 125,000, but they were up against twice as many resistance fighters—mostly Afghans, though some were from neighbouring Arab countries.

Abdul rose through the ranks to command more than three hundred men, and they would use guerrilla tactics to engage the enemy, hitting them hard before fleeing into the mountains. He had over seventy personal kills to his name by the time the last Soviet unit left Afghanistan in February 1989.

He'd returned from his war efforts in the south to discover that his family home and crops in Kabul province had been completely destroyed as part of the Soviet scorched-earth policy, designed to deny resistance fighters shelter and food. His mother, father and twin brother had been victims of the aerial bombardment. The invaders were long gone, leaving him no outlet for his fury. It festered inside him as he set about trying to rebuild his life.

Abdul married a local girl twenty years his junior, and she quickly gave him a son. That child would eventually be joined by four siblings—three of whom were boys who would carry on the family name and inherit his precious farm. Only a small percentage of Afghanistan boasted arable land, meaning his orchards were lucrative and valuable.

It took four years to return the farm to its former glory, during which time the Mujahideen continued its fight against the communist government. Soviet puppet Mohammad Najibullah eventually resigned in 1992, but the civil war raged on. In 1994, the Taliban emerged as a military force, and were supported by Pakistan, who saw them as a way to secure trade routes to Central Asia and establish a government in Kabul friendly to its interests. Led by Mullah Mohammed Omar, the Taliban sequestered power from the Mujahideen warlords whose corruption and despotism they despised. In 1996, the Taliban gained control of the Afghan government, and in Abdul's opinion, their interpretation of Islamic Sharia law was just what the country needed if it were to survive. The lawlessness had gone on for too long, and someone had to take the reins and guide the people along the proper path. The sport that had turned him into a man— Buzkashi—was outlawed, but Abdul didn't see it as a loss. A fragile peace had descended on the region, and he had entertained many Taliban leaders in his home, one of whom had been Mullah Omar himself. Abdul had been quick to pledge his allegiance. Because of his reputation as a Mujahideen fighter, al-Hussain was given a senior position in the region. He enforced the law harshly, and without exception.

However, the events of September 11th, 2001, changed everything.

Kabul fell to anti-Taliban forces, and Pakistan's Inter-Services Intelligence helped the Taliban militia who were in full retreat. Abdul and his family were offered the chance to be spirited out of the country on Pakistani cargo planes, but he wasn't abandoning his country. Instead, he contacted ISI who gave him and his family new papers. He returned to Kabul province as Mukhtar Shah and sold his farm for a less than generous price. His time in the north was at an end, and he relocated to the south, close to the border with Pakistan. There, under his new name, he purchased a smaller holding and set about the pretence of being nothing more than a simple farmer.

Now, nine years on from the first US and British troops landing on his soil, he was able to carry on his insurgent activities right under the noses of the occupying forces.

The boy in the orchard gave up chasing the goat, and had scampered up a tree to pick one of the unripe apricots.

'You'll get stomach ache, Jamal,' al-Hussain warned.

The child looked over at him, noticing his presence for the first time. He bowed his head. 'Sorry, father.'

'In a few more days you can fill your belly, but for now you must be patient.'

It was a virtue Abdul al-Hussain had been blessed with, for his was a waiting game. He knew never to attack the coalition forces until the moment was right and the conditions optimal. If this meant letting targets travel through his land unhindered, so be it.

He also had to wait for the ISI-backed training camp near Quetta to produce able men for his needs. When the Taliban had formed in the mid-nineties they'd had their pick of seasoned Mujahideen veterans, but those days were long gone. Now he was left with a few battle-hardened men and had to rely on the youths from outlying villages to swell his ranks, and many of them had not yet come of age. The more promising ones had been sent to Pakistan for intense training, while the less-capable were used as cannon-fodder, sent on suicide missions in the name of their God.

That was, until now.

A member of the Afghan community in England had passed on news of the American woman of Afghan heritage. She was working in London for a US pharmaceutical company, developing a virus that would ensure pain-free births for all women. To Abdul, such a thing was an abomination. Allah himself had decided how much a woman should bear when bringing forth new life, but that wasn't the part of her research that struck him. The woman had spoken of her frustration at not being able to reduce the side effects of the virus, and these had piqued his interest. He'd instructed the Afghan to find out more about the woman and her work, and word had reached him a month earlier that she would be travelling around the Middle East giving lectures about her discovery.

One of the stops on her tour was Kabul.

The more he'd heard from his man in England, the more it seemed like divine providence; Allah was blessing him with the means to defeat his enemies.

Abdul's wife brought food and tea to his table and then retreated inside. He picked at his Bulani, tearing off a piece of the filled bread, then dipped it in plain homemade yoghurt.

The scientist, Miriam Dagher, had landed in Kabul earlier in the day. All he could do now was wait for news.

It came as he was finishing the last mouthful of his dinner—via a burner cell he'd set up just for this occasion.

'We have the package.'

'You know where to deliver it,' al-Hussain said.

'I do. We'll be there at three tomorrow, *Inshallah.*'

God willing indeed.

Al-Hussain ended the call and removed the battery and SIM card from the phone. He called his son over.

'Take this to the market and—'

'—drop it in the sewer. Yes, father.'

Al-Hussain watched Jamal race off and wondered if his youngest would grow to live a similar life to his own. His eldest son, Omar, was gone; killed in a confrontation with US Special Forces a year earlier. His other two sons were already training in guerrilla tactics, awaiting their turn to face the enemy. It had been his wish that the fighting would be over by now, and the land returned to Taliban rule so that they could live out the remainder of their lives in peace. Sadly, there was no sign of the Western invaders withdrawing.

If the Dagher woman's claims were true, then her virus may just be the difference between defeat and victory. If Allah willed it to be the latter, then perhaps he would live long enough to see his boys grow to be men and have children of their own.

If not... then they would all follow Omar to the grave.

Chapter 6

After six hours in the sack, Gray felt somewhat refreshed. He put on his boots and, wearing just his shorts and a T-shirt, set off for a run around the base. He'd measured out a route that was roughly three-quarters of a mile in length, and tried to get in four circuits each day.

A shade over twenty minutes later, he arrived back at the tent drenched in sweat. Carl Levine was preparing to hit the ablutions, while Sonny was sprawled out on his bunk fast asleep.

'CO wants to see you for a briefing in forty minutes,' Levine said. 'You're to report to the chaos in action suite.'

If the briefing was to be held in the CIA block, it could only mean that Lance Durden had another dubious mission for them.

Gray grabbed a towel. 'Where's Len?'

'Taking a shower,' Levine told him.

'Okay. Wake sleeping ugly and tell him to get his shit together.'

Gray jogged to the shower block, passing Smart on the way.

33

'Briefing in forty,' Smart said.

'Yeah, Carl told me. Looks like we're going out again.'

'Any chance you could ask for a mission based on solid intel instead of greed and make-believe?'

Normally, they received their orders direct from the CO, but now Gray would have the opportunity to question Durden on the source of the information.

'I'll do what I can.'

Gray spent five minutes under the cold water, then walked back to the tent and dressed. Fifteen minutes before the meeting was due to commence, he headed over to the American quarter and bought a coffee from one of the vendors.

'Well, if it isn't the saggy-ass soldier!' A powerful hand slapped Gray on the back, spilling some of his drink.

'Balmer.' Gray growled as he turned to face the Delta Force master sergeant.

'The very same, old chap.'

'You know, when you do an English accent you sound like Dick van Dyke, only without the van Dyke.'

'Man, you're funny. Shame you were born on the wrong side of the pond.' Balmer ordered a drink and a large cookie from the stall owner. 'So, what brings you to the fighting side of the base? Looking for some tips?'

'I'm on my way to see Durden,' Gray said, already bored by the banter. It was the same every time he met Balmer and his squad, and the jokes had long ago started to wear thin.

Gray had met other members of Delta Force through the special forces exchange program, where the US troops would visit Credenhill to cross-train with the SAS. On those occasions the routine had always been the same: rib the yanks for a few hours, put in a few weeks of solid training, then a huge piss-up at the end. It had mostly been good-natured, but Balmer was taking their rivalry to the extreme.

'If you're hoping for a glory mission, forget it,' Balmer said. 'Durden bleeds the stars and stripes. If there's a solid lead on a JPEL target, he'll give it to us. You'll be lucky to get a goose chase or suicide mission.'

'Yeah, that sounds about right.'

'Don't sweat it. You guys were the best for a long time, but warfare evolves. You're still good, but we're the next generation.'

Gray was tempted to cry bullshit, but he didn't have time nor inclination to get into a protracted argument with Balmer. Nothing he said was going to change the man's mindset, but actions spoke louder than words. He finished his coffee and threw the cup in the trash. 'There's only one real way to know who's the best,' he said.

'Yeah? What's that?'

'Your best man against mine.'

A smile spread on Balmer's face. 'We might as well go for it right now.'

'No, this weekend. I'll find somewhere nice and secluded.'

'You're on, Gray. And I suggest you book a furlough to recover. A couple of months should do it.'

'We'll see,' Gray said, as he started his walk towards Durden's office. After a few steps, he noticed that Balmer was still beside him.

'Just so happens I'm going that way, too. Any idea why he'd want to brief both of us?'

Gray shook his head, though one horrific idea was springing in his mind.

For someone who'd spent so much time in the region, Lance Durden hadn't done a good job of acclimatising.

Three powerful electric fans roared as Gray and Balmer entered his office, where Russell and Balmer's CO—Captain Harold Bridges—were already waiting.

Gray was glad of the respite from the heat. He positioned himself in the crosswind and he and Balmer flicked off salutes before Bridges told them to stand at ease.

'Gentlemen,' Durden began, 'thanks for coming.' He wiped his brow with a handkerchief and drank from a bottle of water, condensation dripping from the bottom. 'We've had news that an American citizen was kidnapped in Kabul yesterday.' He pointed to a photograph on a board that showed the Arabic features of a woman in her fifties. 'Miriam Dagher was due to lecture at the Kabul Medical Institute, but her transport was intercepted by hostiles posing as Afghan police. Her three-man protection team was killed, and her whereabouts are currently unknown. As of now, she's our priority.'

'May I ask why, sir?'

All heads turned to Gray.

'I mean, she's hardly the first civilian to be seized by the Taliban,' he added.

'The request to find her comes direct from the PM,' Russell told him. 'She was born in Afghanistan but is now an American citizen, though she's been working on a joint British and US venture in London for the last two years. The prime minister has assumed responsibility for her safety, that's all I know.'

While it wasn't unusual for Gray's team to be made aware of captured British nationals, it was the first time he'd been told to put one at the top of his search list. It could only mean that she was working on something sensitive for both governments.

'What was the purpose of her visit?'

'She was here to lecture on a breakthrough she'd made on painless childbirth,' Durden said.

'Do we know if she was specifically targeted?' Balmer asked.

'Unlikely,' Durden told him. 'Wrong place, wrong time, that's the way we see it.'

Gray and Balmer exchanged glances. Durden knew more than he was sharing, Gray was sure of it.

'Any idea who took her?' he asked.

'It's early days. I've got an asset digging around for information.'

'Is this the same asset who told us Abdul al-Hussain would be hiding in the mountains last night?'

'That's enough,' Russell growled.

Gray wanted to respond, but bit his tongue. Durden was fair game, but he wasn't about to get into a slanging match with his own boss.

'It isn't,' Durden said, ignoring Gray's dig. 'The man looking for Dagher is code-named Sentinel. He's a relatively new acquisition, but the few leads he's given us so far have panned out. Once he's located her, you two will be going in to get her out.'

This was exactly what Gray had feared before the meeting. He had no issues working alongside other team members, except for Balmer. Gray couldn't trust him to leave his ego at the camp.

'You're suggesting a joint mission?' Gray asked.

'It's a possibility,' Bridges said. He was an imposing figure, a buzz cut atop a mound of muscle. 'Whichever team is available gets first crack. If she's being held in a heavily-defended location, you'll go in together.'

'It's not going to be an issue, is it?' Russell directed the question to both Gray and Balmer.

'No, sir. Not at all.'

'Fine by me,' Balmer said, though Gray detected a hint of bitterness in his reply.

'Good,' Durden said, resuming his seat. 'Back to business. We have a couple of leads that I'd like you two to check out. Master Sergeant Balmer, we've picked up radio chatter suggesting Asadi Mansour will be returning from Pakistan in the next twelve hours. He's been on a recruitment mission at the Quetta madrassas looking for fresh blood.'

Gray hadn't been in country long, but he knew that the Taliban often went to the faith schools in Pakistan to recruit young men who had been taught to hate the West.

'Any idea which route he's going to take?' Balmer wanted to know.

'It won't be one of the regular border crossings. I hope to have an exact fix by 2100 hours. Once we have that, you ship out.'

Durden turned to Gray. 'A drone discovered what looks like an arms cache. Four hostiles took several cases into a building in the hills fifteen miles north of here. Captain Russell has the details.'

Durden started writing on a pad, and the two captains made for the door. The meeting was done.

'Good luck finding those pea shooters,' Balmer said to Gray, every word dripping sarcasm. 'You be careful out there. It'll be dark.'

Gray knew he was more likely to find boxes of Christmas decorations and pork scratchings than weapons, but he wasn't about to make Balmer's day by sharing his concerns.

Gray settled for, 'I'll see you on Friday,' then chased after Russell.

'What do you think?'

'Looks to be an arms cache,' Russell said. 'I watched a recording of the drone feed and saw four guys humping boxes from a pick-up truck. I doubt they were delivering pizzas.'

If Russell was sure, that was good enough for Gray, but that wasn't what he was referring to. 'I meant the Dagher woman. It's unusual for a civvy to get top billing, isn't it?'

'Ours is not to reason why—'

'Ours is but to go where no other fucker is stupid enough to go.'

'Amen,' Russell said, and held up a manila envelope. 'I've got the co-ordinates of the cache and a few overhead shots. Let's go put a plan together.'

'Give me fifteen minutes,' Gray said. 'I'll get the team together. Oh, and, sir, permission to do some unarmed combat training this weekend?'

Russell threw a look that told Gray to spit it out.

'I thought we might get together with Balmer's boys and see if there's anything new we might learn from each other. Purely educational, of course.'

'Naturally. And how many of you are going to take part in this… training?'

'I thought just one of us,' Gray said.

Russell thought about it for a minute. 'Okay, but one only. Got it?'

'Crystal, sir.'

Gray turned to leave, but Russell grabbed his arm.

'Make sure he gets a good education,' the captain said, grinning.

Russell headed back to his office while a buoyant Gray returned to his tent. Levine was rubbing lotion on his body, while Smart was lying on his bed, reading a paperback.

'We're on for tonight,' Gray told them. 'Where's Sonny?'

'In the shower,' Levine said. 'What's the objective?'

'A weapons dump.'

'Yay! I finally get to blow shit up!'

Each member of the four-man patrol had a speciality. Levine's was explosives. Sonny was the sharp-shooter. Smart the medic. And Gray was in charge of communications.

'Only if Durden got one right,' Gray cautioned.

Sonny returned with his washing kit. 'What's the news?'

'Weapons dump,' Gray said. 'We're gonna discuss it with the CO in ten minutes. In the meantime I've arranged a little fun activity for the weekend.'

'Don't tell me we get to field-strip a pinkie… again!'

'Even better, Sonny. One of us gets to go toe-to-toe with Balmer's best.'

Sonny and Smart grinned, but Levine wasn't happy.

'Only one of us? How is that fair? Can't we just have a huge dust up, our troop against theirs?'

'The CO wouldn't go for that.'

'But he okayed a one-on-one?' Smart asked.

Gray smiled. 'If you ask me, he's looking forward to it as much as we are.'

Chapter 7

When Commander Sarah Keogh arrived at New Scotland Yard, her stomach was tied in knots. Being summoned to the office of the commissioner meant one of two things—and she hadn't done anything to earn praise nor a promotion in recent months.

She made her way up to the fourth floor and along the corridor to Commissioner Elaine Randall's office. In the reception area she saw a familiar face in Commander David Duke. After introducing herself to the receptionist, Sarah took a seat next to Duke.

'You, too?' he asked.

'Any idea what this is all about?'

'Not a clue,' Duke said. 'My DAC just told me to be here at ten.'

Sarah had been given the same instructions by her own deputy assistant commissioner. She'd pressed for further details, but there had been none.

A buzzing sound came from the receptionist's desk, and then she motioned for Sarah and Duke to step inside.

Elaine Randall sat with her hands clasped on the oak desk in front of her. She was the youngest commissioner in the history of the Metropolitan Police at forty-seven, having bulldozed her way up the ranks. She dyed her long hair black

41

to retain her youthful look, a constant reminder to every one of her achievements.

Sarah and Duke came to attention in front of her. 'Ma'am,' they chorused.

'A woman has disappeared, and I'd like *you two* to investigate it,' Randall said without preamble.

Sarah and Duke glanced at each other.

'Ma'am?' Sarah said again. 'You want two teams to work on the same case?'

Randall pointed at them. 'No, I want you two to work on the same case.' She opened a file and held out a photograph. Sarah leaned forward and took it from her.

'Miriam Dagher,' Randall said. 'She's a US citizen but has been working in London for the past two years. Miriam was kidnapped by at least four armed men yesterday morning. Her three escorts were killed.'

Sarah frowned. A shooting like that would have been all over the news at the very least. 'I didn't hear anything about this. Where did it take place?'

'Kabul,' Randall said. 'Afghanistan.'

It was Duke's turn to voice his concerns. 'You want us to travel to Afghanistan to investigate a kidnapping?'

'No. I need background here. The PM has ordered this personally, but doesn't want a media circus. That's why I'm assigning it to you two. We need to know why she was targeted.'

'Pardon me for sounding dumb, ma'am, but why is the prime minister so interested in her?'

'All I know is that she was working on something that could be of great benefit to the pharmaceutical industry, and both the UK and US have a vested interest in getting her back. By all accounts she's a brilliant virologist, irreplaceable.'

'Yet the PM doesn't know what she was working on?' Sarah asked.

'It appears not. My feeling is he's under pressure from President Arnold to ensure her safe return. Our boys in Afghanistan are doing their bit, but we need to cover all bases.'

Randall handed Duke a file. He opened it, and removed two sheets of paper.

'That's her personal details, place of work and home address. It's all we have at the moment, but the PM is pressing Arnold for more information. You report directly to me—no-one else. And you do not delegate this to anyone. This requires the utmost discretion, understood?'

'Yes, ma'am.'

'Very well. I've already contacted your chief supers to let them know they'll be covering for you for the rest of the day, perhaps tomorrow, too. Get to it.'

Sarah and Duke turned sharply in sync and left the room. As they walked towards the elevator, Sarah took the file from Duke and opened the thin dossier.

'Looks like she lived alone. Why don't we start with her employer?'

'Just like that?' Duke said, stopping dead. 'You don't think something's off here? You don't even want to discuss it?'

'What is there to discuss? We've been given a task—I suggest we complete it as best we can.' She noted Duke's look and sighed. 'What do you want to do? Go back and question Randall's decision to assign the role to us?'

'No, I just...aren't you curious? This woman was obviously working on something top secret, otherwise it would be given to a couple of uniforms.'

'I'm going to view it as a test. Get the information Randall wants, report back and wait for the next promotion to come along.' Sarah had always been career-minded. Not to the same obsessed level as Randall, but she would never pass up an opportunity to get herself a pay rise and one foot higher up the ladder. 'Anyway, any questions you have will be answered once we've completed our investigation.'

Sarah knew she was right. She'd been with the police for close to twelve years but had never encountered anything like this. If she was to progress past the rank of commander, though, she would have to just do her job and move on.

'Okay,' Duke said, walking towards the lift. 'My station's closer. I'll sign out a car and we can visit her place of work.'

'Discretion, remember. Better to go home and change into civvies, then meet up somewhere.'

'Good point. Where is it?'

'Chelsea, just off the King's Road.'

Duke pressed the button for the elevator. 'I used to work that patch. I don't recall any laboratories.'

Sarah handed him a sheet of paper. 'That's what it says.'

'Must have sprung up in the last few years, then.'

They entered the lift and Sarah pressed the button for the ground floor. 'Where do you live?'

'Clapham,' Duke told her.

'I'm in Herne Hill. I'll pick you up on the way.' She took Duke's phone and punched in her mobile number. 'Text me your address.'

When they reached the exit, Sarah said she would be at his place in an hour, and then they split up. She got into the car that was waiting for her and told the uniformed officer to take her home.

Fifteen minutes later, the car pulled up outside her three-bed detached house.

'I'll make my own way back,' Sarah said as she got out. As soon as she got inside she put the kettle on and then headed upstairs to change.

Once she was dressed in a conservative blue suit, Sarah went down to the kitchen and poured a coffee, then threw some ham into a sandwich.

Like Duke, she was curious about the case they'd been assigned, though she really did see it as an opportunity. To be trusted with something so sensitive meant her superiors had every faith in her, and she would do her best to deliver for them.

She finished her snack just as her flip-up Nokia pinged. She squinted at Duke's address.

Sarah locked up and got into her Audi. It took her twenty minutes to reach Duke's place, and when she arrived she parked outside and sent him a text to let him know she was waiting.

Duke was wearing a dark grey suit. It looked good on him, and showed off his well-maintained body. In contrast, Sarah hadn't taken too much care of her body, and she knew it. She promised herself every Monday that she'd start exercising at the weekend, but there were always excuses. A tough week at work, a niggling pain that would put it off for another week, the release of a new film at the cinema. The real problem was she liked beer too much, and if she was going to lose a few pounds, that would have to be removed from her diet. That and the pizzas that went with the four cans. It wasn't that she drank *every* day—three times a week at most—but Sarah had few friends within the force and none outside it. She went home alone every night, and that was how it would be for the rest of her life. She was the first to admit that she wasn't the prettiest flower in the garden, so she'd long ago given up dreams of meeting Mr. Right. A few years ago Mr Barely-Adequate would have done, but these days she only sought the company of her trusted friend Stella Artois.

'Okay,' Duke said as he got in beside her. 'Let's see what Dagher was up to.'

They crossed the Thames on the Albert Bridge, then drove down King's Road and took a right.

Sarah was expecting a modern, white building, but all she saw were red-bricks. Many of them looked residential, apart from one which had a huge black door in the centre of the façade. It was four storeys tall and all of the windows had blinds.

'That's the place, apparently.'

There was no signage outside to confirm that they'd found the laboratory, but Sarah pulled up onto double-yellow lines and killed the engine.

Almost immediately, the large door opened and a man dressed in a security guard uniform trotted down the stairs to her car.

'You can't park here, I'm afraid.'

Sarah showed him her ID. 'Commander Keogh, Commander Duke. We're here to see the person in charge.'

The security guard briefly turned away from them and muttered something into his radio. Then he turned back.

'Okay, through the gates and down the ramp. You'll be met there.'

Sarah looked to where he was pointing and saw a huge metal grille swinging open. She started the car and drove through, and ten yards in she saw the ramp he'd mentioned.

She drove down it and found herself in an underground car park. There were no spaces on the first level, so she went down the next ramp and found a spot in the far corner.

'I wasn't expecting this,' she said to Duke.

'Me neither. I thought this was a residential area.'

As soon as they got out of the car a man in a dark suit approached them. He held out his hand.

'John Farmer,' he said, shaking Sarah's hand first. 'The commissioner told me to expect you. Come, this way.'

Farmer had an American accent, though Sarah couldn't pinpoint whereabouts in the States he was from. He led them through a doorway and into a small chamber, where he pressed a button and the whirring of the elevator's mechanism kicked into life.

'It was so upsetting to hear of Miriam's abduction,' Farmer said. 'Such a brilliant woman.'

'I can imagine,' Sarah said. 'What exactly did she do here?'

'Miriam was the lead virologist for a project that began in the US. For security reasons, the operation moved here. Rival companies had tried unsuccessfully to get access to the research, and it was thought that moving the work here would disrupt their efforts.'

'What was she working on?' Duke asked as they stepped into the elevator.

Farmer pressed a button and they started to rise. 'A virus that makes childbirth virtually pain-free.'

Duke squinted.

'Isn't pain relief already available?'

'It is, but it's not always effective,' Sarah said. She had no children of her own, but her sister had four, and had sworn the pain didn't get any easier with experience.

'There's a big difference between pain relief and pain-free,' Farmer said jovially as the doors opened and they stepped out into a hallway.

The decor wasn't what Sarah was expecting. Instead of plastered walls and carpet, all she saw was white; the floor, walls and ceiling all reflected the light like plastic. She touched the surface, and it confirmed her suspicion.

'The building itself is just an outer shell,' Farmer explained. 'It was completely gutted fifteen years ago, and the new interior was installed. As you can imagine, we work with some pretty serious stuff here, so we have to make sure it's contained. Think of this as one of those interconnected hamster runs. Each node in the laboratory module has a quarantine area, and it's impossible to have both doors open at one time. Kind of like an air lock on a spaceship... if you're into sci-fi.'

Sarah hated sci-fi, but understood the concept. 'Why go to all that trouble when you could build a brand-new place out in the countryside where it wouldn't affect the neighbours?'

'Secrecy,' Farmer said. 'No-one suspects what goes on here, and that's the way we want to keep it.'

'What's so secret about this virus?' Duke asked. 'Doesn't sound very scary to me.'

'It's not so much what it can do, but what it's worth,' Farmer told him. 'At the moment, expectant women have a few choices for labour. There's gas—nitrous oxide, or laughing gas—which as Commander Keogh has pointed out, isn't always effective. Or pethidine, which is injected into the buttocks. The problem with this is that it can depress the unborn baby's breathing as it receives a dose through the umbilical cord. Finally, there's epidural anaesthesia. It's the most effective form of pain relief, but there can be several drawbacks, including the reduced likelihood of a normal vaginal delivery and, in rare cases, blood clots or difficulty breathing.'

'Makes you wonder why anyone would put themselves through it,' Duke said.

'Spoken like a man,' Sarah said. 'So what would this virus be worth?'

'Well, if you consider that over four million babies are born in the US each year, if a quarter of them used the virus at two thousand dollars a go, that's two billion a year from just one country. The states represents about four per cent of the world's population, and two grand per birth is a conservative estimate of the cost… so, you do the math.'

There were a hell of a lot of zeros in that estimation, and it became obvious why other pharmaceutical companies would want to steal the idea.

'Why does it have to be a virus?' Duke wanted to know. It was a question on Sarah's lips, too.

'Normal painkillers can't be used because they would have a negative effect on the child. As I said, pethidine—which is a synthetic opioid—can harm the child's breathing. Other drugs have been tested on animals, but the side effects make them too risky. With a virus, we can target a specific area of the body and avoid contaminating the baby.'

'A virus can do that?'

'Sure. Imagine you stub your toe on the bed post. This causes tissue damage, which is registered by microscopic pain receptors called nociceptors in your skin. Each of these pain receptors forms one end of a nerve cell, or neurone. This is connected to the spinal cord by a long nerve fibre, or axon. When the pain receptor is activated, it sends an electrical signal up the nerve fibre. The nerve fibre is bundled with many others to form a peripheral nerve. The electrical signal passes up the neurone within the peripheral nerve to reach the spinal cord in the neck. Within an area of the spinal cord called the dorsal horn, the electrical signals are transmitted from one neurone to another across synapses by means of neurotransmitters. Signals are then passed up the spinal cord to the brain, where the signals pass to the thalamus. This is a sorting station that relays the signals on to different parts of the brain. Signals are sent to, among other places, the somatosensory cortex, which is responsible for physical sensation. All we do is stop those messages reaching the brain.'

'Sounds great,' Sarah said. 'How close is Miriam to finishing?'

'She's still a few months away,' Farmer told her. 'The project hasn't been without its problems.'

'Oh?'

They reached a door and Farmer pressed his hand onto a pad. The door slid open, and Sarah couldn't help but think back to the earlier sci-fi analogy. She and Duke followed Farmer inside, and their guide pressed a button to seal them in. He placed his hand on another pad, and a door opened into an identical corridor.

'The virus does what it was designed to do,' Farmer continued, 'but there have been some side effects that concern us. There's a release of large amounts of norepinephrine, or noradrenaline as it's called here in the UK, which increases alertness, promotes vigilance, enhances formation and retrieval of memory, as well as focuses attention.'

'That sounds like a good thing,' Duke said.

'It does. In fact, there would be a huge market for that. Athletes would love it, for a start, as would students, chess masters... you name it. Just about every employer in the world would love to have access to it. There would be a huge drop in training time and output would shoot through the roof. The trouble is, it also increases the heart rate and raises blood pressure—neither of which would be good for mother nor child during birth. As yet, we don't know the long-term implications. It could be months, even years, before we get a satisfactory understanding of the lasting effects.'

'Considering how secret this project is, you've been very open to us about it.'

Farmer laughed. 'If only it were that easy. It's like saying 'let's build a rocket and go to the moon', or 'let's create a cure for cancer'. It's easy to identify an objective, another thing to achieve it.'

They reached another door. This time Farmer had to have his palm read and also enter a six-digit code into a keypad on the wall.

'This is where Miriam works.'

The room had the same white plastic composition. Sarah was disappointed to see that there were no petri dishes or flasks bubbling over Bunsen burners, just a computer connected to two monitors. The only other items on the desk were a stack of papers, a pen holder and a phone.

'Do you think her kidnapping could be related to her work?' Sarah asked Farmer.

'It's possible, I suppose. Though why wait until she gets to Afghanistan? Why not kidnap her here if they plan to force her to hand over her research?'

It was a good question—one Sarah had no theory for. Not yet anyway. No part of this case seemed textbook in any way, but all she could do was resort to standard procedure.

'Did you notice anything unusual about Miriam's behaviour in the last few days?'

'No, she was just her usual self. In fact, she was looking forward to the trip. It's the first time she's been back to the place where she was born.'

Sarah had noticed the place of birth in Dagher's file and wondered whether or not it was just a coincidence that she happened to be kidnapped there.

She handed Farmer her card. 'Thank you so much for your time. If you think of anything out of the ordinary, please call me.'

'I will. I just hope this is all resolved soon. She's not a young woman. God knows what they're doing to her over there.'

Sarah was having the same fears.

Once they were back on city streets, Sarah asked Duke what he thought of it all.

'I don't think she was kidnapped for what she knows,' he said. 'I can't see the Afghans having the infrastructure to replicate her work, and even if they could, is anyone likely to buy it, given the circumstances?'

'You think she was just wrong place, wrong time?'

'Looks like it. Let's check out her home, though—for the sake of thoroughness.'

Chapter 8

Sarah stopped off at her office and looked up the address they'd been given for Miriam Dagher. If she was here on secondment from the US, the likelihood was she was renting this property. Within minutes she found that her instinct had been right. She had the name of the rental estate agent and called to arrange for them to be at the house within the hour.

When Sarah and Duke arrived at the home, there was someone waiting at the front door.

'She must have been doing well for herself,' Duke muttered.

Sarah agreed. The house was well outside her own price range. It was a detached red brick in Twickenham, with a short driveway that led to a built-in garage; the kind of place Sarah had on her wish-list. 'We're definitely in the wrong business.'

Sarah opened the glove box and took out two pairs of Latex gloves, handing one pair to Duke. They got out of the car and met the estate agent—a man in his forties in a perfectly cut suit.

'Eddie Howell, Grange and Co.'

Sarah and Duke showed him their ID and introduced themselves.

'Mind telling me what this is about?'

'I'm afraid we can't,' Sarah said. 'It's part of a sensitive ongoing investigation. We shouldn't keep you too long, though.'

Sarah just gestured towards the house and Howell took out a set of keys and opened the front door.

The interior was immaculate, like a show house.

'Nice place,' Duke said.

'Yes, it's one of our more exclusive properties.'

'If you could wait by the door, that would be great,' Sarah said.

Howell seemed happy enough to let them look around on their own. Sarah walked into the living room.

There was nothing out of place, except for a magazine on the coffee table. There was a two-seater sofa and an armchair which faced a giant wall-mounted television. A sideboard completed the furnishings.

Sarah moved from room to room, with Duke in close attendance. The kitchen was spotless, too. Sarah went through it, opening drawers and cupboards, not sure what she was hoping to find. The dishwasher was empty, as was the fridge. It was almost as if Miriam Dagher was planning on being away for some time. Sarah kicked herself for not asking how long the trip was meant to be, but a quick call later could rectify that if necessary.

As she strolled into the dining room, Sarah wondered whether Dagher was a clean-freak or if she actually spent any time here at all.

They ventured upstairs, where one of the three bedrooms had been used as an office. Duke began looking through the drawers, rifling through papers and flicking through notebooks.

'This is all gibberish to me,' he said. 'We're wasting our time. We're not going to find anything that'll explain why she was abducted.'

Frustratingly, Sarah felt the same. This had been a bust from the start.

'Agreed. Let's go.'

All that remained was to inform Commissioner Randall of their findings—or lack of them.

Sarah trudged down the stairs to the front door.

'Thanks,' she said to the estate agent. 'We're done here.'

'You sure? You don't want to see the basement?'

'The basement?'

'Yeah. It's through there, the kitchen.'

Sarah had seen a door in the kitchen but had assumed it was a pantry. She looked at Duke and he shrugged before he strolled forward. Sarah let him go. There was no point both of them checking it out.

She expected him to be gone for a couple of minutes, but when he stuck his head around the door after twenty seconds, she knew he'd found something.

'Stay there,' she said to Howell, before she followed Duke down into the basement.

'Close the door,' Duke told her.

Sarah did as he asked, then walked down a wooden staircase.

The first thing that struck her was the large black cloth hanging on the wall. It was covered in white Arabic writing, and while she didn't know what it said, she'd seen similar setups in the past.

Standing in front of it was a video camera on a tripod.

Sarah squinted behind it, peering at the buttons as she looked for the playback function.

'What are you doing?' Duke asked, his face full of concern.

'I want to see what she recorded.'

'Shouldn't we wait for the SOCO?'

'Utmost discretion, remember?'

Duke still looked unsure, but he came to stand next to Sarah as she pressed the Play button. A woman in her fifties was standing in front of the black background, her greying hair tied back.

'My name is Miriam Dagher. For the last forty years I have been living in the West, but that is all about to change. In the next few hours I will return to Afghanistan, the country of my birth, and do my part to help liberate it from the US and British warmongers.

'When I was growing up I relied, like everyone else, on the news outlets to keep me informed. The reporting was non-partisan for the most part, but in recent years that has all changed. Newspapers and television networks are controlled by the two main political parties, and they tell the people only what they want them to hear. Not only that, but they are used to polarise the population. They constantly pit rich against poor, black against white, but more recently, it has been Christian against Muslim.' She paused, took a breath, then looked back into the camera lens. 'Why? So that the elite can add to their huge wealth, and for no other reason. The American president has said the war in Afghanistan was necessary to find those behind 9/11, but that is a lie. Osama bin Laden was in the country briefly, and the president knows this. His military and intelligence advisors have told him, but he still sends troops to my homeland on this pretence. The only reason America is taking part is regime change. They want their own puppet government in place, one that will hand over mineral, oil and gas concessions to the West. It is estimated that there are almost four billion barrels of oil in one region alone, and the country's mineral wealth is estimated at three *trillion* dollars.' She took another deep breath. 'The US paints itself as the liberator, cleansing us of the Taliban and Al-Qaeda, but there is a pattern emerging that is plainly visible once you have all the facts. The American military-industrial complex is a multi-trillion-dollar industry, and they make no money from peace. More than half of the US government's spending goes to defence, with tens of billions going to private companies who make the planes and bombs that kill innocent Muslims around the world. Simple men are forced to arm themselves to protect their families, but they are no match for the might of the allied armies.' She swallowed. 'Well, I say enough is enough. Over the last few years, I have been tasked with developing a virus to make childbirth pain free, but so far the side effects have delayed progress. What my employer doesn't know is that these unwanted results were of my making. It was the only way I could get access to the right equipment to do my own research. Now that I have completed my work, I will be giving it to the people of Afghanistan so that we can finally rid ourselves of the Western tyrants. With my virus, we will create an invincible army and the ground will turn red with the blood of the invaders.'

'Fuck,' Duke whispered as the screen turned black.

Sarah couldn't have summed it up better. 'We need to tell Randall, right now,' she said.

Duke took his phone out. 'I'll ring her.'

'No. If the call is intercepted, it'll be the end of our careers. Let her know I'm on my way to see her—I'll give her the details in person.'

Sarah trudged back upstairs, where the estate agent was scrolling through his phone. He pocketed it as Sarah approached him.

'What did you find?' he asked.

'I can't tell you. I'm going to need every set of keys you're holding for the property, plus any the owner may have. As of now, this property is a crime scene and no-one sets foot inside.'

'I'm not sure my boss or the landlord will be happy—'

'Is the rent current?'

'What? Yes, it's paid up until the end of the month.'

'Then they don't need access and they won't lose out financially. We'll be here for a few days at the most, then you can have it back. In the meantime, get me the keys and stay out of the way.'

Sarah gestured for Howell to walk out the front door; he reluctantly obeyed. She followed him, locking the door behind her. Then she held out her hand and Howell dropped the keys into her palm.

'You can tell your boss about this, but no-one else. If this reaches the newspapers, I'll know who it came from, and you can't begin to imagine how bad that will be for you.'

Sarah walked to her car before Howell could protest. She drove back to New Scotland Yard, and when she reached Commissioner Randall's office, she was ushered straight in.

'What did you find?'

Sarah explained the discovery in the basement.

'This virus,' Randall said, leaning forward in her seat. 'How would it enhance the Taliban if they got their hands on it?'

'According to Professor Farmer, they would be a lot more focused, and I got the impression it wouldn't take long to train them. It would be like cramming six months of knowledge into a few days. They could probably turn a complete novice into a combat-ready soldier in just a couple of weeks. To get a complete picture of the virus's capabilities, we'd have to bring him in and get an expert to question him.'

Randall nodded. 'I agree. I'll ask the Home Secretary to arrange for someone to speak to Farmer. In the meantime, we have to secure her house.'

'David is there at the moment, and I've told the estate agent to hand over all the keys they hold. Unless you want to bring the forensics team in on this I thought David and I could log everything and take it to a safe storage facility.'

'Yes, do that. I don't want anyone else in on this. Catalogue everything and have a report on my desk this evening.'

'Yes, ma'am.'

Sarah left, preparing herself for a long night.

Chapter 9

Abdul al-Hussain sipped from a cup of tea as he waited patiently for the arrival of his guest. Opposite him in the back room of the textile store sat Farhad Nagi; a ferret-faced man in his twenties who sported the beginnings of a moustache.

'I still think something isn't right.'

Al-Hussain smiled. 'It is good that you are suspicious. Complacency leads to an early grave.'

'But what do we really know about her?' Nagi persisted.

Al-Hussain shrugged. Beyond the information he'd received from his man in London, there was very little in the public domain relating to Miriam Dagher. There were no social media profiles, and internet searches had revealed nothing more than a couple of articles in medical journals—most of which had been written a quarter of a century ago.

The absence of an online profile didn't necessarily mean anything was amiss, but al-Hussain was taking no chances. He'd instructed his men to take the woman into the desert and strip her, discarding the clothes she was travelling in and replacing them with more traditional local garments. The only items she would be allowed to bring with her would be those for work, and they would be transferred to a new bag after being checked for tracking devices.

If the woman was clean, she should arrive in the next few minutes. If not, carrion birds would feast on her for the next few days.

'Sometimes you only learn the truth when it is staring you in the face. We'll soon discover if she is all she promises to be.'

The shop owner poked his head into the room and asked if they required further refreshments, but al-Hussain waved him away. As soon as his men arrived, they would be leaving.

Nagi nibbled a fingernail as they waited—more out of boredom than apprehension. The young man had been in his service for three years now, and his loyalty was unquestioned. The moment he'd been approached by the CIA and asked to provide information on local Taliban movements and plans, he'd come straight to al-Hussain. Promises of wealth and a one-way ticket to the US had not been enough to convince him to betray his countrymen. According to Nagi, the CIA's main objective had been the capture of Abdul al-Hussain, renowned Taliban commander. He'd assured the American that while he knew of the man, he wasn't party to his movements, but for the right money he would ask around and pass any information back to them. Since then, there had been repeated requests for updates, but Nagi would simply tell the CIA that he was still working on it. On a couple of occasions al-Hussain had been in the same room with Nagi as he tried to explain over the phone why his efforts had been fruitless, and afterwards they had both laughed about their enemy's desperation.

Nagi felt the American was losing patience, and al-Hussain had seen an opportunity present itself. It would mean sacrificing a few of his men, but willing bodies were easy to come by. Experienced fighters less so, but there were plenty of young men with heads filled with glory who were eager to pick up a rifle and take on the infidel.

So far, al-Hussain had thrown sixty of his followers to the wolves—half of them in the last week. The attack on forward operating base Tork, twenty kilometres west of Kandahar, was never designed to succeed, and in truth it hadn't come close. That was because Nagi, who had been given the operational name Sentinel by his CIA handler, had warned the Americans three days in advance. He'd lost thirty men while the enemy had suffered no casualties, but it had been a success nonetheless. The Americans now trusted their Sentinel, and in time that would prove costly.

The curtains leading to the shop parted and al-Hussain's bodyguard appeared.

'They are here.'

Al-Hussain rose and followed him outside, where a second SUV was parked behind his own. In the back he could see a figure dressed in black from the head down, flanked by two of his men. Al-Hussain climbed into the back of his own vehicle and Nagi took the front passenger seat. The driver was instructed to take them to the wadi—four miles north of town.

From the moment he'd heard about the woman and her virus, al-Hussain had been anxious to try it out. He wouldn't be satisfied with promises or projections, only verified conclusions on his own terms.

At the wadi—a depression in the ground formed by a river centuries earlier—he saw another of his men waiting, along with a boy who looked no more than fifteen years of age. Al-Hussain got out of his SUV and walked over to the vehicle that had followed his. The back door was being held open and he watched as the black figure emerged

The first thing Miriam Dagher did was remove her niqab, revealing her face.

'I'm sorry,' she said in English. 'It's just too hot. It'll take some getting used to.'

Al-Hussain would normally have exploded at such a blasphemous display, but he remained calm. She was returning to the country after forty years in the West, so she could be forgiven for being affected by the weather. He also needed her expertise, so he let it slide. For now.

If she showed any further disrespect for Islam, he would deal with her harshly once her usefulness had come to an end.

'Welcome to Afghanistan,' he said. 'I hope you weren't too inconvenienced by my... precautions.'

'It has been many years since anyone asked me to take my clothes off, but your men kept a respectful distance.'

'I'm sure you understand my position. The Americans are keen to...how do you say... get their hands on me. I would not like to make that job any easier.'

Dagher smiled. 'If they find you, they'll find me, too. Take all the precautions you feel necessary.'

She seemed at ease, not even slightly nervous, and that was a good sign. If she was here under false pretences, he would have expected her to be a little tense. She also looked younger than he'd expected. Al-Hussain knew her to be the same age as himself, but she appeared less worn. Perhaps if he'd spent his life in a laboratory rather than on the battlefield, he might look as youthful.

'Your men told me you wanted to conduct an experiment as soon as possible. I expect that's why we're here.'

'Correct,' al-Hussain said, looking towards the teenager. 'He is to be the subject of your first demonstration.'

'Then if you'll ask your men to bring my belongings we can begin.'

Al-Hussain barked an order as Dagher approached the boy. She performed some visual checks on him, and when the box containing her equipment was placed next to her she removed a stethoscope and listened to his heart and breathing.

'He'll do fine,' she said, turning to al-Hussain. 'First, we need some control information. This will enable you to see the results clearly. Has he ever fired a weapon before?'

Al-Hussain asked the boy in Pashto, and received a shake of the head in reply. He instructed one of his men to give the boy a crash course, including changing the fire selector of the AK-47 from safe to fully automatic or semi-automatic, replacing a magazine and finally lining up a target and firing. Al-Hussain watched the boy fumble with the unfamiliar weapon. He held it as if it was a live snake about to strike, almost dropping it twice. After a few minutes of instruction and practice, al-Hussain pointed out a gnarled tree trunk that was growing out of the wall of the wadi. It was about thirty yards away and as thick as a man's torso. An easy shot.

'What is your name?' al-Hussain asked.

'Irshad.'

'Okay, Irshad. I want you to shoot at that tree on semi-automatic. Off you go.'

The boy adjusted the fire selector, lined up the sights and pulled at the trigger. The rifle bucked in his hands and the round went high and wide.

'That was your sighter. Think about what you've been told. Squeeze the trigger, don't pull it. Try again.'

Irshad had another go, but his effort was just as feeble as the first. Al-Hussain stood behind him and began shouting. 'Again!'

Bang.

'Switch to fully automatic!'

Irshad had to look down at the selector to make sure which setting was the correct one.

'Faster!'

The boy dropped the weapon in his haste to comply. He picked it up and eventually moved the lever to the correct position and aimed once more at the tree. The gun chattered as a dozen rounds left the barrel, then it fell silent as the firing pin fell on an empty chamber.

'New magazine!' al-Hussain shouted. He watched the boy squirm as he tried to remember how to eject the old mag and insert the new one. All the while, al-Hussain barked orders; screaming at him to hurry up and basically making the boy as nervous as he possibly could.

When Irshad eventually dropped the weapon, his hands unable to stop shaking, al-Hussain put a hand on his shoulder. 'Don't worry, I'm not angry. Come, we have something that will make a real soldier of you.'

Irshad rose and followed al-Hussain over to the woman. She was preparing a syringe—drawing a clear liquid from a phial and pushing the plunger to get rid of any excess air.

'Roll up your sleeve,' she instructed him. Irshad did as she suggested, and looked away as she found the vein in his left arm to stick the point of the needle in.

'How long?' al-Hussain asked.

'About fifteen minutes,' Dagher told him.

Al-Hussain took the time to quiz Dagher on her background. He learned that she had been born in Kandahar, not far from their current location. Her parents had taken her to America in 1960 where her father had enjoyed a successful career in medicine at Johns Hopkins hospital in Baltimore. Miriam had followed in his footsteps, but had opted for research rather than surgery.

Dagher gave al-Hussain a breakdown of her discoveries over the years. Two of them he already knew about; these being detailed in the articles he'd found online. He was surprised to learn that she'd been a big part of the team that had developed the meningitis vaccine in the late seventies and the human growth hormone in the eighties. Her latest work was for a US company but after their systems had been hacked by competitors, they had decided to take the research to England. The relocation had been done under complete secrecy which meant she could conduct her work without fear of prying eyes.

It was a credible story, but al-Hussain was more interested in her motivation.

'What made you decide to come to us with the virus?'

Dagher looked over at the distant mountains. 'Did you ever get the feeling that your life was a lie?' Al-Hussain didn't answer. He simply waited for her to continue. 'Up until fifteen years ago, the only truth we knew was the one offered up by the mainstream media. For decades, the talking heads on our television screens told us *what* was happening and *why* it was happening. There was no reason to doubt them. When they told us that the Iraq war in 2003 was all about seizing Saddam Hussein's weapons of mass destruction, who were we to argue? The thought of the Iraqis launching their nuclear weapons at the USA was enough for people to support government actions…but the internet was beginning to change all that.' She took a bottle of water from her bag and emptied half of it in one go. 'Independent news websites started to spring up, and their stories ran contrary to the official narrative. Of course, they were dismissed as conspiracy theorists. But some of their news items made too much sense. Iraq is a prime example. The US claimed to have detailed intelligence regarding the WMDs, yet after a year of searching, nothing has been found. In the meantime, it emerged that Saddam switched from selling his oil in US dollars to euros. He started doing it in 2001, and that threatened the US economy. Until then, all oil had been purchased in dollars. If a country didn't have enough dollars, they had to borrow it from the world bank, incurring dollar interest. Meanwhile, the US could print as many dollars as it wished. The currency had been pegged to gold until the 1970s, but soon after US energy resources began to deplete, and the government struck a secret deal with Saudi Arabia—who accounted for a large slice of their oil imports—to sell in dollars in return for US protection. Since then, the dollar has been pegged to oil, which is the only reason Saddam was toppled.'

She finished off the rest of the water, then let out a sigh. 'A million people died just to prop up a failing economy, and it's going to happen again. Muammar Gaddafi wants to sell oil with a gold-backed dinar, so expect him to be gone in the next couple of years. The US will make up some story about human rights abuses or other such nonsense as the reason for ousting him, while their Saudi friends continue to publicly execute people for being homosexual. The hypocrisy stinks. To answer your question, I'm giving you the virus because America is a country built on lies; a country happy to kill millions of foreigners just to ensure the elite few can continue to rape the economy for their own benefit. They deserve everything coming to them.'

Dagher looked at her watch. 'It's time.'

She walked over to Irshad and checked his signs once more.

'He's all yours,' she declared.

Al-Hussain could see a difference in the boy already. He seemed more confident, his posture more assured. He handed Irshad the rifle and a spare magazine.

'Remember what you were told. See if you can hit the tree now.'

Irshad took a knee. Then he brought the AK-47 up to his shoulder, flicked the selector to semi-automatic and squeezed off a round. It whistled past the tree, but the next shot struck the trunk, as did the one after that.

'That's good,' al-Hussain said. 'Let's try something a little more difficult. Do you see that white rock at the end of the wadi?'

Irshad nodded.

'Okay, that's your new target.'

The stone was nearly two hundred metres away and about the size of a crouched man. A testing shot for a lot of fighters—it would have been well beyond Irshad's capabilities twenty minutes earlier.

The first attempt fell short, but Irshad composed himself and tried again. This time his aim was high, but he nailed it with the third.

Al-Hussain was impressed with the transformation, but the test wasn't over.

'Fully automatic! Fire!'

Irshad peppered the target, and when the magazine ran dry, he nimbly switched it for the spare before al-Hussain had time to prompt him. After chambering a round, he sent a two-second burst toward the target, then reverted to single-shot until the second magazine was empty.

When al-Hussain turned to Dagher, he was grinning from ear to ear. 'That is most impressive,' he said.

'I thought you'd like it.'

'How long does it last?'

Dagher shrugged. 'Basically forever. It was initially designed to be triggered by the hormones released during a woman's labour, but I modified it to be stimulated by increases in adrenaline. Whenever Irshad gets into a fight or flight situation, the virus will kick in, making him calm and focused.'

This news was beyond al-Hussain's dreams, but he reined in his excitement. He'd only just met the woman, and despite her convincing background story and the remarkable display he'd just witnessed, he wasn't about to get carried away. He would wait a few days and see if the virus had any adverse side effects. He would have Irshad brought to him within a week, and if the boy was alive and well, he would be shipped off to the camp in Pakistan for rigorous training, and the next experiment would be conducted.

Five men had already been earmarked for phase two, and he couldn't imagine a sorrier bunch of subjects. They were barely any better than Irshad had been prior to his exposure to the virus, so it would be interesting to see how they performed under battle conditions.

'Come,' he said to Dagher. 'You must be tired after your journey. I have prepared accommodation for you in a nearby town, a walled compound to keep you hidden from curious neighbours. I'm sure the Americans will be doing all they can to get you back, so remain inside as much as you can. If you wish to leave the building, please wear the niqab—otherwise you might be spotted by their drones. I'm afraid I can't allow you to leave the compound without my express permission.'

'I quite understand. Will this place have electricity?' she asked as she massaged the area under her breast.

'It has its own generator, so you should be able to start mass production of the virus immediately.' He noted her discomfort. 'Are you okay? You seem to be in some pain.'

'I'm fine, just an insect bite.' Dagher said. 'I will also need some extra equipment. It would have looked too suspicious if I'd brought everything with me. But the items I require are common enough, even here in Afghanistan.'

'Then prepare a list and give it to Samir. He owns the house and has been instructed to provide you with whatever you need, including privacy. Your work will not be interrupted.'

Dagher nodded a thank you.

'I do have one other task for you.'

Al-Hussain explained what he required, then led Dagher back to her vehicle and watched it drive away. So far, she had been everything he'd been hoping for, but something inside him still dictated caution, and he was prepared to be patient.

For a man who had spent half of his life fighting foreign invaders, another few days was not going to matter.

Chapter 10

Cataloguing Miriam Dagher's belongings didn't take long. She lived alone, and apart from her clothes, make-up, toiletries and cooking utensils, there wasn't much to look through. She had a handful of books, a couple of them cookbooks, the rest on virology.

'Didn't this woman have any kind of life?' Duke asked as he wrote down the name of another heavy tome. He flicked through the pages in case anything had been slipped in between them, but like the rest it was empty. He placed it in the box with the others.

'Would you rather be sorting through a pile of used needles and pizza boxes?'

'Good point,' Duke said. 'You'd just expect a few DVDs or CDs for relaxation. It's like she never switches off.'

'Some people are driven, others plod through life,' Sarah shrugged.

'I guess.'

Sarah wrote down the name, date and supplier of the gas bill and slipped it into a clear plastic evidence pouch, writing

71

the corresponding log number on the front of the bag. She dropped it in a box, then moved on to the next document.

'This proves it wasn't a spur of the moment decision,' she said to Duke. 'It's confirmation of the sale of her property in the US. It went through a couple of weeks ago.'

'How much did she get for it?'

'Just over nine hundred grand. Dollars, of course.'

'Any idea what she did with the money?'

'Not yet.'

Sarah put the completion document aside and leafed through the rest of the papers she'd found in the sideboard drawer.

'Here it is,' she said, holding up a bank statement. 'She received the money in her local NatWest account four days ago. Two days later it was gone, transferred to another account. I'll have to speak to the bank to find out where it was sent.'

Sarah noted down the date and amount of the transaction plus the sort code and account number in her notebook, then bagged the bank statement and logged the details.

She was halfway through cataloguing the next document when her phone rang.

'Keogh.'

'It's Randall. I'm sending a forensics team to relieve you.'

'What? Why? I thought you wanted this to be compartmentalised.'

'It's too late for that. Dagher recorded another video and Al Jazeera have been showing it non-stop for the last half hour. The cat's out of the bag.'

'Shit!'

'Exactly,' Randall said. 'Just drop everything and get back to my office as soon as they arrive. I'm going to be giving a press conference in an hour.'

The phone went dead and Sarah fed Duke the gist of the conversation.

'It's a relief, to be honest,' he said. 'With these things you always worry that if news gets out you'll be the one accused of talking to the press. Now that it's all over the news, we can probably get back to normal duties.'

Sarah had to agree, though she'd enjoyed delving back into some real police work.

They only had to wait ten minutes for the forensics unit to arrive. Sarah showed them what they'd done so far then left it to them, handing over the house keys. She drove Duke back to the station.

'Looks like the shit just hit the fan,' Duke said as they pulled up outside New Scotland Yard. A gaggle of reporters was gathered outside the front entrance, and several news network vans were parked up nearby.

'Let's go in the back way,' Sarah said, before she drove around the building.

Five minutes later they were in Randall's office once more.

'Well, this is a royal pain in the arse,' the commissioner said.

'At least the leak didn't come from inside,' Duke offered. 'The PM can't apportion blame to anyone.'

'There's that,' Randall conceded, 'but who knows what else the press will dig up.'

'If they look hard enough, they'll find out that Dagher sold her house in the US a couple of weeks ago and transferred the funds a couple of days after they hit her bank here in London. Apart from that, we didn't find anything.'

'Where did she send it?' Randall asked.

'We don't know yet. I'll have to go to the bank when it opens in the morning.'

'Okay, but when you have something it stays between us. I'm going to feed the wolves the bare minimum for now. Professor Farmer arrived at Paddington Green an hour ago, and we soon hope to have an idea as to what this virus can do.'

'In the video she claims it'll be a huge boost to the Taliban,' Duke said.

'Yes, Sarah told me. I've already passed that on to the Home Secretary and he said he would keep the MoD informed.' Randall sighed, then stood and adjusted her jacket. 'Okay, let's go face the press.'

Chapter 11

Word of the match-up had spread throughout the camp and by the time Gray and his team arrived there were at least a hundred observers eagerly awaiting the action. They'd formed a large circle around a patch of dirt roughly the size of a boxing ring, and there was a big US contingent, plus the other three four-man teams from 8 Troop. Captain Russell was nowhere to be seen, but Gray had a feeling he would be close by.

Gray went over to the area where the rest of the SAS contingent had gathered.

'Give 'em hell,' Sergeant Bob Jones said as he slapped Gray on the shoulder. 'Fucking yanks need taking down a peg or two.'

'I know,' Gray said, 'but it won't be me doing it.'

'No? Len, then?'

Gray winked at him and smiled. 'Watch and see.'

Balmer emerged from the throng of American soldiers. He turned and waved his arms around, whipping them into a frenzy, then turned again and approached Gray.

'You ready to do this?'

'Sure am,' Gray said. 'Who've you chosen?'

Balmer whistled, and the American ranks parted once more to allow Hank Lomax into the arena. He was shirtless, his vast chest glistening with sweat.

'Fancy your chances?' Balmer asked.

Gray chuckled. 'Against him? No way. But I know a man who does.'

Sonny stepped forward and removed his T-shirt.

It was Balmer's turn to burst out laughing. 'You're kidding. You're pitching Tiny against the bear?'

'If your man wants to back out, now's his chance.'

Balmer shook his head in astonishment. 'It's his funeral. What about the rules?'

'No biting, no gouging, no hitting below the belt,' Gray said.

'You got it.'

Balmer walked over to Lomax and whispered something in his ear, earning a malicious grin from the big man.

'He's gonna fight dirty,' Gray warned Sonny.

'Wouldn't have it any other way.'

Gray patted him on the back and retreated to the British lines.

A roar erupted as the two combatants walked towards each other, Lomax flexing his muscles while Sonny whirled his arms to loosen up.

'You ready to feel some pain, little guy?'

'Bring it on,' Sonny taunted. He danced on the balls of his feet, waiting for Lomax to make the first move.

Gray watched on as Lomax launched his attack, and he was shocked at how quickly the big man moved. Lomax's fist shot towards Sonny's head, but he ducked under the swinging arm and jinked to the right, delivering a punch to the big man's kidney before dancing out of reach. Lomax didn't seem to notice the contact. He faced Sonny once more, took a couple of steps towards him, then lashed out with a leg the size of a tree trunk. Sonny put his arms out to protect his stomach, but it was like trying to stop a moving train. Sonny was lifted off his feet and landed on his back.

'Get up!' Gray shouted, while from the other side of the crude circle shouts of 'Kill him!' and 'Finish him off!' rang out.

Sonny got back to his feet and Gray was glad to see he didn't look injured.

'Should have stayed down,' Lomax said, as he came in for more. He feigned another kick, then pirouetted and caught his opponent with a roundhouse to the head. A mad cheer went up from the American contingent as Sonny crashed to the ground, drowning out the groans from the British side.

While Lomax walked around with his arms raised in victory, Sonny pushed himself onto his knees and shook his head. He got to his feet and brushed the sand from his body, then adopted a boxer's stance and waited for Lomax to come at him once more.

'You've got spunk, I'll give you that,' Lomax said as he paced towards Sonny. He kicked out again with his left, which Sonny blocked easily, then scissor-kicked with his right. Sonny took a step back, anticipating the move, and when Lomax's foot was level with his head, Sonny grabbed his boot and twisted. Lomax had no option but to go with it, and he landed heavily on his back, much to the elation of the British in the crowd.

Lomax bounced back to his feet and started to circle Sonny, looking for an angle. Sonny let him get to his nine o'clock, and Lomax aimed a kick at his lower back. Sonny jumped back—the heavy boot missing his kidneys by millimetres—and as Lomax's impetus spun him around, Sonny pounced. He leapt towards the big man and landed a punch to the side of his face. Lomax stumbled backwards, and Sonny followed up with another strike to the face and a combination to the body. He looked to be gaining the upper hand when Lomax lashed out with a right and caught Sonny high on the head. It wasn't a devastating blow, but enough to knock Sonny off balance, and Lomax sought to push the advantage. He lunged at Sonny, his right arm pulled back to deliver a piledriver. He swung, but Sonny stepped inside and crouched, pushing his body into Lomax's abdomen to make the most of the American's momentum. Lomax rolled over Sonny and landed on his back and Sonny went in for the kill. He jumped and landed on Lomax's chest with one knee, knocking the wind out of the giant, then hit him twice in the face. Sonny wrapped his legs around one of the massive arms and started bending it backwards.

'Yield, or I'll break the fucker.'

Lomax tried to punch Sonny with his free arm, but the way his body was contorted meant he could barely move more than a couple of inches.

'Fuck… you!' Lomax spat, his face going purple as he used all his energy to keep his arm from snapping at the elbow.

'That's enough!'

The crowd was immediately silenced as Captain Russell walked into the ersatz arena.

'Corporal Baines, let him up. That's an order.'

Sonny released his grip and kicked Lomax away, then got to his feet and dusted himself off.

Russell waited to ensure the fight wasn't going to flare up again, then started walking away. 'Master Sergeant Balmer, Sergeant Gray, on me.'

The two men followed the captain as the crowd scattered in different directions.

'Lomax was just about to kick his ass,' Balmer whispered.

'Bollocks,' Gray responded. 'He was lucky the CO came along when he did.'

'That's enough, gentlemen. I call it a draw.'

Russell led them to the American section of the camp, and as they approached the office of Lance Durden, Gray had a sinking feeling.

The last mission he'd been given had been another bust. The packages that had been filmed being unloaded into the small village had gone by the time Gray and his team arrived on the scene, and the old men and women who lived there claimed to know nothing. Balmer, on the other hand, had managed to engage Asadi Mansour and his men, resulting in six confirmed kills—including the main target.

When they entered the office, Gray positioned himself once more near one of the electric fans. Durden was sitting behind his desk with Captain Bridges of Delta Force who was leafing through a folder.

'Gentlemen, we've received word about Miriam Dagher,' Durden told them.

'Let me guess,' Gray said. 'They killed her already.'

'I wish.'

That wasn't what Gray was expecting to hear. 'What do you mean?'

'We got word from home that she was in on the abduction,' Durden said. 'The childbirth virus was a cover for her real work, which was to create something that would enhance the Taliban soldiers... some sort of magical instant training potion. Once infected, a kid who's never even seen a rifle can be transformed into an experienced soldier in a matter of weeks, sometimes even days.'

Gray stole a glance at Balmer, who appeared as shocked as he was.

'How do we know this?' Balmer asked.

'She made a couple of videos; one before she left London, the other soon after her staged kidnapping. The British government has authenticated her claims.'

'What this means,' Russell added as he sat back in his chair, 'is that you can expect to come up against a better prepared enemy in the coming weeks and months. Since we arrived here over a year ago, we've been fighting a war of attrition. We've taken out a lot of their most experienced fighters, but now it looks like they can replace them at will.'

'Is there a cure?' Gray asked, still reeling from the revelation. 'An antidote?'

Bridges shot him a look that had *Dumbass* written all over it. 'Even if there was, you'd have to get close enough to the enemy fighters to administer it intravenously. Might as well shoot them while you have the chance.'

'Do we have any idea how much of this stuff she has?' Balmer asked.

'As yet we don't. It's believed she took a small amount with her, and from what I gather, it wouldn't be too hard to create more in a home laboratory. Let's just assume there's a lot of it out there.'

'What about contamination?'

'It can't be passed from person to person through physical contact,' Durden said, 'and we've been able to rule out airborne transmission. The only way to get it is intravenously.'

'Our priority,' Russell said, taking over from Durden, 'is to find her before she can create enough of the virus to cause us any problems.'

'Any idea where she is?' Gray asked.

'Unknown,' Durden said. 'Sentinel is probing, but he can't push too hard in case it raises suspicion. We'll just have to bide our time.'

'And in the meantime, our men are in the firing line,' Russell pointed out.

Bridges concurred. 'It would be nice to know exactly what this virus could do before sending my men out to face them. Are we talking super-soldiers? Invincible warriors?'

'Nothing like that,' Durden assured him. 'It focuses the mind and enhances memory, allowing training to be conducted over a much shorter time. It also makes them more alert. You men know what it's like in battle; it takes years of experience to remain calm and do your job under heavy fire. While the bad guys are panicking and firing blindly, you're able to remain in control, and that's your advantage. Now imagine injecting that capability into a raw recruit.'

It sounded ominous. Gray had never come up against elite troops; men whose skills were on a par with his own. The Taliban fighters were fierce warriors, all willing to give their lives for what they believed in, but few had what it took to succeed in combat. Now it looked as if the balance of power was shifting in the wrong direction.

'You mentioned before that she was born in Afghanistan. Was she a sleeper agent all this time?'

'It doesn't appear so. In the videos she mentions her growing disdain for the Western governments. I think she just decided to switch sides.' Durden wiped his forehead with his handkerchief. 'Be careful out there. We have no idea how long it'll be before they start testing this thing in the field. It could be tomorrow, or a couple of weeks. Just be prepared.'

Russell took that as his cue to leave, and Gray followed him out the door.

'Unbe-fucking-lievable,' Gray said as they walked back to the British quarter.

'My thoughts exactly, but it doesn't change the fact that the enemy has evolved. As the senior NCO for 8 Troop, I want you to brief the other team leaders. Do it now, before we get our new mission orders.'

Russell broke off towards the coffee stand, and Gray went back to the area where the rest of 8 Troop were stationed.

There were sixteen men in the troop, which consisted of four 4-man patrols, also known as bricks. They rarely operated together, though when they had to they worked as a cohesive unit. Each patrol was led by a sergeant, and Gray gathered them together to give them the shocking news.

Chapter 12

The solitude of the night desert was a great comfort to Saif Ahmadi—always reminding him of more peaceful times. But today wasn't going to be one of them; today was going to be about war. About violence. About death.

By the light of a midnight waning crescent moon, Ahmadi began to dig. The sound of the shovel hitting hard ground seemed to travel for miles, but he knew there was no-one around to hear it. His men were scattered over a wide expanse, looking out for signs of unwanted visitors. They would call him as soon as an enemy patrol was spotted, giving him ample time to reach a hiding place. His biggest concern was the drones that plagued the skies, invisible to the eye, ready to deliver death without warning. That was why he was working underneath a thermal canvas that would hide his body heat from the onboard infrared cameras. It made the work hot and difficult, but it was preferable to having half a ton of ordnance dropped on his head.

Ahmadi stopped digging every minute to take on water, but eventually he had a hole big enough to accommodate the improvised explosive device he'd created. It consisted of four artillery rounds connected with a series of wires which would ultimately be attached to a satellite telephone.

Ahmadi placed the four shells in the hole, making the shape of a cross—the tips of each round facing into the centre. He had already primed them and connected the wires before setting off from his camp, and all that remained was to link the pieces together. Using electrical tape, he bound fresh wire to the pieces sticking out of the shells then twisted all four strands together. He had to constantly pause to wipe the sweat from his hands, and it took a lot longer than expected to have everything in place. The last part of the puzzle was the satellite phone. He dialled the number from his own phone, and seconds later the screen on the detonator phone lit up. He ended the call and turned his phone off, just in case he triggered the device by mistake. Then performed the final step. Once the sat phone was in place, Ahmadi began to carefully fill the hole in. By the time he'd finished, there was still a pile of dirt left over on the plastic sheet he'd brought along. He carefully pulled the corners together and tied them up. He would take the excess soil with him and hide it in the hills overlooking his current location so as not to leave any tell-tale markers.

After covering the darker soil with fine dust from nearby, Ahmadi turned on his torch and admired his handiwork. It was almost perfect. All he needed to do was obliterate any sign that he had been there and the trap would be set.

An hour later Ahmadi was back in the hills, six hundred yards from the IED. Spread out around him and well-hidden were his men; forty young fighters who had trained exclusively in Pakistan for the last two years. This was to be their first engagement with the enemy; their blooding. Most carried AK-47s, but their number included two snipers, one equipped with a Russian-made Dragunov and the other a Barrett M107.

They would lie in position all day long, waiting for the Western forces to take the bait. Later that morning, Abdul al-

Hussain would pass word of a stockpile of anti-aircraft rockets to the Americans via a trusted contact—and this was the only road leading to the fictitious cache. The invaders would no doubt send a drone over to ensure it wasn't a trap, hoping to catch Ahmadi and his men out in the open, but they would be too late. Every one of his soldiers was equipped with a sand-coloured thermal blanket, rendering them invisible to the airborne eyes. And they would remain hidden until word came that the enemy had been sighted. In the meantime, they would eat dry rations and relieve themselves in plastic bags. No-one was to leave their position until the mission was complete.

Ahmadi's spot was around a hundred yards up the slope, giving him a good view of the kill zone and his men below him. He nestled between two large rocks and spread the blanket over them, forming a crude shelter. He used his backpack as a pillow after taking out his worn copy of the Qur'an and clutching it to his chest. It was too dark to read it now, but after he woke, it would provide him with comfort while he waited to do Allah's work.

Chapter 13

Saif Ahmadi scanned the heavens once more, but there was still no sign of any enemy aircraft preceding the expected patrol. Darkness had fallen an hour earlier, so tonight's combat would take place through the green tinge of his night vision glasses.

He looked around the hillside but found it difficult to spot his men who were hunkered down in their positions awaiting the single vehicle that had set out from Kandahar a couple of hours prior. His spotter had confirmed that there were four soldiers aboard, though there was no telling which unit they were with. They could be special forces or plain infantry, but it would make little difference. They wouldn't know about the ambush until it was far too late.

Ahmadi had walked the route the enemy would take, just to ensure his men were invisible from the road, dragging a tree branch behind him to obfuscate his tracks. He needn't have worried. His men were so well hidden that not even the dreaded drones would be able to spot them. There were forty men on the hillside. And they had the advantage of numbers, the high ground and the element of surprise.

The enemy wouldn't stand a chance.

It was approaching midnight when he saw the vehicle in the distance, a plume of dust heralding its arrival. It was still around two miles away, but he was already dialling the number that would trigger the IED buried under the dirt road. It would take a shade under four seconds for the device to go off once he hit the Send button, so timing was crucial. Too late, and the vehicle would pass out of harm's way. It would then come down to hitting a moving target driven by someone alerted to danger, which levelled the odds a little.

Ahmadi's thumb hovered over the button as he studied the approaching target and tried to gauge the speed. The success of the attack was all down to him, now. His men wouldn't open fire until the device exploded, so if it failed to go off, the patrol would escape.

As the enemy reached the hundred-metre mark, it was time to find out if they would live or die.

Saif Ahmadi pressed the button on the satellite phone and began a mental count.

One...two...

It was going to go off too early, he could feel it. He'd misjudged the speed. No, that wasn't it—the vehicle was slowing.

When he reached and passed the count of four with no detonation, his heart sank.

* * *

For sergeant Joshua 'Josh' Miller, the boring part of the patrol was over. Very little usually happened on the heavily-travelled highways, but now that they were off-road and a few miles from their target, it was time to sit up and pay attention.

Like the other three members of the patrol, Miller was looking at the world through his NVGs. The lights of the Land Rover Defender were off, leaving the driver to navigate the dirt road using the artificial light enhanced by the quarter-moon above them.

'Billy, slow down,' Miller told the driver.

To their left was endless desert, while to the right the ground began to rise as they neared the base of a mountain. The mission to locate and destroy the weapons cache would take them into the hills; Miller saw it as the perfect place to set an ambush.

'I don't like it,' he told the rest of the team. In truth, he'd had a bad feeling since the hillside had come into view, but hadn't wanted to say anything in case he sounded jumpy; he didn't want his men thinking he wasn't up to the task.

'I'm with you on that,' Mick Donaldson replied from the back seat. 'Do you want me to scout ahead?'

It was the sensible thing to do, Miller knew. Donaldson could jog along the route and report any signs of the Taliban, if any were indeed in the area. In the meantime, the rest of the patrol would follow a few hundred metres behind him in the Land Rover, ready to provide support if he was engaged by the enemy.

'Sounds like a plan,' Miller said to Donaldson. 'Billy, stop here.'

As the driver eased his foot onto the brake pedal, the ground beneath them erupted. The nose of the vehicle was thrown violently upwards and it flipped onto its back. The trooper manning the .50 machine gun atop the roll bars didn't stand a chance, his body crushed by over 4000lbs of metal.

Before the dust had even settled, Miller was taking stock. Like himself, the driver was hanging upside down, his harness pinning him to his seat.

'Billy, you okay?'

The response was a groan, but that meant he was still alive.

Liquid dripped in front of Miller's face, and he looked up to see that the source was his own feet. Both boots where shredded, and one of them was hanging at an unnatural angle.

'Mick, Simmo, talk to me.'

'Simmo's dead, Josh. We gotta get outta here.'

Donaldson had already dropped out of his harness, and he eased between the roll bars and crawled forward to Miller's side. He mouthed a curse when he saw the state of the sergeant's feet.

'Brace yourself, I'm gonna hit the release.'

Miller put his hands in the dirt as Donaldson undid the catch. The sudden shift in his weight caught him off guard, and his damaged feet struck the dashboard as he fell to the ground. Miller uttered a few of the choicer swear words he knew as Donaldson dragged him free of the vehicle and then handed him his rifle.

'I'm gonna get Billy. Call it in.'

As Donaldson disappeared under the Defender, Miller—through gritted teeth—radioed the base to let them know about their situation. He'd barely told them about the IED when bullets started thudding into the body of the vehicle.

'Contact! Contact!' he yelled into the mic, then threw himself onto his stomach. He crawled to the front of the upturned vehicle and saw dozens of flashes in the hills above him. He answered them with his own rifle, and as he paused to replace his empty magazine, he realised that he was the only one returning fire.

'Mick, what the hell are you playing at?'

When he got no answer, Miller sent a few more rounds into the hills, then crawled back to see exactly what Donaldson was playing at.

The reason he hadn't received a response was because half of Donaldson's head was missing. Miller had seen a similar wound before, when a sniper armed with a .50 Barrett had taken out a Taliban fighter as he was preparing an IED.

Facing such firepower, he knew the battle would soon be over.

The driver, still secured in his harness, moaned again.

'Stay still, Billy.'

He hoped that if the driver appeared to be dead, he wouldn't attract any more fire, but that still left Miller facing impossible odds.

'I need immediate air support,' he shouted into his mic. He had to wait a few seconds for the reply—it wasn't what he wanted to hear.

'Nearest bird is sixteen minutes out.'

Miller knew that he'd be lucky to last another two minutes. By now, the enemy would know that he was the only survivor and would be preparing to flank him. He was trapped—death was a matter of moments away.

Dying wasn't the issue. He felt he'd let his team down by getting too close to the high ground. If only he'd spoken up a few minutes earlier, they'd all still be here.

More incoming fire made him snap out of it. All that remained was to take a few of them out before the reaper came calling.

He dragged Donaldson's headless corpse out from under the vehicle and went through the dead man's pouches, snatching at six magazines and a supply of four hand grenades.

Miller screamed as he flipped himself onto his back; his mangled feet determined to taunt him while he still had breath in his body. When the pain subsided a little, he eased himself up against the body of the stricken Land Rover and waited for the fat lady to begin her solo.

* * *

Saif Ahmadi saw the open-topped vehicle leap into the sky as its front wheels caught the full impact of the blast. He watched it flip as if in slow motion and it was clear that the soldier standing behind the machine gun had taken his last breath.

For some time, the scene was obscured by dust thrown up by the explosion, and he and his men waited patiently for targets to present themselves. When the air finally cleared, Ahmadi could see the driver hanging lifelessly upside down in his seat. That left just two to deal with.

In a bid to get them to reveal their positions, Ahmadi sent a volley into the side of the wreck. His men soon joined in. The response was a burst of fire from the front of the vehicle, so at least one survived the blast.

Then he saw the second, making a foolhardy effort to help the unconscious driver. His sniper had also seen him, because a second later the soldier's head vaporised.

That left one, and Ahmadi wasn't content with putting a few bullets into him. Over the years he'd seen many close friends die at the hands of the invaders, and it was time that he and his men got some payback—up close and personal.

Casting aside his own orders to maintain radio silence, Ahmadi instructed some of his men to surround the vehicle and take the last one alive. It had to be done quickly, because there had been plenty of time to call for help, and those reinforcements would no doubt arrive by air.

Below him, the mountain came alive as half of his men emerged from their hiding places to make their way down the hill and towards the target. The rest covered their advance, sending a hail of bullets into the bodywork of the upturned vehicle.

It wasn't long before a dozen men were within a few metres of the surviving enemy soldier, who was hidden from view by the wreckage.

'Cease fire!' Ahmadi ordered, and the night fell quiet.

'Take him! Now!'

Ahmadi watched as two of his men, who had been crouching at the rear of the ruined Land Rover, stood up and aimed their rifles at the unseen target. Faint shouts reached him as they turned and started to run in the opposite direction. A second later, they were enveloped in a fountain of dust—the small explosion reaching Ahmadi's ears moments later. More detonations followed as the hidden soldier threw grenades over his vehicle. Two more of his men went down before the rest backed off to a safe distance.

'What are you doing?' Ahmadi screamed over the radio. 'Get in there and take him!'

His men regrouped once the explosions stopped. Ahmadi saw one of them point to either end of the wreckage before he slowly climbed on top of it. One man went to the rear of the car and fired a couple of rounds, and when it was answered by a burst from the enemy, the one on top of the wreck grabbed his AK-47 by the barrel and swung it like a golf club.

'We have him!' Ahmadi heard over the airwaves.

'Hurry,' he ordered, and as an afterthought added: 'check the driver.'

There might be some fight left in the one suspended in his harness. Two men carried out his orders, checking for signs of life, then released the man's restraints and dragged him behind them.

'He's alive!'

Ahmadi managed a humourless smile. Allah had truly blessed them this night, and there would be more pleasure to come once they got back to their base.

His men had already picked the wreck clean and, loaded up with weapons, ammunition and the vehicle's radio, they began to climb the hill once more. When they reached the summit, they started the descent down the other side, where their own vehicles had been camouflaged under sand-coloured tarpaulins.

A glance at his watch informed Ahmadi that six minutes had passed since the IED had exploded. Aircraft would be on their way, and he and his men needed to get under cover before they arrived.

He urged his men to hurry, warning of harsh consequences if they were caught out in the open once the helicopters—or worse, the heavily-armed C-130—arrived. Both of these aircraft had infrared cameras to detect heat signatures against the rapidly cooling landscape, and once caught in their crosshairs there was no escape.

Within two minutes, everyone was underneath the huge tarpaulins. They had been erected earlier in the day, and by now they were the same temperature as the surrounding hills. The material, like the personal blankets each man carried, would shield Ahmadi and his soldiers from the prying eyes in the sky. It wasn't long before he heard the sound of rotor blades ripping the night apart, and it felt strangely satisfying to know that he was hiding within spitting distance of the enemy.

The helicopter spent a few minutes overflying the area, then the pitch changed as it climbed and headed southeast towards the border with Pakistan. It was obviously searching for them, but the effort would be in vain. Ahmadi and his men were situated west of the ambush site, and would remain there for the next hour until the search team exhausted its fuel supply and was forced to return to base. He knew from experience that a recovery team would be setting out by road to investigate the attack, but they wouldn't arrive for some time. When they eventually turned up, it would be with adequate air cover, so it was pointless leaving a small team behind to tackle them. That would be a more one-sided encounter than the one he'd just orchestrated. No, the battle had already been won. It was time to melt back into the countryside and get to know their prisoners.

A couple of hours before first light Ahmadi instructed his people to dismantle the overhead covering. The material was split between four trucks, and it was used to cover the two captured soldiers in the flatbed on Ahmadi's Toyota. The group then dispersed; nine vehicles in total on different southerly trajectories. In time they would meet up again near Quetta, and while the enemy were searching for a large attacking force, the individual trucks would be overlooked.

It wouldn't be long before Ahmadi was back in the relative safety of the Chiltan mountains—his prisoners would soon learn the price for daring to set foot on his land.

Chapter 14

'Looks deserted,' Len Smart whispered.

Gray had to agree. Through the green tinge of his NVGs, he couldn't see any movement. It had been like that for the last twenty minutes, and Gray was beginning to believe it was yet another night wasted.

To get to the target house they'd travelled over forty klicks in the chopper, then ridden eight more on the bikes before walking the last two kilometres. The building was believed to be owned by a local Taliban leader—Farzad Shah. And a drone had pictured two vehicles dropping eight men off the previous afternoon. Shah himself hadn't been positively identified, but it was assumed there was a high likelihood he was among them. Gray and his team had been tasked with taking him out.

The house was one of just three buildings that nestled between two mountains. It was three storeys tall while the others looked like they were just used for storage. Probably farm equipment, Gray surmised, judging by the neatly-arranged crops farther up the valley.

'Anything?' Gray whispered into his mic.

The replies from Levine and Sonny were negative.

'Let's give it another half hour,' Gray said over comms. 'If we don't see anything, we'll go and take a look.'

It wasn't like they had any other plans for the evening.

Ten minutes before they were due to give up and call it a day, Sonny's voice came over the air.

'Movement.'

'What you got?' Gray asked.

'One X-ray just came out the back door. Looks like he's heading to one of the outbuildings.'

'Armed?'

'AK,' Sonny said.

Gray acknowledged the report with two clicks of his mic.

'Let's give it twenty minutes, then go in,' Gray suggested to Smart, who nodded his agreement.

Gray passed on instructions to the other two members of the team who were watching the rear of the main building. Sonny was to stay in position, covering them with his suppressed sniper rifle. Levine would make his way to the rear, while Gray and Smart would go in the front way. The signal for Levine to go in was the sound of all hell breaking loose.

Clearing a house was a tricky business at best. Gray would have preferred to look at the blueprints beforehand so that they knew the layout and could assign everyone their role, but in these circumstances that was impossible. They would be going in blind, against an unknown number of threats, with only their exceptional training to fall back on.

As Gray's watch ticked over to a quarter to one in the morning he tapped Smart on the shoulder and began to make his way towards Farzad Shah's house. He dropped to the ground after twenty yards and fixed his rifle on the building while Smart leapfrogged him, then repeated the manoeuvre until they were within a hundred yards of the target. They waited there, scanning the house for signs that they'd been spotted, but it remained shrouded in darkness.

They probably had black curtains to prevent the light from escaping, but that would work both ways. If Gray couldn't see in, they couldn't see out.

'We're a hundred yards out... going in now.'

Levine replied with two clicks, and Gray set off at a fast crouch. When he reached the front door Smart was a second behind him, his shotgun out and ready. Gray stood aside and readied a grenade, then gave Smart the signal to kick things off.

Two *Booms* in quick succession shattered the silence as Smart blew the door off its hinges. He kicked the remains inwards and Gray threw his grenade into the opening. A second later, another thunderous explosion rocked the wall Gray was leaning against. He stepped inside while the sound was still reverberating around the room, and was welcomed by a thick cloud of dust. Gray stepped away from the doorway so as not to present an inviting target just as a volley from deep inside the room flew past his head. Gray answered with a three-round burst, and heard the satisfying sound of screams and a body thudding to the floor.

Smart also opened up, hitting a man who had run into the room with a Kalashnikov up to his shoulder. The man crumpled to the floor without managing to get a shot off.

More AK-47 fire was heard from another room, and Gray knew that Levine had sneaked inside while everyone was pre-occupied with the frontal assault.

Gray indicated a doorway and pulled a grenade from his webbing. Using sign language, he instructed Smart to go in first and take the left. As soon as they heard the explosion, both men piled in. Gray saw a figure on the ground, blood seeping from numerous shrapnel wounds. He put a round in the back of his head to make sure he was out of the fight.

More gunfire erupted from another room, then quickly died away.

'Report,' Gray said into his mic.

'Two down,' Levine replied as he stepped into the hallway.

With the three Gray and Smart had killed, it meant three more were left. Somewhere.

They quickly cleared the remaining rooms on the ground floor, then headed for the stairs.

'Send a grenade up,' Gray whispered to Smart. Then he stepped forward and fired a few rounds towards the top of the stairs.

The big man unhooked one and tossed it up to the landing at the top of the steps. It bounced once, then fired hot metal fragments in all directions. Gray was on his way up before the ricochets had died away, and he saw that only two bad guys remained.

He stepped over the shredded corpse and told Levine to cover the stairs to the top floor. Gray and Smart then headed for the first door on the right just as a figure stepped out of another room and opened fire on them. Bullets pierced the wall next to Gray, but they stopped short when Smart sent three rounds into the Afghan.

One to go.

None of the dead were Farzad Shah, so the main prize still eluded them.

'We've got a runner,' Sonny said over the air. 'Guy climbing out of the rear window, top floor. He's using a rope.'

'It has to be Shah,' Gray replied, running back towards the stairs. 'We need him alive.'

'Roger that. I'll slow him down.'

Gray raced down to the ground floor and out the back of the building just as the last of the Taliban sprinted into the darkness. He was heading for one of the outbuildings, but stopped dead when Sonny put a round into the ground just in front of him. He turned and saw Gray chasing after him, then started running again.

He didn't get far. Sonny was done with warning shots—the next round buried itself in his foot. The man crashed to the ground screaming, and Gray was on him seconds later. After a cursory pat down, he flipped the injured man onto his front and pulled his arms behind his back. By this time Smart and Levine had joined Gray, and between them they applied plastic cuffs and turned him onto his back so that they could do a proper search for weapons. They found only a knife, which Sonny confiscated.

'It's Shah alright,' Smart said. He pulled out a roll of tape and covered Shah's mouth. Then Levine took a black nylon bag from a pocket in his webbing. He put it over the struggling Shah's head and pulled the noose tight.

'Let's get moving,' Gray said. 'They might have called it in.'

Shah cried out as they hoisted him to his feet. He tried to collapse to the ground, but Gray and Smart held an arm each and kept him upright.

'You don't wanna walk, fine.'

They let him go limp, then began to drag him. Shah fought their efforts, and Gray knew it would be a long journey back to the transport if he kept it up.

'Do the honours, Len.'

Smart pulled back his arm and delivered a hammer blow to Shah's temple. The prisoner immediately sagged, and

Smart threw him over his shoulder. Fortunately, Shah wasn't a big man.

Gray reported in, informing Captain Russell they had their prize, but that he needed medical attention. The CO said he would send the bird out to pick them up.

Shah was still out when they reached the vehicles, and Gray cut the plastic cuffs and placed the unconscious man on the back of Sonny's Honda. He then wrapped Shah's arms around Sonny's waist and applied fresh cuffs. It should only take them around twelve minutes to reach the LZ— Gray hoped the prisoner wouldn't wake before they got there. Just in case, Gray let Smart take point and rode at the back so that he could keep an eye on Sonny and his baggage.

They got to the landing zone a few minutes ahead of the chopper. Gray waited until he could hear the sound of the rotors slicing through the night air before cutting Shah's restraints and pulling him off the back of Sonny's bike. The Taliban leader groaned as Gray dumped him on the ground.

The moment the Chinook touched down, Smart and Sonny rode their bikes up the ramp, then ran back to collect Shah while Gray drove his own bike aboard the aircraft. A deck hand took the Honda from him and started to secure it as the ramp began to rise and the chopper lifted into the air.

'Finally got one,' Smart said, wiping his brow with the sleeve of his jacket.

'Maybe it'll be enough to get us a day off,' Sonny said with a resigned smile.

'Dream on. We'll be the golden boys and get every mission going.'

That suited Gray down to the ground. There was nothing to do in camp, anyway—it wasn't as if they could walk into town to enjoy a few cold beers and the delights of the local girls. As the adrenalin from the battle wore off, a wave of fatigue washed over him. All he was interested in right now was a shower and bed.

It was a short flight back to the base, and Captain Russell had arranged for a pair of medics to take Farzad Shah off their hands. The CO himself was there, and he grabbed Gray as soon as he deplaned.

'We've got a major problem.'

Russell wasn't one for histrionics, so Gray knew it must be serious. 'What is it?'

'Josh Miller's patrol got hit about an hour ago. We sent a chopper out when he called it in, but there's no sign of anyone. It looks like one dead, but we need to send a team out to take a look.'

'We're ready to go,' Gray said, his weariness immediately evaporating.

'Good. The other two patrols are still out, so it's just you four. I've readied a Land Rover. It's waiting for you.'

'Give us five minutes to grab some gear,' Gray said, before he ran off to fill the others in.

Three minutes later, they were driving out of the camp gates, their water and ammo replenished and fresh batteries in their NVGs.

No-one said a word during the journey. They all knew that there was little chance of finding anyone alive, and their thoughts were with those who might have been captured. The Taliban were not great advocates of the Geneva Convention, and Gray had heard the horror stories of what happened to soldiers who went missing. Many were found without heads or limbs, and a few were found with their skin flayed from their bodies—presumably while still alive.

'Two minutes,' Smart said as he studied the GPS in his hand.

Usually that signal would have put Gray on alert, but he'd been that way since they left the camp. As they approached the base of the mountain—tall, dark and menacing—a chill came over him.

'Pull over,' Gray said to Sonny, who pressed on the brake.

Gray got out and surveyed the area. As the sun breached the horizon, he could see the outline of Miller's upturned vehicle in the distance, but the rest of the area looked clear.

That didn't mean they were alone.

'Sonny... give us a fifty-yard start, then tail us. Carl, with me.'

Levine got out and set off beside Gray, allowing twenty yards between them. Both had an eye out for threats from the hills as well as underfoot.

Gray took them off-road where there was less likelihood of encountering another IED. He kept a decent pace, but not so fast that he might miss a tell-tale mound or patch of disturbed earth.

When he eventually got to the wreck it was worse than first thought. The body of Mick Donaldson had already attracted a swarm of flies, and another cloud of them was gathered inside the roll cage of the Land Rover. Gray stuck his head inside and saw an arm with a dagger tattoo. Paul Simmons, or Simmo. And from the discolouration, it was clear he'd been dead for some time.

Gray checked the vehicle for booby-traps, then radioed the team in. When he was done with that call he walked around the vehicle while he contacted the CO. On the ground he could see dozens of footprints, as well as blood trails.

'Mick and Simmo are dead. No sign of Josh or Billy. Looks like they were taken away.'

'Roger that. Can you bring the bodies home?'

'Affirmative, but I want to follow the tracks and see if we can catch up with them.'

'That's a negative. I can't risk losing a second brick. Bag 'em up and return to base.'

'But you know what they'll be—'

'I said negative!' Russell said, finality in his tone.

Gray launched a vicious kick at the side of the Land Rover, disturbing the flies. They swarmed around him and he walked away, batting them away as best he could.

There was a strong temptation to disobey the captain's orders and go and find his friends. He'd passed selection at the same time as Josh Miller and aside from being an excellent soldier, he was a top bloke. What really choked Gray was the fact that Josh was married, with a three-year-old daughter. Gray knew Karen Miller well—it was going to break his heart to visit her once he rotated back home. But the CO was right. The Taliban would be long gone by now, and even if they managed to track them they would be heavily outnumbered judging by the number of footprints he'd seen around the vehicle.

'What did Russell say?' Smart asked.

'We grab these two and head home.'

'What about Billy and Josh?' Sonny asked.

'They're gone, and you know it. Let's get to work.'

Gray went back to the Land Rover to fetch the body bags, then rejoined the others. They wrapped Mick Donaldson in his plastic shroud and, together, they pushed the overturned vehicle onto its side and retrieved what was left of Simmo's body. They worked in silence, no-one commenting on the state of the deceased.

Chapter 15

Gray woke from a troubled sleep and looked at his watch. It was just after ten in the morning, barely three hours after he'd hit the sack. But he couldn't face any further dreams.

He got up and threw on a T-shirt and a pair of shorts, then went for a wakeup run.

It was still hard to believe that Josh and his patrol were gone, and in such terrible circumstances, too.

Simmo had been the lucky one. His death would have been instant, whereas the rest of them... it didn't bear thinking about.

Gray tried to put them out of his mind, but part of him wouldn't let go. He hated himself for not trying to track his friends down, for giving up on them so easily. Josh wouldn't have listened to the captain; he would have cut comms and followed the tracks until he either rescued his brothers in arms or died trying.

As Gray began his second circuit, Sonny fell in step.

'Couldn't sleep either?'

Gray shook his head. 'Don't think I will for a long time.'

Sonny looked at his sergeant as they jogged past a row of tents. 'It's not like they were the first dead bodies you've seen.'

'It's not that. We should have looked for them.'

'You'd have been RTU'd the minute we got back to base. We all would.'

Sonny was right. All four of them—had they made it back alive—would have been shipped back to Hereford before being returned to their original units. There was no greater shame for a member of the SAS.

'Besides,' Sonny continued, 'you saw how many footprints there were around that Land Rover. There must have been twenty of them at least. We'd have been well outnumbered.'

'That doesn't change anything. I feel like a real shit.'

'You preserved the life of your men when the alternative was to push a bad position, that's all you did. You can't beat yourself up about it, Tom.'

But Gray knew he would.

After finishing his run, Gray hit the shower, then dressed and went to find food.

After loading his plate with sausage, eggs, chips and beans, he found a table and started tucking in. His thoughts immediately turned to Josh Miller, but before he managed to bury himself in self-recrimination, another tray landed opposite him.

'Mind if I join you?'

Gray looked up to see Balmer's huge frame. He was tempted to tell the American to piss off and leave him to wallow in his own self-pity, but that would have been churlish. And the last thing he wanted to do at that moment was fight. Instead, he pointed towards the empty seat with his fork.

'I heard about your guys,' Balmer said, slicing off a chunk of steak. 'That sucks ass, man.'

Not the most eloquent words of commiseration Gray had ever heard, but they summed up his mood perfectly.

'Thanks,' Gray said, then stuffed half a sausage into his mouth.

'When's the service?'

Gray held up three fingers as he chewed.

Balmer nodded. He put a thick slice of steak in his mouth and they both chewed in silence for a while.

'Is this the first time you've lost men?' Balmer eventually asked.

'As patrol leader, yes. But I lost a couple of mates in Sierra Leone.'

That hadn't been quite the same. It had hurt to lose friends in battle, but they'd died quickly—one with a bullet to the head, the other ripped apart by a grenade.

They hadn't been abandoned.

'Three years ago, I led my team into the White Mountains,' Balmer said. 'Tora Bora. We were told Bin Laden was there, and we wanted to be the ones to catch him. Intel said there were hundreds of fighters protecting the caves, but that estimate was way low. I was in charge of seven men, and I sent two ahead to scout out a trail that looked like it hadn't been used in years. They were maybe a klick ahead of us when the Taliban opened up on them. We ran to their position, but it was too late. We expected a full-on engagement but it was a lightning raid. We found one dead, and the other guy had disappeared. Of course, everyone wanted to go and find him, but I wouldn't let them. We were on their territory and they knew the landscape well. And if I was in their shoes, I would do what I could to suck us in to a trap.'

'What happened to him?' Gray asked.

'We found him five days later. The B-52s had pounded that hill for three days straight, and by the time we made our way inside the network of tunnels there was no-one left alive. What was left of Tarkowski was unrecognisable, so we had no idea what they did to him. I guess that was a blessing.'

Balmer stabbed a carrot with his fork and took a bite. 'I guess what I'm saying is, you've got to see the bigger picture. You probably wanted to hunt them down, but you did the right thing by bringing your men home. There's nothing you could have done.'

'I could have at least tried to get a general direction of travel and call in air support.'

'That's just what they would have wanted. You're lucky they didn't have men waiting for you to show up. No... you did what was best for your team.' Balmer popped the last of the steak into his mouth and stood, picking up his tray. 'Take it easy, Gray.'

* * *

The service for the fallen men took place at three that afternoon. Four coffins draped with the Union Jack—two full, two empty—sat on the dusty ground as the remaining twelve men of 8 Troop, plus the CO, stood to attention in front of them. A chaplain borrowed from the NATO-ISAF contingent was to conduct the proceedings.

As they waited for the clergyman to turn up, Gray spotted Balmer and his men. They were decked out in dress uniforms, and marched past the coffins before standing to attention off to the left of the SAS ranks. Gray looked over and caught Balmer's eye. The American nodded imperceptibly, and Gray returned the gesture.

Moments later, the chaplain arrived. He exchanged whispers briefly with Captain Russell, then launched into his sermon. He spoke of the valour and sacrifice of the fallen, about how their memories would live on forever in the hearts of those touched by their presence

Gray missed most of it. His head was still full of thoughts of Josh and Billy and what they were going through. As much as it hurt, he hoped they were already dead. A quick end was the best they could hope for in their situation, and Gray knew they wouldn't be afraid of death—few members of the regiment ever were. It came with the territory and was something they faced on every mission. If you let it play on your mind you wouldn't be able to do the job, period.

'Our father, who art in heaven, hallowed be thy name...'

Gray found himself mumbling along to the Lord's prayer, but all the while a picture of Josh's wife, Karen, stuck in his head. She would never know the truth about her husband's death, that he was sure of. The official line would be that he was killed in action, a quick end and his body unrecoverable. Telling her the truth would just torture her, just as it was doing right now to him.

He was jerked out of his thoughts as a bugler played the Last Post, and his eyes were watering by the time the last chord echoed around the camp.

Captain Russell saluted the coffins, then turned smartly and dismissed the men. Each in turn went over to the wooden boxes and said their own words before they solemnly walked away, carrying the guilt of the living.

When Gray had said his final goodbyes, Balmer approached him.

'Thanks for coming,' Gray said. 'I appreciate it. We all do.'

'I'd say any time, but I hope we never have to do this again.'

It wasn't something Gray wanted to repeat, either.

'You think Dagher's virus had anything to do with this?' Gray asked in order to break an awkward silence.

'Too soon, I think. But in the coming weeks we can all expect to get acquainted with their super-warriors. Interesting times ahead.'

Gray clapped Balmer on the arm. 'Yeah, well, you be lucky out there.' He walked away, all of a sudden desperate to get back to his dreams.

Chapter 16

A lone cloud hung in the sky, a white cirrus island in a cobalt sea. It passed out of sight as the SUV carrying Abdul al-Hussain left the highway and headed into the desert along a seldom used dirt track. A few minutes later it arrived at the wadi where, a week earlier, the Dagher woman had given her first demonstration of her virus.

The driver parked next to a similar vehicle and al-Hussain got out. Irshad was there, sitting on a rock and sipping from a bottle. He rose as al-Hussain approached.

'Sit,' the Taliban commander said, flapping his hand to reinforce the order. Irshad complied, and al-Hussain took a seat next to him.

Though it had only been a few days since they'd last met, Irshad seemed a different person. The awkward teenager was gone; replaced by a confident young man.

'You're looking well,' al-Hussain noted. 'How have you been feeling?'

Irshad considered his response with a furrowed brow, as if searching for the right word.

'Invincible.'

It wasn't what al-Hussain was expecting to hear, but a pleasing reply nonetheless. 'Oh? Why do you say that?'

'I just… I'm not scared anymore. There is another boy in my village—Aktar—and he belittles me every day. He has been doing it for many years. Mostly it is just name calling to make himself look tough in front of the other children, but when he is in a particularly bad mood he beats me. Sometimes with his fists, but mostly with a stick that he always carries around. He hits me and calls me ugly, saying I will never find a wife because I look like a goat and smell even worse.'

'And you've never fought back?'

'No,' Irshad said. 'He is bigger than me.'

'But you're no longer scared of him?'

'No. Two days ago, as I was walking to the market, Aktar was with a group of boys. They hang around him because they are also afraid of him, but by being in his gang they are given his protection. Sometimes he makes the smaller and younger ones beat me, and if I fight back, Aktar beats me even harder. Anyway, Aktar threw a stone at my head. Normally I would have run away, but this time it was different. Instead of running, I just turned to face him. I felt… powerful. Aktar didn't seem as big any more. In fact, he seemed to shrink with every step he took towards me. He was carrying his stick and grinning as he approached me. Not a happy grin, but one full of evil and malice.'

When Irshad paused, al-Hussain asked what happened next.

'Aktar raised the stick to hit me, but instead of cowering, I lunged for him.' Irshad smiled as he recalled the incident. 'I've never seen such a look of surprise. I hit him with my right fist, then the left, and he fell onto his back. I just remember landing on top of him and hitting him as hard as I could. I don't know how many times I struck him, but when two adults pulled me off him, his face was a bloody mess.'

Al-Hussain had called Irshad to the wadi to see if the boy had suffered any ill effects since being injected with the virus, but this news suggested Dagher's creation was even better than she had described. If it could transform this weakling into a fighter, what could it do to better men?

The Taliban had become a dwindling force in recent years. The enemy were better equipped and had air superiority which had led to many deaths on the side of the defenders. It wasn't the number that was the issue, though. It was the quality. Men who had gained combat experience fighting for the Mujahideen against the Russians in the 80s had been in plentiful supply fifteen years earlier, but now most were gone. Instead, he had to plan attacks that would be carried out by boys who weren't yet old enough to sprout facial hair. Now, though, there was the possibility of a Taliban renaissance. What could he achieve with a hundred like Irshad? A thousand? Ten thousand? The foreign warmongers believed they were in control, but they were about to witness a resurgence they could only have imagined in their worst nightmares.

'What about your health,' al-Hussain asked. 'Have you noticed anything different? Headaches, anything like that?'

'Nothing,' Irshad assured him. 'I just feel better than before.'

Al-Hussain was elated, but tempered his excitement. It had only been a handful of days since Irshad had been infected and there was still a chance that he might develop some adverse reaction. Still, based on what he'd seen so far, he felt it appropriate to move on to the next phase of testing.

First, though, he wanted to see if Irshad had lost any of his newfound prowess.

'Time for some target practice,' al-Hussain said. He instructed his driver to give Irshad an AK-47, then asked the boy to hit the same target.

Irshad accepted the weapon, checked the chamber to ensure the rifle was ready to fire, then took a knee and focused on the white stone two hundred metres down range. Round after round found the mark, even with al-Hussain shouting instructions to try to put him off.

'Automatic fire! Change magazine! Single shot!'

Irshad carried out the instructions flawlessly, much to al-Hussain's delight. To get someone to this level of competence would usually take months of training, and even then the recruit would have to have started with the proper aptitude and temperament.

'You have done remarkably well, Irshad. Do you think you could do the same if it was a person standing in front of your rifle?'

Irshad's mood darkened. 'My father was killed by the American scum. It would be an honor to avenge him.'

'And avenge him you will,' al-Hussain smiled. 'Malik will take you back to the village. Gather what belongings you need and say goodbye to your mother. You are going to Quetta to train with the few elite soldiers we have left. Learn from them. Follow their lead, and you will soon get the vengeance you seek.'

Irshad thanked him and walked to the SUV that had brought him to the wadi. Al-Hussain watched it pull away, then turned to his driver.

'Make the call.'

It would be over an hour before the next visitors arrived, so al-Hussain took a bag from his car and ate a meagre breakfast as he pondered what the future might hold.

Dagher's virus would make a difference, of that there was no doubt, but would it be enough to see off the coalition forces once and for all? On its own, no. To win this war, he needed men who believed in what they were fighting for, and those were in plentiful supply. The British and Americans, by comparison, had no idea why they had been sent halfway around the world to die. It certainly wasn't about freedom, security in the region or the war on terror.

As Dagher had said, it was all about money.

The Afghan president, Hamid Karzai, was nothing more than an American puppet. When the Taliban ruled the country, poppy harvests were almost zero. Anyone caught growing the plants faced immediate death; usually by decapitation. Following the arrival of the Americans, including the CIA, opium production soared. It was now estimated that ninety per cent of the world's heroin supply originated in Afghanistan, with the US profiteering to the tune of $200bn a year.

The opioid wasn't the only thing that attracted the Americans to Afghanistan. Geological surveys indicated that Afghanistan was rich in several valuable minerals. Huge veins of copper, cobalt, gold and iron had been discovered, along with critical industrial materials such as lithium—essential for modern technology to exist. Conservative estimates valued the mineral reserves at over two trillion dollars.

Al-Hussain had seen a recent online article in the *New York Times* that claimed the deposits were 'previously unknown', but he knew that to be a complete lie. The Soviets had discovered the pegmatite fields east of Kabul as early as the 1960s, which contained precious stones including rubies, emeralds, beryllium and kunzites. That was just the tip of the iceberg. Geological reports seen during the Taliban reign confirmed the presence of the precious minerals, and these had been written a couple of decades earlier by American exploration teams. The only reason they were kept out of the media was because the US needed an excuse to overthrow the Afghan government and install one that would give them cheap access to the country's riches.

The events of 9/11 gave them that excuse.

Once their troops landed, Karzai was catapulted into power. He immediately began auctioning off the mining rights and while some went to China, the US was a major beneficiary. Hundreds of thousands of Afghans died so that the Americans could add to their pile.

The sound of an approaching vehicle brought al-Hussain out of his ruminations. The SUV stopped near his own transport and six men got out, including the driver. The five passengers varied from a short stocky man to a stick figure with arms like knotted string.

Al-Hussain was waiting for one more guest to arrive, so he had time to see what they were capable of. They were all part of his local militia, though they were far from the cream of the crop.

A small pile of rocks had been set up a hundred paces down the wadi, and al-Hussain watched as one by one they expended their ammunition while his driver screamed instructions at them. It was vital to see how they coped under pressure. The answer was *poorly*. Not one of them got close to the target, which left plenty of room for improvement.

Al-Hussain was doling out more ammunition when the car carrying Miriam Dagher pulled up. She emerged covered from head to toe in black, and this time she removed just her face veil rather than abandoning the niqab. He was pleased that she was at last respecting the religion. Dagher had obviously grown used to the heat after a week in country.

'Your patients await,' he smiled, gesturing towards five men who were inserting bullets into magazines.

Dagher carried a medical bag over to them and checked each man's vitals. She declared one of them to have extreme hypertension, but al-Hussain insisted she continue.

'If these experiments are successful,' he said, 'we will soon infect every soldier we can get our hands on. I'd like to know what effect it will have on those with high blood pressure. If he reacts badly, then we will need to screen everyone in future... but if he is fine, it will save us a lot of time.'

'Whatever you say.' Dagher prepared a syringe and applied a rubber tourniquet to the first subject's bicep. She located the vein, then injected him with the clear liquid. Once the other four were dealt with she retreated into the air-conditioned SUV.

Al-Hussain climbed in beside her. 'Any regrets?' he asked.

'Only that it took me so long to see America for what it really is; a slave nation ruled by unseen masters. For so long, I lived under the illusion of choice, but it was all a fabrication. They decide which crops we can grow, what food we can eat, how our children will be educated. Even elections are a sham. No matter which side wins, there's always someone in the background pulling their strings.'

Dagher looked down at her hands. 'I chose to forsake Allah in search of fame and material gain. I hope he can forgive me.'

'He already has,' al-Hussain told her. 'He gave you the gift of knowledge, and you have used it wisely. Perhaps it was his plan that you should experience the corruption in the West so that our victory will be all the sweeter.'

'Perhaps,' Dagher conceded.

Al-Hussain asked how preparation of the virus was progressing.

'A little slower than I anticipated,' Dagher admitted. 'If I had proper facilities I could create it a lot quicker. I have enough for about five hundred doses, but it took four days to get all the equipment I needed and to set it all up. Now that everything is in place, I should be able to create around six hundred doses a day.'

A quick calculation and al-Hussain knew he would have enough for ten thousand recruits in just over two weeks' time. With that kind of army at his disposal, it would level the odds considerably. The Taliban would no longer be David to the West's Goliath. Instead, battles would be fought on an even footing. For too long, his men had gone into battle as lambs to the slaughter, but with Allah's deliverance, they would become the wolves—the Americans would be their prey.

But only if the virus worked its magic on the battlefield.

'Let's see if it transforms these five as it did Irshad,' al-Hussain said as he got out of the SUV.

The guinea pigs were waiting, and Dagher checked them over.

'This one's blood pressure is still high, but it hasn't increased since I administered the dose. He should be fine.'

'We'll see,' al-Hussain said.

He put the men through their paces once more and, as with Irshad the week before, their performance was much improved. Once the test was over, al-Hussain instructed them to return to their town and not speak a word to anyone about what had happened that morning.

'If I hear even the smallest rumour you will all be executed, as will your families. Do you understand?'

All nodded solemnly.

'Good. It will soon be time to show your worth on the battlefield. *Inshallah*, you will live to tell the tale.'

The men returned to their vehicle and were driven away. Dagher was also in her SUV, and al-Hussain opened her door and enjoyed the cool hit of air-conditioning.

'I'm grateful for your efforts so far,' he told her. 'There will be a field test in the next few days and if that is successful we will roll out the virus to all of our soldiers. Please ensure you have at least three thousand doses ready for transportation by the end of the week. You will be travelling for a few days, so please pack any personal belongings you need.'

Dagher promised to meet his requirements, and al-Hussain closed the door and returned to his own vehicle.

The journey back to his home took forty minutes and when he stepped out of the car he saw Farhad Nagi sitting at an outside table, enjoying the first apricots of the harvest.

'How did it go?' Sentinel asked as al-Hussain took a seat and inspected one of the fruits of his labour.

'As well as I could have hoped for. We'll know more once we test them under battle conditions.'

'When will that be?'

'Soon. I want you to tell your CIA handler that an arms shipment will be crossing the border in four days' time. They will send out an ambush team the day before, but my men will already be waiting for them. I am sending them out this evening. You're familiar with the pass at Jebbel al-Jabr?'

'I am,' Sentinel confirmed.

'I want you to go with them. There is a cave overlooking the pass. From there you will observe the confrontation and then let me know how the men handled themselves. I'm not concerned with how many they kill; I just need to know if they fight like true soldiers. They should be focused, disciplined. If you see any sign of panic, I want to know about it.'

'I will travel to the cave today, before your men arrive. If they know that I am watching, it might influence their behaviour. It is better if they do not know that I am there.'

'You are wise beyond your years, Farhad.'

Al-Hussain called his son over and told him to prepare a bag of fruit for his guest.

'The next time I see you, I hope it is with favourable news.'

When Nagi left to pass the information to the Americans, al-Hussain allowed himself the luxury of daydreaming about the battles that lay ahead. In the next few days he would know the virus's true potential, but even now he could feel the tide turning in his favour.

Chapter 17

John Balmer had just returned from PT when Captain Bridges stuck his head inside the hut and yelled his name.

'Sir.'

'Durden's office, five minutes.'

The master sergeant quickly dried the sweat from his body and threw on some fatigues before he double-timed it over to the CIA quarters. When Bridges said five minutes, it meant two.

A new sheen had broken out on Balmer's forehead by the time he arrived though he was relieved by the numerous fans Durden constantly had spinning. He found a spot on the edge of a breeze and flicked off a salute. Bridges returned it and told him to stand at ease.

'We've got a job for you,' Durden said to Balmer. 'An arms shipment is coming over the border from Pakistan in four days' time. I want you to take a team to intercept it.'

'What are we talking? A couple of AKs on a mule, or a fleet of trucks?'

'We know that it's big,' Durden told him, 'but we don't have specifics.'

That was enough to put Balmer on edge; only weak intel could be so vague. Most of his missions had been based on credible evidence from drones or the manned surveillance aircraft that roamed the skies over Afghanistan. This must

121

have been humint—human intelligence—which meant one of Durden's snitches. It was this kind of intel that had led to Josh Miller's patrol being wiped out, and Tom Gray's team had spent many wasted nights in the wilderness chasing shadows due to poor information.

'What's the source?' Balmer asked, although he already knew the answer.

'Sentinel,' Durden said.

'The same guy who told you about the attack on FOB Tork?'

'That's him.'

That gave Balmer a little reassurance, but not total confidence. The guy had been right before, but it didn't mean he would be on the money every time. And while Durden might trust his informer, it didn't mean Balmer had to. He was wary before any mission, but more so since the SAS patrol had stumbled into a trap. If he was going to avoid a similar fate, he had to be proactive.

'What route are they expected to take?'

Durden got up and walked over to a large map pinned to the wall. He pointed to a spot on the Afghan-Pakistan border. 'Here, at the Jebbel al-Jabr pass—about forty-five klicks south of the Angoor Ada border crossing. The ultimate destination is unknown, but it's believed to be a cache within five klicks of the border.'

'So our only option is to take them at the crossing in the mountains,' Balmer said. 'Does it smell like an ambush to anyone else, or just me?'

'I see your point,' Durden said, 'but you have to appreciate that Sentinel isn't at the top of the tree. He can only pass on the information he's able to gather.'

Or that's fed to him, Balmer thought.

Durden's problem was that he thought money was the be-all and end-all. Throw a few grand at some poor soul and hope he rats on his family, friends and neighbours. Balmer knew it wasn't as easy as that. He had studied the local culture intensely, and he understood that loyalty and religion were the cornerstones of the Afghan ethos. While there might be a few willing to abandon those principles in the pursuit of material gain, they were by far the exceptions.

'Just to be sure, I'd like to set out early. If they are planning a trap, we'll be there when they show.'

'I concur,' Bridges said. 'Take seven men tomorrow night. That'll give you plenty of time to dig in.'

Two nights camped out in the mountains wasn't Balmer's idea of fun, but it beat walking into a barrage of lead. He took down the co-ordinates of the crossing point, then asked about transport.

'I'll arrange for a chopper to drop you off seven klicks from the base of the mountain.'

That meant ten kilometres on foot, the last three uphill. Just a Sunday stroll for Balmer and his men.

Once he had all the information he needed to brief his men, Balmer made to leave. But when he reached the door, he paused and turned back.

'Any news on the Dagher woman?' he asked Durden.

'Not yet. Sentinel is still working on it.'

'But when do we expect her virus to be in play? Any day now? A few weeks?'

'I expect it'll be soon,' Durden said. 'If it works as she predicts it will, they'll want to test it out as soon as possible.'

Balmer sucked on his lips.

'That's just what I was thinking,' he said.

* * *

When the crew chief gave the two-minute warning, Balmer picked up his pack and threw it on. It weighed close to eighty pounds and had enough supplies to see him through the next two nights out in the open. They would be tucking into nothing but MREs—meals ready to eat—but had prepared for it by taking double portions at chow time. It had added a few pounds to their frames, but they would burn that off in no time.

'One minute!'

Balmer checked the chamber on his weapon and pulled down his NVGs before he and the seven other men from the Operational Detachment Alpha descended the ramp. The moment the bird touched down he was out, running at a crouch for twenty yards before throwing himself to the ground and sweeping the horizon. Behind him he heard the pitch of the rotors change as the helicopter climbed rapidly into the night.

He waited until silence fell once more, then radioed his team members. All reported in—none had enemy sightings to report. Balmer ordered Lomax to take the lead, and they followed in single file, leaving twenty yards between each man. After a quick course check, the big man set off.

Lomax set a moderate pace, but by the time they reached the base of the mountains, most of the team were already blowing hard. Balmer allowed them a five-minute rest as he shed his load and checked out the surrounding hills.

It all looked quiet, but then the Taliban were hardly likely to advertise their presence.

Having studied a map of the area in detail prior to setting off, Balmer knew the scale of the climb ahead. Several trails had been worn into the mountain over the years, but he was keen to avoid them, preferring to cover the rocky ground where it was harder to lay mines.

After taking a bearing to the spot where they would set up camp, Balmer picked up his pack and threw it on again. 'Let's go... Liebowitz, you take point. We're heading for the base of that outcrop.'

Liebowitz nodded and set off. Balmer gave him a small head start, then followed.

It was hard going. The lower slope of the mountain was a soft shale that sapped the strength from Balmer's legs, and by the time they got to the rockier part he was drenched with sweat. They still had a couple of kilometres to climb to reach the summit, but time wasn't pressing on them. Balmer gave them another rest.

He was in the middle of drinking from his water bottle when the mountain erupted in small arms fire. The canteen jumped from his hand as a round struck it—Balmer ducked behind a boulder and brought his rifle up. Through his NVGs he could see muzzle flashes from higher up the mountain—roughly two hundred yards from his position. He answered back just as the rest of his team opened up, firing three-round bursts up the slope.

The incoming fire was as precise as he'd ever come across, and the enemy fighters weren't wasting ammunition as they usually did. None of them were spraying and praying, but sending short, accurate bursts Balmer's way. These were seasoned professionals holding the high ground, and they had his men pinned down. Retreat was impossible, and pushing forward would be suicidal.

'Jacobs! We need air support!'

More bullets pinged off the rock Balmer was using for cover. He heard Jacobs scream instructions into the radio as the enemy fire intensified, but the sound was drowned out as an explosion shook the ground. Shale was thrown into the air and came down in a thunderous rain.

'Twelve minutes!' Jacobs shouted.

We'll be lucky to last two, Balmer thought as he sent more rounds up the mountain. His reservations about the mission were now justified, and he cursed himself for not demanding air support from the start. If a plane had been in the sky from the moment the chopper touched down in the desert, the fight would be over by now.

He spotted a figure breaking ranks and climbing slowly down the hill to his right.

'They're trying to flank us!' Balmer snapped off a three-round burst and watched the enemy fighter fall, but another was soon heading in the same direction. Balmer was just taking aim when another grenade detonated just yards from him.

'Harper's hit!'

'How bad?' Balmer shouted back.

'I'm okay,' Harper responded, though Balmer could hear the strain in his voice.

Harper was as tough as old boots—they all were—so his wound must be pretty serious. Whatever it was, it would have to wait until the battle was over.

Balmer returned his attention to the guy who had tried to get down their left flank, and took him out with his second burst. But it wasn't enough to deter the attackers. Two more men started down the same route, while the grenade attacks became more frequent. If they were going to get out of this, Balmer knew he had to go on the offensive.

'Lomax, I'm going right. Cover me.'

Balmer chambered a round in his underslung M203, then took two smoke grenades from his webbing. He pulled the pins and tossed them in the direction he was about to move in before firing the grenade launcher. The projectile arced into the air and came down above the dug-in Taliban, but it was enough to give him a couple of seconds of breathing space. He ran to his right while the rest of the team laid down suppressing fire, then threw himself behind a rock to gather his bearings.

The two Taliban were still making their way down the mountain, and Balmer picked them off before edging farther right and beginning his climb. He immediately came under heavy fire, and had no alternative but to hunker down behind a rock and mount a lone defence.

'How long on the air support?' he shouted into his throat mic.

'Nine minutes.'

Fuck!

'Tell Hubble to keep an eye on the left flank. We can't let these bastards get around us.'

More smoke grenades exploded, throwing a thick grey blanket over the battlefield, but they hadn't come from his men. Balmer knew it had to be a prelude to an attack. The enemy would be advancing on his position at this very moment, probably hoping to neutralise the threat of air cover by being up close.

'Hit 'em with the 203s,' Balmer shouted into the radio. 'One hundred and seventy yards.'

Moments later he heard the *crump* of the first grenade firing, followed shortly by the explosion. Balmer added his own rounds into the mix, and was rewarded with the sound of enemy screaming. His guess had been right, but whether the barrage was enough to deter the Taliban remained to be seen. Until the smoke cleared, all they could do was keep firing blindly in the hope of hitting targets.

'Bring it in, a hundred and fifty yards!'

More shells shot into the sky, falling onto the rocks and lighting up the night. There were no cries this time, so Balmer told his men to hold off on the grenades. Rounds continued to pour down from above, but the smoke worked both ways, and the incoming fire was now ineffective.

Balmer wanted to move his men, but options were limited. To retreat meant relinquishing cover, and advancing would put them within spitting distance of the enemy—not good if they planned to call in an air strike.

Before he could make a decision, the smoke began to clear and the Taliban once again laid down intense and accurate fire. A scream erupted from farther along the lines, and Hubble reported that Johnson had been hit in the shoulder. Not a life-threatening wound, but it meant they were another man down.

Balmer found a target and put a burst into the enemy soldier's chest, then ducked back behind cover as more bullets flew his way.

'Jacobs, how long?'

Balmer fired at another Taliban target as he waited the reply.

'Six minutes!'

It didn't sound like much, but it was plenty of time for the enemy to get in close enough to ruin his day.

More smoke grenades popped seventy yards from the Delta Force lines, signalling another Taliban advance. If they carried on like this, they'd be on top of Balmer's men before the cavalry arrived.

You wanna get up close and personal? Fine by me!

'Move up, now!'

Balmer was already advancing when he gave the order, flitting from rock to rock as he sprinted up the hill. From the corner of his eye he could see the huge silhouette of Lomax making short work of the terrain, leaping up the incline like a gazelle. Five yards from the dissipating line of smoke, they both stopped. The remaining active members of the team were close behind them.

Between the spurts of automatic rifle fire, Balmer caught the sound of loose pebbles being crunched underfoot. The Taliban were closing, fast. He hunkered down behind a rock and swapped his magazine for a full one, then aimed up the hill as the last of the smoke curled away in a gentle breeze.

The enemy were a lot closer than Balmer had envisaged. They were still advancing when the smokescreen cleared, making them easy targets. Balmer opened fire, and his men joined in. Fifteen of the enemy fighters fell within seconds— easy targets at just thirty yards. The remaining handful dived for cover.

'Cover me!'

Balmer broke away and ran forward as the others laid down suppressing fire. A head appeared over a rock twenty yards from Balmer but before he could take aim one of his team mates blew a hole in it. Balmer jogged on, getting level with the last of the Taliban. He shot one through the side of the head as he cowered in a small depression, then sought out another kill.

The moment he turned he was punched in the chest and thrown onto his back by an invisible force. He knew immediately that he'd been shot, and his hands went to his rib cage in search of blood. They came up clean. The Kevlar in his jacket had served its purpose—and not for the first time—which left him still in the fight. He spun onto his front just as his assailant was fumbling with a new magazine.

Balmer put an end to his struggles.

'One minute out!' Jacobs announced, but Balmer knew the plane had arrived too late to make a difference. There were only three Taliban left, and while half of his men kept them pinned down, the others crept closer until, inevitably, the battlefield fell silent.

'Call them off before the tardy fuckers mistake us for the bad guys,' Balmer told Jacobs. 'And call in transport.'

After assigning two men to take care of their wounded, Balmer began the task of ensuring there were no fakers among the dead. He went from body to body, kicking them to elicit a reaction, but all had been sent to their maker. What he did notice was that none of them were the veterans he'd imagined they were during the onslaught. These were… kids. A few might have been in their twenties, but most looked like teenagers. To have fought so well meant only one thing.

Balmer took out his spare canteen and drank the contents, then called Lomax over.

'Give me a hand with this one.'

He instructed Lomax to hold the dead kid up by his feet, then crouched down and put the canteen up against the corpse's neck before making a small incision. Once a small amount of blood had trickled into the flask, he screwed the lid back on and told Lomax to drop him.

'Looks like the virus is in play,' Balmer told Lomax. 'There's no way these guys learned to fight that well in a training camp. I'll take this back to camp and have the captain analyse it.'

The big Texan spat on the ground. 'What concerns me more is that the fuckers knew we were coming. I think Durden's mole is playing us.'

Alan McDermott

Chapter 18

From his vantage point five hundred yards north-west of the ambush site, Farhad Nagi observed the virus in action for the first time. He was shielded from the skies by an overhanging rock, lying underneath a thermal blanket dyed the same colour as the surrounding landscape. It provided the perfect camouflage. Through green-tinted binoculars, he watched the battle unfold.

It started off badly. The young men were patient as the enemy patrol approached, and when the distance closed to within four hundred yards, he willed the leader of the group to open fire while the targets were stuck out in the open.

It didn't happen. Instead, they let the Americans get close to the cover of rocks before they decided to engage them.

A fatal mistake.

What the boys lacked in tactical knowledge, they more than made up for in aggression and determination. Their weapons handling and discipline was exceptional for such novices; they didn't waste ammunition. And the use of smoke to advance on the Americans was also a smart move. But in the end it was all for nothing. They did manage to

132

inflict a couple of injuries, but from what Nagi could see, none were serious.

It was a pity that they hadn't managed to secure at least one kill, but that wasn't the purpose of the exercise. Nagi had witnessed some heroic actions, tactical discipline—for the most part—and resolution from a bunch of boys who just a couple of weeks earlier had never even seen a rifle, never mind taken on some of the finest soldiers the West had to offer. All in all, it was a pleasing demonstration of the Dagher woman's gift.

He was keen to report back to Abdul al-Hussain, though he would have to remain in position until the Americans were clear of the area.

Twenty minutes after all the gun fire had stalled, a helicopter came to whisk the enemy away, and he waited until the thudding of rotors faded into the distance before creeping out from his cover. He did so slowly, moving like a sloth with the thermal blanket still on his back. He expected the enemy to leave a drone high in the sky to monitor those who came to claim the dead, and the last thing he wanted was to be caught in its sights.

It took three hours to crawl a kilometre to the east, which he considered to be well outside the scope of view of any airborne cameras. He finally stood, but still moved deliberately as he walked towards the lower slopes of the mountain. Once he reached the desert floor, he knew it was just another two kilometres to the wadi. That's where he'd hidden his motorcycle.

When he finally threw his weary leg over the machine, Nagi wished he had a faster mode of transport. He couldn't wait to tell al-Hussain what he'd seen.

It was almost lunchtime when he arrived at the market. He parked the bike outside a café and went inside, ordering a tea and glass of water. He was an hour early for his pre-arranged meeting with al-Hussain, and spent that time reading a newspaper provided by the owner.

Nagi was on his third tea when al-Hussain appeared. They were both immediately shown into a back room, and the owner promised to bring refreshments before leaving them alone.

'How did it go?' al-Hussain asked.

'Beyond our wildest expectations,' Sentinel grinned. 'Our boys fought courageously to the very end, and they acted like seasoned professionals throughout. I had only one negative observation to make.'

'Which was?'

'If they had engaged the enemy sooner, the outcome might have been more favourable.'

Nagi explained how the fighters had let the Americans get too close before launching their attack. 'If they had opened fire at four hundred yards, we would be celebrating a great victory. As it is, the Americans were able to find cover and launch a counterattack. It was... devastating.'

Abdul al-Hussain held up a hand as the door opened and the café proprietor brought in a tray of drinks and some finger food. He waited until the man had disappeared again before responding.

'How many of our men survived?'

'None,' Nagi said, tearing off a piece of flatbread and popping it in his mouth.

The news didn't seem to faze the warlord, his face remaining impassive.

'That is unfortunate.'

Nagi nodded his agreement. 'With a little further training, they might have been victorious. It is just a shame that this virus doesn't give them added intelligence. They followed the combat manoeuvres exactly as they had been shown, it was just that the decision-making was lacking.'

'I will ensure that is addressed,' al-Hussain promised. 'And speaking of which… you need to contact your CIA handler.'

'Of course. What should I tell him?'

'That fifty men will attack forward operating base Vincent in three days' time.'

'And will they?' Nagi asked. 'I'm sure I am getting very close to losing the American's trust. Leading his men into one trap is something I can explain away, but two in a row? At the very least it would put an end to our relationship.'

'Fear not. The attack will take place at two o'clock on Saturday morning. It has been planned for some time. The men who will launch the assault have been training hard these last few days, and I will send one of my most experienced soldiers to lead them.'

Nagi took a sip of tea. 'If they fight half as well as our men did last night, then a great victory awaits us.'

'*Inshallah.*'

* * *

John Balmer stormed into Durden's office without knocking. The CIA operative didn't flinch as the door slammed against the wall, then bounced back to softly click closed.

'What the fuck is Sentinel playing at?'

'I wish I knew,' Durden said, gesturing for Balmer to take a seat.

The master sergeant remained standing. 'What the hell does that mean? You're supposed to be running this guy. Are you telling me you don't trust him?'

'No intel is ever going to be a hundred per cent accurate,' Durden said. 'We act on what we consider to be reliable. And up to now, Sentinel has delivered.'

'Yeah, that fucker just delivered two of my men to the hospital!'

'So I heard,' Durden grimaced. 'How are they doing?'

'They'll live. Tell me, the SAS patrol that got hit…. did that intel come from Sentinel?'

Durden shifted in his seat and the look on his face answered Balmer's question for him.

'You mean he caused the death of four good men, and you still believe he's on our side?'

'There's no proof that he lied to us,' Durden said defensively. 'There wasn't enough information available to prove that it was an ambush.'

'You're telling me the patrol tripped an IED and there just happened to be twenty Taliban cruising by? Are you fucking serious?'

'Stranger things have happened. I have to make judgement calls, and perhaps I might have got this one wrong.'

'Might have?' Balmer growled, furious with the civilian. One thing he despised was people who were happy to sit behind a desk and send his men into harm's way. The officers did it, but at least many of them had seen action themselves. They wouldn't take unnecessary risks with the lives of the soldiers under their command.

Durden raised his hands. 'Okay, I made a bad call. But if it had been a genuine shipment and we let the weapons fall into the hands of the Taliban, many more could have been killed as a result. I was just looking at the bigger picture.'

'Well, picture this: you leaning over that desk while Sentinel is fucking you in the ass! Because that's what I see!'

'Not anymore,' Durden said. 'I won't know for sure until I speak to him, but if he hasn't got a damn fine excuse, he's out.'

'Out as in he walks away?'

'Give me credit. If he *is* playing us and we let him get away with it, we'll have hundreds of them knocking on the door offering to sell themselves. No, we'd need to make an example of him.'

'If it comes to that,' Balmer said, 'I'm your man.'

'Yours was the second name that came into my head. The Brits deserve first crack.'

Balmer couldn't argue with that. While his team had suffered two relatively minor injuries, the SAS had lost an entire patrol, with two of their men still unaccounted for. It was only right that they should be the ones to give Sentinel what was coming to him.

'So, tell me about the ambush,' Durden said. 'Captain Bridges gave me a brief heads-up, but no details.'

Some of Balmer's anger had dissipated at the thought of Sentinel getting what he deserved, but he was still a little pissed at Durden for not being more diligent.

'We counted thirty—all of them early twenties or younger. But they fought like pros. I think Dagher's virus is in play. We brought back a blood sample, just to be sure. It's with the Captain.'

'Good work,' Durden told him. 'If we can confirm that suspicion, I'll need you to give us a full briefing.'

'I'll have something prepared by—'

Durden's phone rang, cutting Balmer short.

'Durden... aha... yeah... no... okay, but not over the phone. We have to meet. The same place as last time. Two hours.'

He ended the call and looked at Balmer. 'Speak of the devil. Sentinel has news about an attack planned for this weekend. I'm going to see him.'

Balmer puffed a smarmy laugh from his nostrils.

'I'll inform Gray. He can go with you, or tag along close behind.'

'No need. We're not going to get this done today. Don't worry. If he's not on the level, he'll pay for it.'

Chapter 19

The nearby village of Karz was bristling with a mixture of US and Afghan troops, giving Lance Durden a little comfort about being beyond the safety of the camp gates. Although he'd been in country for some time—since before 9/11 and the start of the war on terror—he wasn't naïve enough to believe that he wouldn't be a valuable target for the local warlords. A couple of years earlier he would have walked these streets without fear. But following the Western invasion he might as well have painted a target on his forehead. In recent months he'd mainly restricted himself to camp, but this wasn't something he could do over the phone.

He told the private behind the wheel to park the pool car by the kerb opposite a grain store and then walked thirty yards down the street to the café. By the time he got inside, his cotton shirt was forming wet patches.

Sentinel was already waiting.

'Can I get you anything?' Farhad Nagi asked.

Durden sat down opposite him and shook his head. 'What the hell happened last night? I almost lost eight men.'

He took out a handkerchief and wiped moisture from the back of his neck.

'So I heard. Abdul al-Hussain is also aggrieved.'

'He is?' Durden looked surprised. 'Why?'

'He was anticipating a rival crossing into Pakistan to tie up an arms deal. Al-Hussain had put his men there to intercept him. Instead, your men turned up. In the darkness they must have been mistaken for the warlord and his entourage.'

'That explains the encounter they had. They thought they'd been led into a trap.'

'No, no,' Nagi said, emphasising his words with extravagant hand gestures, 'they just wandered into the wrong area. I personally had no idea that al-Hussain was planning to hit his competitor. If I did, I would have warned you to avoid that route.'

Durden studied Sentinel's face and saw deceit etched all over it.

'In that case, you wouldn't mind me looking at your phone for a moment.'

'My phone?' Nagi asked. 'What...What for?'

'I'd like to download the text message logs to study back at base. Just to convince my superiors that you're playing straight with us.'

Sentinel sat back in his chair and smiled as he reached into his pocket for his cell. Then he handed it over to Durden. 'Of course.'

Durden took out a memory card and inserted it into the Siemens SL45. He already knew the phone's make and model, having seen it at a previous meeting and had brought along a multimedia card that would fit. Once inserted, he clicked a few buttons, occasionally gazing up at Sentinel.

After a couple of minutes he removed the card and handed the phone back.

'I'll have the messages translated and analysed. If they tell me you're being less than honest, there will be consequences.'

Nagi put his hand on his heart. 'As Allah is my witness, I have always been truthful with you.'

Durden stared at him for a few moments, then sat back in his chair and offered a thin smile. 'Okay, I believe you. So what's the information you desperately wanted to pass to me?'

Nagi looked around the room, then leaned in closer. Durden couldn't help thinking Nagi had watched too many spy movies.

'There will be an attack on forward operating base Vincent this Saturday. Two o'clock in the morning. At least fifty heavily-armed fighters will be sent.'

That was music to Durden's ears. If the intel had meant sending men out into the wilderness, Durden would have dismissed it out of hand. All this would entail, though, was a reassigning of resources; a few extra men to repel the attack, perhaps the beefing-up of the base's structural defences. If the attack didn't come it would cement Sentinel's fate, but if the informer was being truthful, then he would actually save lives.

'Who exactly will be carrying out the attack?' Durden asked.

Sentinel looked confused. 'You want the names of the fighters?'

'No, I just want to know if these are seasoned veterans, or if al-Hussain has brought people in from outside…or maybe he's going to throw a lot of kids at us again. The more information I have, the better we can prepare.'

'Ah. That, I do not know. When Abdul was discussing the attack, I was outside the room. I could only hear bits of the conversation.'

Durden leaned back in his seat and stared at Nagi, making the informer fidget with his fingers. Eventually, he sat up straight again. 'Okay, but next time, I want details.' He took a roll of money from his pocket and slipped it under the table to Sentinel. The notes quickly disappeared inside Nagi's clothing.

'How is my visa progressing?' Nagi asked, his voice still low.

'As I told you, these things take time. It's with the State Department as we speak, but there's not much I can do to rush them along. In the meantime, you need to keep feeding me information on al-Hussain. The more you help me thwart his plans, the easier it will be to convince my superiors that you should be relocated to the States.'

When Nagi had first come to Durden, he had asked for more than was on offer. Alongside the cash payments, he wanted to be given passage to the United States, with settlement rights. Quite a few of the informers asked for the same thing, and Durden's response was always the same: provide me with enough worthwhile information and I'll make it happen. In most cases it was an empty promise; the informer gave him intel that was a couple of days old, the target was long gone, and the snitch never returned.

Sentinel, though, had delivered from day one.

He'd come to Durden with news of an IED planted on the main road just outside of Kandahar. It was designed to destroy a passing coalition convoy and would be remotely detonated. He gave Durden the locations of both the device and the man tasked with detonating it. A snatch team had been sent in and the threat verified. EOD technicians from the 184th Ordnance Battalion had neutralised the bomb and the 72-year-old holding the phone had been picked up. He'd claimed to have been forced into it by local militias on pain of death and had been released a few days later.

Durden had arranged another meeting with Nagi to dig into his background. When he discovered that the Afghan was on the fringes of Abdul al-Hussain's network, he immediately agreed to help him leave the country once he'd proven his worth. Durden had actually started the paperwork, something he rarely did at such an early stage.

He'd be cancelling it now, though.

In his fifty years on the planet, he'd fine-tuned what he liked to call his bullshit detector—right now it was telling him that Sentinel was full of it.

Even though he'd provided information that had saved a few lives, Durden knew that Nagi's real alliance lay with Abdul al-Hussain.

Durden ran his hands through his bleached-blond hair, now thick with perspiration. 'What I really need from you is al-Hussain's itinerary.'

'You've asked me for that before—I told you it is impossible. I am not close enough to him to gain access to it, and if I try they will kill me. I am already risking my life by meeting with you.'

Durden doubted that very much, but it didn't matter. Thanks to Nagi's stupidity, he would soon have Abdul al-Hussain. The tracking software he'd uploaded to Nagi's phone would let the CIA know where it was to within five metres, whether it was powered on or not. And when in use, it would record all conversations which would be sent to Langley for analysis. He'd told Nagi on his second meeting that he should get a new phone, one to be used for contact between the two of them and no-one else. Nagi had done so, but judging by his reaction when Durden had asked for the handset, he hadn't followed the instructions to the letter. The fearful look when he'd handed over his cell informed him he'd used it to call others, possibly al-Hussain himself. Unfortunately, Durden hadn't had time to note down all the numbers in the call log. He'd made a mental note though, to contact Langley and suggest a dual-purpose virus; one that would grab the phone's contents while uploading the tracking software.

'I understand how difficult it would be,' Durden told him, 'but he's the man we really want. If you can hand him to us on a plate, I'm sure your resettlement application could be fast-tracked.'

He knew Nagi had no intention of moving to the US, but it was a game that had to be played.

'I will see what I can do, but I make no promises.'

'That's all I ask,' Durden assured him. 'In the meantime, tell me what you know about a woman called Miriam Dagher.'

Again, Nagi's face betrayed him. 'I have heard the name mentioned.'

'What was said?'

'I don't know,' Nagi replied, regaining his composure. 'I was standing in a hallway when al-Hussain walked by, and he mentioned that name.'

Durden nodded thoughtfully. 'And what about a virus that makes men invincible? Have you heard anything about that?'

Nagi managed a laugh. 'Yes, but it is fanciful stuff; the kind of stories you tell children at bedtime. There is no such thing.'

'There is,' Durden told him, 'and I want you to find out all you can about it. In particular I need to know where the Dagher woman is right now. It is imperative we get her back.'

Nagi leaned forward. 'Really? I thought they were simply tales.'

'Far from it. We think al-Hussain has her, and if she gives him the virus it could tip the war in the Taliban's favour. I can't stress how important it is that we prevent that from happening.'

'Again, I will do all I can.'

'Do more,' Durden said. Then he got up and left, pacing back to his car. The armed driver opened the door for him, then got back behind the wheel.

As the car headed back to the base, Durden wondered if the attack on FOB Vincent would be carried out by fighters infected with Dagher's virus. It would be prudent to film it, just in case. Balmer was preparing a report on the firefight the previous evening, but to see it in action would give him a much better idea of the virus's capabilities. His paymasters at Langley were also keen to get first-hand accounts—and there was nothing more reliable than video evidence.

Chapter 20

'Who's the kid?' Sonny Baines asked, looking over Tom Gray's shoulder.

Gray looked up from the picture of his nephew he'd received in the post—one of the highlights of his week. 'That's Sean. He's Dina's sister's son.'

'Poor sod,' Sonny said. 'Looks a lot like you. You been playing away from home?'

'Cheeky bastard,' Gray said, pushing him away. 'He's nothing like me.'

'It's the eyes. He's got your eyes. And the ears. He's definitely got some Gray in him.'

Gray didn't bite. Arguing with Sonny was always a pointless exercise. 'Dina says she wants one, too,' he said to Len Smart.

'And what about you… you ready to be a dad?'

Gray lay back on his bunk, his hands behind his head. 'You know what? I am.'

'You serious.' Sonny chuckled. 'You want to make a little version of you? Why would you intentionally create something that's gonna grow up with a tiny dick and questionable hygiene.'

Sonny was silenced by a paperback hitting the crown of his head. 'Better that than no dick and a questionable IQ,'

Smart said as he stooped to pick up his book. 'It's gotta be hard for Dina, you being over here.'

'It's hard for both of us,' Gray admitted. He was the only one in the entire troop who was married. The others either had casual girlfriends or, like Len, were single. Life in the SAS often meant being deployed to dangerous situations at a moment's notice, and not many women were comfortable with that. Gray's wife Dina was an exception. Before proposing, he'd made it clear that the SAS was his career and he wouldn't be giving it up, and she'd been fine with that. She'd promised never to ask him to choose between the army and their relationship and had stuck to her word.

Recently, though, it was Gray who had been torn. This wasn't the first time she'd suggested starting a family, and he'd been thinking about it a lot over the past months. On the plus side, he wanted a child as much as Dina did, but it wouldn't be fair to his wife nor the baby for him to remain in the SAS. It was a profession fraught with risk, and he hated the thought of his wife having to bring up a child alone. Gray's parents had put him up for adoption at a tender age, and as a result he'd spent his entire childhood moving from one foster family to another. He wasn't about to let that happen to any child of his.

'This could be my last tour. I'm getting out.'

Sonny flopped down on the bed next to his sergeant, his jaw ajar. 'You're quitting the regiment?'

'Eventually. Once I get back home we're gonna try for a kid. The moment she gets pregnant, I'm out.'

'But…what will you do? BG work?'

'Sort of,' Gray said. 'But instead of being the bodyguard, I'm going to hire them out. I'm gonna start my own security business. I've already got the name: Viking Security Services.'

'Waste of time,' Sonny said. 'The market's already flooded. Everyone that leaves the regiment starts their own security firm.'

'Not everyone,' Smart said. 'Danny Stillman didn't. Paul Burgess didn't.'

'Okay, not everyone. But there are so many around that you'd have to be damn lucky to get a foothold in the market.'

'Lucky... or clever.' Gray grinned. 'My plan is to hire the best and go in dirt cheap. I've got a bit put aside to survive a couple of years with a minimal income, and once I've established my reputation I can bump up the prices.'

'Yeah, and I'm sure no-one ever thought of that before.'

'Why do you have to be so negative?' Smart asked. 'At least he's got a plan for when he leaves the army. What about you? What great scheme have you got lined up? Get pissed and fall asleep in a ditch?'

'That was plan B.' Sonny smiled. 'First, I'm gonna go contracting. No overheads and a decent income.'

'You'll never get rich working for someone else,' Smart snorted. 'Tom's got the right idea. He won't have to face any danger, so he'll always be there to support his family. On top of that, his clients will be paying a grand a day to hire schmucks like you, and he'll keep half of it. I say good luck to him.'

'Me, too, obviously,' Sonny said, 'but I'm just saying it isn't guaranteed to pay off, so don't get your hopes up.'

'I won't,' Gray assured him as he got up from his bunk. 'Gotta go see the CO. No fighting while I'm gone.'

Gray threw on a T-shirt and made the short walk over to Russell's tent. Just as he got there, the captain emerged.

'Ah Tom, perfect timing. We're off to see Durden. Seems he has a job for us.'

'Great. Another wasted night in the mountains, no doubt.'

'Apparently not. He didn't give me details, but it sounds like you're going to see some action.'

'I'll believe that when I see it.'

They entered Durden's wooden office to find Balmer and his CO already there. Balmer was standing in Gray's favourite spot, in the crossfire from the electric fans. The Delta Force master sergeant grinned knowingly at Gray, who ignored the unspoken challenge and stood facing the CIA operative.

'Gentlemen, we have an op for you. We've received intel that Abdul al-Hussain plans to attack FOB—'

'Intel from who?' Gray interrupted. Russell threw him a glare that said 'shut it'. 'Sorry,' Gray dipped his chin. 'Carry on.'

'As I was saying, there are plans for fifty of Abdul al-Hussain's men to attack FOB Vincent at oh-two-hundred on Saturday.'

'How many men are stationed there?' Balmer asked.

'It's a work in progress. Vincent is home to B company, 3rd Battalion of the 654th Infantry Regiment, plus Seabees from Naval Mobile Construction Battalion 111 who are doing the building work. There are also civilian contractors preparing the restaurants, shops, coffee houses, laundry, field hospital… everything you would need for a base that will eventually house three thousand men and women. In terms of combat-ready defensive personnel though, we're talking a hundred and twenty-five men.'

'Should be enough to repel fifty Taliban,' Gray said.

'If it was a small base, I'd agree,' Durden said, 'but Vincent is the size of three hundred football fields. There's no way one hundred and twenty-five men can guard a perimeter that big. They'd be spread too thin.'

Gray hadn't known that. He'd operated out of a couple of FOBs, but these were existing structures like old forts—less than a third of the size of a football stadium. The construction of new bases wasn't something he was regularly briefed on, so it was unsurprising he hadn't heard of this one.

As Durden had said, there was no way one hundred and twenty-five men could hope to cover a perimeter so large, especially if the attack came from all sides. Figure six miles of fencing or walls, divided by a hundred and twenty-five men, meant about eighty-five yards between each man. Not ideal in the best of circumstances. But if the Taliban somehow managed to breach the boundary, it would soon turn into a shitstorm.

'I assume you're sending reinforcements,' Gray said to Durden.

'We're trying. I've managed to get another two hundred men from the 667th and the 698th, but that's all they can spare. The brass thinks that's enough, given the perceived threat.'

'But you don't?' Balmer said, squinting.

'No, I don't. Especially after reading your report on the mission last night. If the people you killed were as young as you say, they had to have been exposed to Dagher's virus. If that's the case, we can expect more of the same on Saturday.'

'If you're right, then three hundred and twenty-five men still wouldn't be enough.'

'That's why we're sending you guys in,' Captain Bridges said.

'Both of us?' Gray asked.

'Both of us, *sir*!' Bridges growled.

'Both of us, *sir*!' Gray conceded. He could get away with informalities with Captain Russell, but the American was clearly of a different breed.

'Yes,' Durden said, trying to get the room back. 'I want you *both* to head over there today and co-ordinate the defensive strategy. Work only began on the camp a couple of months ago, but the basic infrastructure is in place. The wall is complete; guard towers at each corner, shelter, water and electricity. I've already spoken with Major Tanner of the 654th and he'll be expecting you.'

'And who'll be in overall command?' Balmer asked.

'You mean, who's going to be in charge between you two?'

'Yes, sir.'

'Neither,' Russell said. 'You're big boys now. We need you to put your heads together, use your vast experience and come up with a joint plan that everyone's happy with.'

Gray wasn't sure that was a good idea, but Russell's expression informed him he'd better make it work. Balmer didn't look too happy at the arrangement, either.

'The Pentagon is keen to know more about how this virus—they've designated it AR, for Afghan Rogue—affects the recipients. Your report was thorough, master sergeant, but they want more. So I'd like you to ensure we have comprehensive video coverage of any attack.'

Gray surmised that 'keen to know more' was a euphemism for 'want to weaponise it for their own use'.

'How many men do you want me to take?' Gray asked Russell, deliberately omitting the honorific for Bridges' sake.

'Your patrol as well as Sergeant Campbell's should do it.'

'Same for you,' Bridges told Balmer. 'Eight men in each team should be enough.'

'Transport has been arranged for twenty hundred hours,' Durden told them. 'I'll have the CCTV equipment ready and waiting.'

'What about air support?' Balmer asked. 'We could have done with a plane overhead last night.'

'I'm working on that,' Durden said. 'We won't know what assets we have available until a couple of hours before it all kicks off. When I know, you'll know.'

When the meeting was called to a halt, Gray walked out with Russell in his wake.

'How come we both have to go?' Gray asked his captain.

'Politics,' Russell answered. 'The PM wants to know just as much about this virus as the president, and the top brass insisted you guys work together for the time being. From what I understand, Balmer already has a blood sample from one of the guys he killed last night. Our government would like the same, if you can.'

'And do you think they'll use it?'

Russell shrugged. 'Hard to tell. Certainly not in the next few years. It would have to undergo rigorous testing before it was used on our own men. In the meantime, be alert. I read Balmer's report—I think you're going to be in for an interesting weekend.'

Chapter 21

Balmer's team was waiting next to a pile of metal boxes when Gray and his men reached the chopper.

'Thought you weren't going to make it.' Lomax laughed. 'Couldn't blame you. It's gonna be hairy.'

'Like your momma's upper lip?' Sonny said, dumping his Bergen on the floor.

'Cool it,' Smart said. 'We gotta play nice… captain's orders.'

'Yeah, quit it,' Gray added. He walked over to Balmer and put his backpack on the ground. 'Durden said you came up against the virus last night. How was it?'

'Scary. Like taking ourselves on. They were kids, but fought like they'd been at war all their lives. They made a couple of mistakes, but if they can iron them out we're in for a rough time.'

Gray was used to being the best in any battle—if the odds were no longer going to be heavily in his favour, he'd have to up his game. They all would.

A crew chief came over and pointed to a nearby transport helicopter—a huge Chinook. And the sixteen men started loading up. Ten minutes later, they were heading south in the darkness.

It was a short flight to Vincent, located sixty miles from Kandahar, with the Pakistan border thirty miles to the east.

As they approached the camp, Gray asked the pilot to circle once so that he could get an idea of the layout and surrounding landscape.

Although work had only just begun, the US Navy Seabees had made excellent progress. A wall had been erected around the entire perimeter and, as Durden had promised, there were guard towers at each corner of the rectangular camp. Around fifty sand-coloured tents stood in neat rows and the foundations had been laid for a lot more. Elsewhere, permanent buildings were taking shape, too. Beyond the walls lay nothing but flat desert for miles in all directions.

When Gray had seen enough, the pilot guided the helicopter to a makeshift landing pad at the northern end of the compound and touched down gently. Gray was waiting at the ramp as it began to open and a private was there to greet them.

'Sergeant Gray, Major Tanner is expecting you. I'll show your men to their quarters on the way.'

They followed the soldier past aviation fuel bowsers and mountains of construction material to the accommodation area. Two tents had been allocated; one each for the SAS and Delta Force. As the rest of the men stowed their gear, Gray and Balmer went to see the camp's commanding officer.

If Major Chuck Tanner was glad to see them, it didn't show. He remained seated when they were led into his office and he left them standing to attention while he scribbled on a notepad. When he eventually looked up, his face contorted to a blend of anger and disdain.

'So you're the cavalry, eh?'

Gray and Balmer said nothing.

'Well, in my opinion, you've had a wasted journey. Whoever decided my men couldn't defend this compound from a handful of insurgents has underestimated the 654th. We're fighting men. We shit bullets and piss napalm—God help anyone who gets in our way. We sure ain't scared of a few raghead goat fuckers.'

'What about facing fifty Delta Force?' Gray asked. 'Would you still be so confident?' As a pause, he tagged on, 'sir?' He didn't like the situation any more than the Major did, but they wouldn't get anywhere if they were at each other's throats for the next three days. Best not to kick off on the wrong foot.

'That would be different,' Tanner conceded.

'Not really, sir. Master Sergeant Balmer here faced similar troops only last night. He can tell you what you're up against.'

Balmer gave Gray a nod of thanks. 'He's right, sir. Last night my patrol was attacked by thirty insurgents. They kept us pinned down for almost fifteen minutes and put two of my men out of action. At first we thought we were taking on old Mujihadeen—they were so good—but they turned out to be kids, mostly teenagers. I tell you, they had us rattled for a while.'

Tanner didn't even bother trying to hide his contempt, huffing out a sarcastic snigger. 'America's finest, scared of a bunch of little boys?'

'Have you heard of Miriam Dagher, sir?' Gray asked.

'I have. Bunch of hooey if you ask me. There ain't no superman virus, it's just Taliban propaganda.'

'I beg to differ,' Balmer said. 'Gray lost an entire patrol to it last week, and there's no way the kids we fought last night have been training all their lives. The virus is real, and that's what we'll be facing come o-two-hundred on Saturday.'

'I'll believe that when I see it. Until then, I have my orders—no matter how much I disagree with them. I'm assigning Lieutenant Green to you. Whatever you need, he'll provide it.'

Tanner flicked a dismissive hand at them. Gary and Balmer offered smart salutes in return, then walked out of the Major's office.

'Went about as well as I expected,' Gray said as they walked back to their tent.

'Can't blame the guy. If a couple of grunts came and told me how to do my job, I'd be pissed off, too.'

They had bigger concerns than the hurt feelings of an infantry major. The attack was due in a little over fifty-three hours, and they had a lot of work to do.

'I'll get Bennett to set up the cameras,' Gray told Balmer. 'Why don't you ask the LT what ordnance they have here. A few Claymores would be a good start.'

'Can do. After that, I'll walk the perimeter and meet you in your quarters at midnight to discuss options.'

'Sounds good. See you then.'

Gray went off to find Paul Bennett—the comms expert of Jeff Campbell's squad. He was in his tent looking through one of the boxes they'd brought along on the chopper.

'What have we got?' Gray asked him.

'Eight cameras and digital recorders. Decent-looking kit. Should get some nice shots.'

'How long to install them?'

'About an hour for each one,' Bennett told him. 'I thought about putting them on the guard towers, but they would be the first thing I'd hit if I were leading an assault on the camp. I'll see what angles we get from some of the taller buildings, but failing that I'll just mount them along the perimeter wall.'

'Good idea,' Gray said. 'Start at first light.'

* * *

After a hearty breakfast provided by one of the civilian contractors, Gray met up with the other six members of his troop and the eight men of Balmer's Delta Force ODA inside a briefing hut. Bennett was already working on getting the cameras set up; Gray would fill him in afterwards. He'd spent a couple of hours with Balmer the previous night, thrashing out the workings of a defensive plan and how they were going to put it to the rest of the men for a Chinese parliament. All input was welcome and encouraged, though it had been decided that Gray and Balmer would have the final say.

Gray let Balmer kick things off by running through a list of resources they had available.

'We've got three hundred and twenty-five men from the 654th, 667th and the 698th, plus sixty Seabees we can call on at a push. There are also seventy civilians, but they'll be choppered out on Saturday afternoon. As for heavy weapons, we have ten mortars with thirty rounds apiece, and two-dozen Stingers. On top of all the small arms we have three hundred grenades, twenty-four Claymores and a shitload of flares.'

While Balmer talked through the list, Gray pinned an A3 drawing of the camp to the board.

'This is as close to scale as I can get,' Gray told the assembled men. 'As you know, the intel we have is minimal.

The Taliban will be sending fifty men at oh-two-hundred on Saturday, and that's all we know. We have no idea if they have transport, what weapons they'll be carrying, or which direction they'll be coming from. That's why I thought it best to spread the men evenly around the perimeter, with a reserve force to tackle any breaches. Balmer and his men will cover the north and east walls, my patrols will take the south and west.'

'We've got NVGs,' Carl Levine pointed out. 'We should see them coming a mile off.'

'You'd think,' Balmer said, 'but two weeks ago a couple of dozen attacked FOB Tork and got within two hundred yards before we spotted them. They approached slowly, blending in with the landscape, and that was before the AR virus was in play. Now they'll be even more disciplined.'

'Trip flares are out,' Gray added. 'If they're moving so slowly, they'd spot them easily.'

'That's if they adopt the same tactics,' Len Smart said. 'They might decide on a more direct approach this time.'

'Maybe… but it's still too large an area to cover effectively. There'll be huge gaps that they could slip through.'

'We only need one of them to trip it, not all of them.'

'He's got a point,' Carl Levine agreed. 'Might as well set a few up, far enough out that they won't be so switched on. A mile should do it. That would at least tell us where they're coming from.'

Gray looked at Balmer, who nodded back at him. 'Okay… Carl and Len, that's your job today. Take two men from Delta.'

'Rees and Hubble, that's you.'

'Who's going to be posted in the towers?' Lomax asked. 'That's the first thing I'd hit.'

'My thoughts entirely,' Gray said. 'That's why we're not gonna use them. I've asked the Seabees to build four viewing platforms for us. They'll be twenty yards inside the wall and just tall enough to give us a good view out without presenting a tempting target.'

Liebowitz raised a hand. 'What about air support?'

'We won't know until nearer the time,' Balmer told him. 'Hopefully, we're not going to need it.'

Gray turned to the map and pointed out where he wanted to deploy the Claymores and the mortar teams, and where the men would be stationed. Suggestions were thrown his way; some of which he agreed with, others he dismissed. But after half an hour they had their defences defined.

'I hope they turn up after all this.' Tristram Barker-Fink laughed.

Balmer looked him in the eye. 'Careful what you wish for.'

Chapter 22

It was just after eleven p.m. when the flare shot into the sky a mile from the south wall.

'Contact south,' Gray said over comms. 'One mile out, sector seven.'

The area around the camp had been broken into twelve sections to mirror a clock face, dead north being twelve, dead south, six. Gray looked through his binoculars as the flare parachuted leisurely to the ground, but couldn't see any movement. Once it died, he switched to the night vision glasses. But still nothing stirred. The playbook said that if a flare was fired into the air, you hit the ground. If you tripped one, you ran like the wind. Either these guys didn't know or were ultra-disciplined and hoping it was chalked up to a stray animal.

'Three hours early,' Balmer replied. 'Looks like they planned another stealthy approach.'

'Let's see what they do now that that plan's gone to shit.'

The immediate answer was a resounding nothing. The entire camp was on alert, everyone tense with pre-battle nerves, but the night remained silent.

After fifteen minutes, Gray still wasn't convinced that a wandering animal had tripped the flare. It could have been a wild rabbit or something of a similar size, too small to be seen at such a distance. But his gut told him it was the prelude to an assault.

'Mike-zero-seven,' Gray said. 'Give me one round, seventeen hundred yards, bearing two-one-five.'

The team manning the L16 81mm mortar at the southwest corner of the base acknowledged the order, and twenty seconds later a shell shot into the air. When it exploded a mile away, Gray was watching for movement in the blast vicinity.

Nothing.

'Looks like a false alarm,' he told Balmer. No-one was disciplined enough to remain calm and lie still while bombs fell around them.

Gray checked in with the other teams. They'd divided the available men into four units; one for each wall, with the longer north and south aspects getting a larger allotment. Gray was heading Alpha. Balmer, Bravo. Smart, Charlie. And Lomax was in charge of Delta. None of them had anything to report.

Something was afoot, though—Gray could feel it. A sixth sense that told him danger was close by.

An hour passed, and the feeling still hadn't deserted him. He'd considered sending up flares at irregular intervals, but that would have told the Taliban that they were expected— not that the mortar round wouldn't have given them a heads-up if they'd been within sight of the compound at the time. He'd decided against it, instead relying on the keen eyes of the men manning the walls. They only had forty pairs of NVGs between them, and every set was focused on the desolate land surrounding them.

Gray tucked into a chocolate bar as his eyes swept the horizon for the thousandth time, frustrated at the lack of movement. If they were going to repeat the tactics used at FOB Tork, then with under two hours to go he expected to see something. Perhaps that had been a trial, to see if it was possible to get in close to a fortified base without being seen. And after that failure they'd written it off as impractical. That seemed the most likely scenario at present, which meant there was just over an hour and half until it all kicked off. Plenty of time to take a piss.

He was halfway through emptying his bladder in the nearest toilet block when a shout came over the radio. He stopped in mid-stream and started running back, only for it to be declared a false alarm. Someone had seen movement in the far distance. But it turned out to be a dog, or possibly a wolf, on a nocturnal hunting trip.

Gray had to wait another eighty-two minutes before things got real.

At seven minutes to two, one of the men on the south wall noticed a dust cloud. Gray spotted it moments later, and within a minute he could see that it was preceded by at least two vehicles—Toyota trucks by the look of them. He informed the other team leaders, warning them to concentrate on their own sectors in case it was a multi-pronged attack.

By the time the tiny convoy closed to within four hundred yards, a hundred weapons were focused on the fast-moving targets. But the rules of engagement said Gray couldn't give the order to open fire. The vehicles were not on a collision course with the base, but angled to miss the south-west corner by a couple of hundred metres. If he destroyed both trucks, there would be hell to pay if it turned out the occupants were unarmed. There had to be clear, unequivocal aggression towards the compound before he could even consider firing upon them.

That said, it was too much of a coincidence that they should just happen to be there at that exact moment in time, and if just one of the men currently under his command died because he hesitated, it would haunt him forever.

Sometimes you just had to say, 'fuck the rulebook' and follow your gut.

He was about to give the order to light them up when a figure popped up from the lead truck's flatbed, took a knee and threw something onto its shoulder.

'RPG!' Gray screamed. He sent a couple of bursts towards the vehicle and was immediately joined by dozens of other small arms from within the camp wall. A deadly stream of lead slammed into both trucks, putting them out of commission and shredding the occupants, but not before two projectiles—one from each vehicle—were sent hurtling towards the base. One of them hit the main structure of the tower in the south-west corner—blowing the roof off. While the other flew high over Gray's head and landed harmlessly on a pile of timber.

'Check your sectors!'

The three team leads reported no movement, but Gray knew this was just the start.

After thirty seconds of silence, he was proved right when the night erupted.

The timer connected to the banks of C4 hidden in the side panels of the trucks counted down to zero. The bullets striking the explosives hadn't provided enough of a shockwave to set it off, but the blasting caps did. The fifty pounds of plastic explosive in each vehicle had thousands of steel ball bearings pressed into the surface, turning the

Toyotas into giant Claymore mines. The explosion lit up the night, and seventeen soldiers from the 667th didn't live long enough to see the intense flashes of light die away. They'd been looking over the wall and into the night seconds before their corpses collapsed to the ground—most of them headless.

Gray was grateful to the Seabees for providing makeshift armour-plating for the observation towers they'd built. Without it, he too would have been ripped apart. He'd instinctively ducked when the trucks exploded, a natural movement that saved his life.

As Gray stuck his head over the wall of the platform, he could hear the cries of those injured in the blasts. He quickly ordered medics to attend to the wounded and the remaining men to be vigilant. 'Next time you see anything, open up immediately. Don't let them bastards get that close again!'

He didn't have to wait long for the next wave. More vehicles were spotted, this time advancing from the west. Gray spread the word, then instructed the sergeant from the 698th who was coordinating the fire mission to lay down a curtain of fire. Mortar teams Mike-Zero-Seven and Mike-Zero-Eight immediately popped off sighting rounds, their warheads dropping almost a mile away. The sergeant corrected the fire a couple of degrees to the left, then told the teams to dial it back a hundred yards and fire at will. The result was one kill and a vehicle thrown on its side. But two more kept coming. The mortars adjusted their range with every delivery, but the two approaching trucks zig-zagged erratically, making themselves impossible targets to hit. When they got to a thousand yards from the western wall the two vehicles split up, heading north and south respectively. As they raced along at a fair clip, Gray could see men in the flatbed readying shoulder-launched missiles.

'More RPGs!' he warned.

The maximum effective range for an RPG-7 round against stationary objects was five hundred yards, but it was possible to extend that range to nine hundred and twenty by removing the self-destruct mechanism. If the vehicles managed to get a couple of hundred yards closer, any accurate rounds would be exploding inside the base walls.

'Sniper, take 'em out!'

* * *

Jeff Campbell and Tristram Barker-Fink were lying on the roof of one of the shops being built in the centre of the base. From their vantage point they could see for miles in any direction, and Campbell had the southbound truck in his sights.

'Distance nine-sixty, speed fifty,' Barker-Fink said, spotting for the shooter. 'No wind.'

With a moving target, Campbell had to lead it. That meant shooting where he expected the target to be by the time the bullet got there. Also, the vehicle wasn't heading across the horizon, but approaching at an angle which made the shot more difficult to calculate. He set the crosshairs just forward of the truck's nose, breathed out, then squeezed the trigger. The .50 calibre round took a shade over one second to travel to the target, but the man kneeling in the back didn't flinch.

'Reduce your lead by five yards,' Barker-Fink said.

Campbell made the adjustment, and his second shot found its mark. He immediately turned his attention to the other vehicle; the RPG was the immediate threat.

'Distance nine hundred, speed…sixty-five, no wind.'

Campbell fired, and his spotter reported his shot to be a few inches high and three yards wide. The second round was much closer.

'Come on, you prick… die…' Campbell squeezed once more, and the third found its mark.

Campbell now focused on stopping the vehicles. He put four rounds in the engine block of the first one, bringing it to a halt seven hundred yards from the base perimeter. The second managed to get closer, just under five hundred yards from the wall before a thumb-sized bullet took the driver's head off.

* * *

Gray called upon the mortar teams to neutralise the remaining threat, and it only took a handful of rounds to reduce the two Toyotas to burning hulks. They hadn't been packed with explosives like the first wave.

'I make that ten down,' Gray told Balmer. 'There's plenty more out there.'

'We'll keep 'em peeled.'

Gray then asked for updates from the corporal tending the wounded. He confirmed eighteen fatalities, including one who'd just passed away. Another twelve being stretchered to the base hospital by the Seabees of the naval construction battalion. It wasn't yet fully operational, but there were two military surgeons on standby.

What have you got planned? Gray wondered. The Taliban wouldn't keep throwing men and vehicles at the base, now that the element of surprise was gone. It would be a dreadful waste of resources. But then, what option did they have? The allied forces ruled the skies—the Afghan Air Force consisted of little more than a few helicopters, and none were in rebel hands—so they couldn't attack from above. And it would take years to dig a tunnel long enough to penetrate the base from below. All they could do was continue to send men across the desert floor to die.

That was fine with Gray.

'Durden wanted an update, so I told him what we've had so far,' Balmer said over the air. 'He's also asking if we need air support.'

'Negative,' Gray replied. 'If they do come at us again, we've got them covered.'

'I concur. I'll let him know.'

To anticipate the enemy's actions, you had to think like them, so Gray put himself in their shoes. It didn't help much. In this situation he would call off the attack, recognising the futility. There was nothing to gain from going up against greater numbers, with strong defences and superior firepower.

'Movement south.'

Gray picked up his night vision binoculars and looked out over the wall. Yet another vehicle was entering the fray. It was around two miles out and heading directly for the base.

'Target acquired,' Gray told the two mortar teams. He gave them the rough bearing and distance as well as the rate of closure, but before they could get a round away, the truck pulled to the right and stopped.

'Hold,' Gray instructed them.

Four men climbed out of the truck. The figures were hazy because of the distance, but Gray could see them put weapons over their shoulders and he squinted as he shook his head.

They were a mile beyond the maximum range of an RPG-7. Firing from that position would just be a waste of ammo.

'What are they up to?' he mumbled to himself.

He adjusted the magnification until the targets were in focus. That's when he spotted something wrong.

Whatever they were carrying, it wasn't RPGs. Those had a warhead that was roughly the thickness of his arm, but these weapons were much larger. The only thing he could think of that was that size and capable of firing a missile two miles was the FGM-148 Javelin—a US-built fire-and-forget anti-tank missile.

His fear was confirmed when four streaks of light flashed into the sky.

'Incoming!'

Gray threw himself off the platform and landed in the dirt. He repeated his warning over comms, then screamed at Mike-Zero-Seven and Mike-Zero-Eight to throw all they had at the last given distance and bearing. Seconds ticked by as Gray scrambled for cover. He found a spot behind a pile of aluminium panels just as the first explosion shook the base.

* * *

Jammas Gulwal heard the series of four quick explosions and knew his time had come. There was a strong chance that he would die in the next few minutes, but that could have happened at any time in the last five hours. That was how long it had taken him to crawl a mile across the desert floor with the camouflaged sheet over his body. His body ached from the relentlessly slow deliberate movements, but he cast his discomfort aside as his time for glory dawned.

Three weeks earlier he'd been working for his grandfather, transporting the crop from the farm to sell in the local town. Now he was about to attack the people who had killed his father the previous year. He'd never even held a rifle until the moment he'd been taken to see Abdul al-Hussain along with four others. That was when he'd been given the injection that had changed his life.

The rockets fired into the south side of the camp would keep the Americans occupied while Jammas and the other thirty men would launch their attack from the north. The Javelins had a feature called top attack mode, where the missile would rise five hundred feet into the air before racing downwards to strike its target. It was designed to hit tanks at their most vulnerable point—from above. That method had been deployed this evening, so that the rounds fell inside the base rather than just hitting the outer wall. As the Americans fought to deal with the resulting carnage, Jammas and the others would strike.

They were now just two hundred yards from the base, and Jammas knew from the intense week of training that he could cover that distance in twenty-five seconds. First, though, he had to assemble the RPG that was strapped to his side. It had made his trek all the more difficult, but it was a necessary price to pay. He slowly untied the four pieces of cloth strapping and carefully pulled the launcher and projectile in front of him, then mated them together. After cocking the weapon, he removed the plastic safety covering on the impact fuse at the nose of the missile. His final act of preparation was to remove his AK-47 from the bag on his back and unfold the stock.

He was set.

Jammas said a silent prayer to Allah then jumped to his feet, casting his camouflaged covering aside. He lifted the RPG to his shoulder, sighted on the wall and squeezed the trigger. The moment the round flew out of the tube, he abandoned it, picked up the rifle and began running.

Within seconds, his lungs were bursting. More RPGs were fired; some from around him, others from between seven and eight hundred yards from the camp. The latter were well outside the effective range of the weapon, but the intention was to make use of the built-in self-destruct mechanism. The rounds would blow themselves up after travelling 950 yards, creating air bursts over the camp and sending shrapnel down to kill or maim anyone in their path.

Jammas could see the opening he'd blown in the wall, and he was only seventy yards from it.

Sixty…

Fifty…

Bullets chewed up the ground in front of him, but Jammas continued, unrelenting—firing back as he ran. He saw one of his bursts take out an American, but according to the intelligence that had been gathered, there were still over a hundred left to deal with. He looked forward to doing his part.

But for Jammas, that kill would be his last. When he got to within forty yards of the compound, the earth in front of him opened up and he slammed into a wall.

* * *

'Get that fire out before we all go up!'

Balmer pointed to the fuel bowser. The cab was ablaze, flames licking out through the smashed windows. The missile had struck just in front of the truck, and the fire threatened to ignite the thousands of litres of jet fuel in the main tank. Men ran from the wall to help put out the flames, some carrying fire extinguishers, others grabbing shovels to throw dirt at the fire. One of the Seabees jumped on an excavator, jabbed the bucket into the ground to fill it with earth and sand, then trundled over to the truck and dumped the contents on top of the cab. It helped a little, but the fire still raged.

'Again!' Balmer shouted from atop his observation platform, as more men rushed forward to help.

Balmer was watching the digger scoop up another bucket of dirt when his earpiece exploded into life.

'Contact north!'

Balmer spun just as three explosions rocked the north wall. From nowhere, thirty figures emerged as if from out of the sand, racing towards the gaps they'd created in the perimeter.

'Take them down!' Balmer bellowed sighting on his first target. His initial burst missed, but the second struck the sprinting figure in the chest.

They were now within a hundred yards of the wall, and with half his men firefighting, the rest were spread thin.

'Get on the Claymores!' He ordered the remaining defenders—men from the 667th.

The mines were configured to be detonated remotely by an M57 firing device, known as a clacker, rather than by trip wire. Balmer saw a trio of men pick up the clackers and squeeze them.

Sand exploded from the desert floor as the three mines spat out thousands of steel ball bearings. They'd been placed thirty yards outside the wall, pushed into the ground and hidden under a loose covering of sand. In all, five enemy combatants were caught in the blasts, leaving nothing more than bloody stains on the ground to mark their passing.

That still left around two dozen, and Balmer and his men laid down heavy fire as the enemy sprinted onwards.

One made it to a hole in the wall created by the RPGs. He let rip with his AK-47, taking down two infantrymen and three Seabees before he was stopped by concentrated fire from two angles.

Another two drove through a similar gap a hundred yards away and they managed to take seven more American lives before being cut down.

More Claymores tore the night apart, claiming another six kills, but the remaining Taliban were undeterred. They piled forward, seemingly impervious to the hundreds of rounds streaking their way. Ten were cut down in mid-sprint, but another four made it to the wall.

'Breach, north wall!' Balmer announced over comms.

* * *

'Len, Sonny—get over there and help!' Smart heard in his earpiece.

He acknowledged Gray's instructions and ordered the men on the west wall to keep their eyes peeled before he sprinted towards the fire burning to the north. When he got there he saw a Seabee in a digger about to dump a load of dirt on the truck, but before he could empty the bucket, a burst from an AK-47 hit him in the chest. He fell forward, the arm of the excavator hanging impotently over the flames.

Smart got the shooter in his sights and hit him in the chest with a short burst, then yelled for someone to get on the digger and dump its load just as more rounds chewed up the ground at his feet. Smart ran, throwing himself behind a pile of timber. He stuck his head out and saw that the three remaining Taliban had also found cover—but they were in a hopeless position. They were heavily outnumbered, and the American troops were already beginning to flank them. One was killed by small arms fire, and another took the full force of a hand grenade.

The last of the insurgents made a brave last stand, taking two American lives before he stuck his head out too far and Smart nonchalantly sent him to meet his maker.

* * *

'Cease fire!' Balmer bellowed, as the infantry took pot-shots at shadows. He ordered a few of the men to look after the wounded, while the rest were instructed to keep an eye on the perimeter in case there was more to come. He told them to report any movement, no matter how insignificant.

Gray trotted over. 'How bad?'

'We lost twenty seven in all, plus about fifteen wounded. It would have been a lot worse if that missile had hit the fuel truck. What about your team?' Balmer's men were all accounted for.

'All made it.' Gray glanced over as the last of the flames were extinguished in the cab of the bowser after a dozen men had run relay to carry buckets of water to cool down the main tank. 'I think they used Javelins.'

'I think you're right,' Balmer said. 'Where the hell did they get them from?'

'A few of the Gulf States purchase them, including the Saudis. I reckon they were either stolen or sold to the Taliban.'

'I'll mention it to Durden. He can find out if any of our allies have reported any missing.'

'They're hardly likely to admit it,' Gray said. 'It would jeopardise any further sales if it's thought they can't keep hold of them.'

'The CIA have their ways. Come on, let's take a look at who we were up against.'

Gray followed Balmer over to the body of one of the attackers.

'He looks like a school kid,' Gray told Balmer, who nodded in return.

'Same as the ones who ambushed us a few nights ago. This is Dagher's doing.'

They wandered the camp, checking each of the dead. Like the first one, they were all young—most of them still in their teens.

'I have to admit, that was a pretty slick attack.'

Gray agreed. 'I was expecting them to just rush the gates. How the hell did they get so close to you?'

'They must have crawled across the desert. We were so busy watching the horizon we didn't see what was under our noses. Well… that won't happen again.'

Chapter 23

Abdul al-Hussain got out of the 4x4 and cast his eyes around the camp. It was set on a plateau high in the mountains, with rock formations protecting both sides, in the middle of which was a single track that led to the gate. He was immediately met, inside that gate, by Ali Kamal—a man who had served with him for over thirty years.

'As-salamu alaykum,' al-Hussain greeted him.

'Wa-alaykumu salam. Come, we have much to discuss.'

Kamal led the way to a sand-coloured tent and then Dagher emerged from the vehicle and followed. Inside, tea had already been prepared and Kamal barked instructions for food to be brought in. A soldier at the entrance ran off to fulfil his wishes.

Al-Hussain took a seat in a folding chair that faced a collapsible table; Dagher sat next to him. Like everything else at the camp, the furniture was ready to be packed away at a moment's notice. There were no permanent structures, just temporary shelters that could be bundled into vehicles should the need arise.

'What do you make of the boy I sent you?' al-Hussain asked.

'Irshad? A blessing from Allah himself. Please tell me there are more like him.'

'I thought you'd be pleased,' al-Hussain smiled. 'And yes, there are more. Tens of thousands more.'

Kamal's eyes betrayed his shock. 'And you only tell me now? I thought we were friends!'

They were more than just friends. Ever since they'd first fought together in the Mujahideen against the Soviets, the bond had been strong. After surviving that conflict, they teamed up again when the new invaders arrived. Kamal had been his first port of call as he set about building up a militia to deal with the allied forces. In one of his first engagements with the Americans, Kamal had lost a hand. Although it was enough to take him off active duty, al-Hussain wasn't about to cast him aside. With so much combat experience, Kamal had been the perfect choice to head up the training camp just outside Quetta in Pakistan. Al-Hussain had been sending promising recruits there for the last seven years, but he doubted any of them had been like Irshad.

'Would you believe me if I told you Irshad had never seen a rifle until two weeks ago?'

Kamal looked puzzled, then laughed. 'Right now, if I had to pick my best three soldiers, Irshad would be among them. Nobody becomes that good in a few days.'

'They do now,' al-Hussain said, turning to his companion for the first time. 'This is Professor Miriam Dagher. She is the one responsible for Irshad's remarkable progression.'

Kamal now looked downright confused. 'A woman?'

'A particularly gifted woman,' al-Hussain corrected him.

Between him and Dagher, it took fifteen minutes to explain how they had turned a timid teen into a killing machine, and when they'd finished, Kamal looked as excited as a child about to receive his first horse.

'How much of this virus do you have?'

'Enough for a few thousand doses, and that is just the beginning. We have forty litres with us, plus a few thousand needles. The professor will show your men how to administer it so she doesn't have to be here every time I send you new recruits. Her time is better spent in the laboratory.'

'When will the first batch of boys arrive?' Kamal asked.

'In the next couple of hours,' the Taliban commander said. 'There will be around two hundred at first, but my men are scouring the countryside for anyone capable of holding a weapon. You will soon have more than you can handle. I have spoken to ISI and they will be bringing you tents and equipment in the coming days.'

'It would be better if we leave the camp at its current size,' Kamal suggested. 'Any larger and we risk drawing attention to ourselves. I will instruct my second-in-command to create more camps in the area and I will oversee them all.'

'That would be wise. Another thing we need to establish is the need for secrecy. The Americans are desperate to find the professor, but more importantly they will want to prevent us from using her creation. If they discover that the virus is here, nothing will prevent them from attacking.'

'Even though we are in Pakistan?' Kamal asked.

'They will not hesitate launching an attack on a sovereign nation to halt our plans. No-one must know you have it.'

'I will make sure my men understand,' Kamal assured him.

'Excellent. Now, while we wait for the new intake to arrive, tell me about your recent victories.'

Reports of Kamal's battles had filtered through to him, but al-Hussain enjoyed hearing the details from someone who had first-hand knowledge—he knew his old friend wouldn't have any need for embellishment.

They chatted for a couple of hours, mostly about the virus and al-Hussain's plans for it, until the first truck packed with new recruits wheel-spun its way into the camp. It parked under a huge awning alongside several other vehicles and Kamal led his superior and guest outside to welcome them.

'They are barely teenagers,' Kamal noted, the disappointment evident in his delivery. 'Look! That one's shaking like a leaf in the wind!'

'Trust me,' al-Hussain said, his hand on his friend's shoulder. 'What you are about to witness will be the most amazing thing you will ever see in your life.'

Thirty minutes later, Kamal stood with his mouth open, trying to find words to describe his amazement.

'It's impressive, isn't it?' al-Hussain laughed.

'It's… I can't… If I hadn't seen it with my own eyes I would have called any man a fool who claimed such a potion existed. It is truly astounding.'

'Just imagine what we could achieve with ten thousand warriors of that calibre.'

'I dare not think,' Kamal said. 'Please tell me this isn't a dream.'

'Far from it, my friend. Though in the days and weeks to come, our enemy will endure many nightmares. However, there is more to be done. The virus gives them focus and eliminates fear, but it does not make them true soldiers. They still have to be taught the art of warfare.'

'Then they are in the right place. What do you have planned for their first mission?'

'A repeat of the attack on the compound they call Vincent.'

Kamal looked concerned. 'I heard about the last attempt. It was a crushing defeat,' he said. 'Are you sure you want to waste good men on such an impenetrable target?'

'I can think of no better test for them. We sent fifty men to attack Vincent, and used four of the Javelins. This time we will use the remaining eight and send four hundred men. They won't stop until they are dead or victorious. At the weekend, thirty men managed to crawl to within two hundred yards of the base before they attacked it. Those tactics worked even though the Americans knew we were coming and had reinforced the base. We can do the same again, but this time we will catch them unawares.'

Kamal bowed his head slightly. 'I will teach them well. When do you wish to strike?'

'Two weeks from today. Set up a new camp specifically for this mission, and ensure no-one knows the target until the very last moment. I will provide everything you need.'

A smile crept across Kamal's face. 'If this works, if these boys manage to overrun the Americans and capture their base, it could be the turning point in the war.'

'*Inshallah.*'

Chapter 24

Miriam Dagher was exhausted. She'd been working non-stop creating her virus and injecting subjects for almost a fortnight, surviving on just five hours of sleep a night. It was all beginning to catch up with her.

Thankfully, her job was almost done.

With her hands inside the rubber gloves of the hermetically-sealed Perspex chamber, she secured the stopper on the last of the phials and put the glass container through the decontamination process. Again. Probably for the three-thousandth time—enough for approximately ten thousand doses.

She wanted her bed—not the hard, unforgiving one that had been provided by her hosts. She wanted the luxurious dual-sprung, super-king-size mattress that had cost her over a thousand British pounds—the one that was lying unused in her rented London home. She also missed her wardrobe; the cool breeze of a British autumn; the occasional glass of wine.

She'd known when she'd made the decision to come to Afghanistan that she'd have to make sacrifices, but it was eye-opening to discover how different her birth country was from her adopted home. Still, she reminded herself, she was doing this for the country she loved—that made it all worthwhile.

After packing the last phial in the box along with the others, Miriam closed the lid and carried it to the cooled storage room. She placed it with the other boxes that were all ready to be shipped out and administered in the next twenty-one days. That was the shelf-life she'd given al-Hussain. Beyond that, it was doubtful the virus would be as effective, if at all. How he was going to find ten thousand volunteers to infect was not her concern. She'd played her part, and only one thing remained.

Miriam went to the main house, where her host Samir was reading to his two young children. She recognised the passages from the Qur'an and waited patiently for him to finish.

'How may I help you?' Samir eventually asked. He'd been a pleasant enough host, but like everything else in this country, she would soon be glad to see the back of him.

'I am finished for today,' she replied. 'The next consignment of boxes is ready to go.'

'I will arrange a collection later this evening. Would you like something to eat?'

'That would be wonderful. I'll take it in my room, if that's okay. I'd like to shower first.'

Samir nodded his acceptance, then called for his wife and told her to prepare supper for their guest.

Miriam thanked him before heading to a bedroom that had the luxury—if it could be called that—of an en-suite toilet and shower; though both were functional at best. Miriam locked the bathroom door, quickly stripped and got under the drizzle of tepid water.

Her final act was to let her masters know where she was. She did this by putting her hand under her large left breast and locating the tracking device that had been sewn into her body prior to her flying to Afghanistan. The instructions were to squeeze the unit, which was an inch long and three millimetres wide, until the casing cracked in the middle. This would activate the tracker and pass her exact location to the coalition forces designated to rescue her.

Miriam hesitated with her thumb and forefinger pressed lightly on the device. Although the entire mission was fraught with danger, this was the most unnerving part. British and American troops would be sent to rescue her, the finest soldiers available, by all accounts. The trouble was, they wouldn't know her true role in Afghanistan. To them, she would be the traitor who provided the Taliban with the deadly weapon that had probably resulted in the deaths of their friends. She'd been told that there was a small chance that rather than rescue her, they would be seeking revenge.

'We'll do all we can to get you home safely,' they'd said at the final briefing. 'We can't divulge the details of your mission to the insertion team, but they'll be told that you are needed alive at all costs.'

'And what if they disobey orders?' she'd asked. 'What if they decide to concoct a story? They could say I was killed by the Taliban before they could rescue me, or I died in an explosion—one of their making. Why not just tell them the truth and swear them to secrecy?'

'Because at the moment, maybe ten people know about this mission, including you, me, the president and the British prime minister. We all have top-secret clearance. If we start adding a few grunts into the mix, it'll be in the papers before we know it, and that puts all of us—you especially—in a dangerous situation.'

It had been spelled out specifically how much danger— revenge attacks from Taliban supporters in the US, for one.

The possibility of the allied forces killing her first was real. She'd heard al-Hussain talking to his men, bragging of great victories brought about by her virus. That news had crushed her. Deep down, she'd hoped it wouldn't work as well as it was designed to, but her worst fears had been realised. She'd been complicit in the deaths of American and British soldiers, proud young men who wouldn't be returning home to wives, parents, children...

She'd tried to tell herself that it wasn't entirely her fault, that they were there to fight and had been given a fighting chance, and that it had all been for the greater good. Though, it still made her physically sick as she thought about it each night. She might have done some good for her country, but she would have to bear the pain for the rest of her life.

Perhaps if her rescuers decided to put a bullet in her brain they would be doing her a favour.

She took a deep breath, then squeezed the capsule and felt it break in the middle. All she could do now was wait.

Chapter 25

When Gray got the summons to see the CO he hoped it was for news of replacements for Josh Miller's team. It had been three weeks since his friend's patrol had been wiped out, and Gray had been short since then. The first four men sent out to reinforce the troop had been caught up in a quarantine situation at the staging area in Kuwait. They'd arrived just as the flu had spread through the base and in an effort to prevent it reaching the front-line troops in Afghanistan, no personnel were allowed to complete the last leg of their journey to Kandahar. That had meant Gray and his patrol doing the job of two teams, and the fun was beginning to wear off.

As Gray approached Russell's office, the captain strode out through the door. 'Follow me. We're going to see Durden.'

That put paid to any hopes of reinforcements. Visiting Durden meant only one thing— another mission. Gray silently cursed. His men were close to exhaustion. They'd been out every night for fifteen days, clocking up over a hundred kilometres on foot. If they didn't get some R & R soon, their ability to function efficiently would be severely impaired.

'Please tell me you've got some good news on reinforcements.'

'Three days,' Russell told Gray. 'They're shipping via Incirlik this time.'

'Great. Any chance me and the boys can have a few days off once they get here?'

'No problem,' Russell assured him. 'I'll sort something out.'

'Thanks. Did Durden say what this was all about?'

'They've located the Dagher woman—looks like you're going in to get her.'

Gray perked up. The only thing he wanted more than a sumptuous meal and a week in bed was to get his hands on that woman. She was responsible for many deaths, including, he suspected, those of Josh Miller and his patrol.

'Let's just hope it's a 'dead or alive' deal, 'cos I know which I'd prefer.'

'I know what you mean,' Russell told him, 'but that's not my call.'

When they got to Durden's office, they found that Balmer and Bridges were already there. The American captain made a show of looking at his watch, then at the British pair. Gray ignored him.

'What do we have?' Russell asked the CIA officer.

'Miriam Dagher's location,' Durden said, rising from his desk and walking over to a wall map. 'She's here, thirty miles from the Pakistan border. It's a small village, no more than twenty dwellings.' From his desk, he picked up two files and gave them to the senior officers. 'As you'll see from the satellite imagery, there are just five people in the house marked with the big X. That's where she's being held.'

Russell opened the file and saw the photo taken from miles above the planet. The blurred outlines of five white figures could be clearly seen against the dark background.

'How come we've never had this type of intel before?' Gray asked. 'Up until now, we've been given a location by some shady character and worked from that.'

'None of the other targets have been high enough on the JPEL to warrant it,' Durden told him. 'This bird was only launched eight days ago and is supposed to be over Russia right now, but JSOC had it moved to watch over her. We have to go in tonight and bring her home.'

'Why not just bomb the bitch?' Balmer asked. 'Drop a couple of Hellfires on her head… job done.'

'We need her alive,' Durden told him. 'That's non-negotiable.'

'We can't guarantee that,' Russell said. 'Things happen in battle—the situation is fluid. A stray round, misplaced grenade, things can go tits-up pretty quickly.'

'Then you'd better make sure it doesn't. She has to get out alive, and that comes direct from the oval office. If we wanted 'maybe' or 'might', we'd have got the Albanians to do it. You guys are the best on the planet, so either tell me you'll bring her home, or I'll have you relieved and find someone else who can.'

The captain was right; a multitude of things could happen during the operation, many of them out of Gray's control. However, he wasn't about to step aside to let someone else go in his place. It would be the ultimate humiliation, one that would see him kicked out of the army for good. While he planned to leave anyway, once Dina became pregnant, he'd prefer to do so with a pension. More importantly, he'd lose the respect of his only friends. His reputation in the service would be tarnished forever, and he could kiss goodbye to any chance of making a name for himself in the private security market. Though the clincher was his own pride—it would never allow him to walk away from a challenge.

'We'll get her out,' Gray said.

Balmer nodded. 'Yeah, we'll bring her back.'

'Good,' Durden said. 'And if you're thinking of concocting a story about her catching an unfortunate bullet, don't bother. If you don't bring her back in one piece, you'll spend the rest of your lives in Fort Leavenworth. And no interrogation. You don't so much as ask her how she feels, you got that?'

Both men acknowledged that they understood the instructions, but something didn't sit right with Gray. Over the years he'd been on a few snatch missions, but the brief had always been to bring them back alive 'if possible'. Now he was being asked—*told*—to put Dagher's life before him and the team.

This was all supposition, though. Dagher had to actually be there before Durden's orders came into play.

'What's the source?' Gray asked the spook.

'That's classified.'

'Classified?' Gray had never heard that one before. Vague hints at elint—electronic intelligence—or humint—human intelligence—but never classified.

'Need to know,' Durden added, 'and that's all you need to know.'

The mission was getting stranger by the minute, but Gray knew he wouldn't get answers here.

'We've had a drone up for the last few hours,' Durden said, changing the direction of the conversation, 'and we've spotted just two hostiles. They alternate; one inside the house, one patrolling outside. We don't expect that to change by the time you go in.'

'When will that be?' Balmer asked him.

'Zero-two-hundred. I'll leave the team structure and roles to you guys, but the chopper will be ready at zero-one-hundred, and a Predator and AC-130 will be on station throughout. The satellite will be overhead at all times, so we'll have a real-time view of the operation. All eyes will be on you.'

Gray wasn't expecting that, either. Normally he had to beg for air support, and the answer was usually 'if it's available at the time'. This time, they would have a drone stuffed with Hellfire missiles and a Hercules gunship boasting more firepower than the average battle tank watching over them. On top of that, they would be able to see if anyone put a bullet in Dagher.

It seemed like a hell of a lot of effort and resources to find one person. It was certainly more than had been available to tackle the Taliban leadership.

'Why do you want her alive so bad?' Gray couldn't help asking.

'We want all our targets alive,' Durden glared at him, 'but you guys much prefer to bring us bodies instead. As I said, though, this comes from the president. Fuck this up, you answer to him.'

Russell slapped Gray on the arm with the file, then nodded to Durden and Bridges. 'Captain, let's meet at nineteen-hundred hours to discuss.'

Gray followed his CO out the door and after walking ten yards, he leaned towards him and whispered.

'Was it just me, or was that strange as hell?'

'Lots of unanswered questions,' Russell agreed. 'My guess? They want what's inside her head.'

'The virus,' Gray said. He suspected that his earlier thoughts about the US and British wanting to weaponise the virus for their own use was bang on the money. 'You think the government would use it on our own troops?'

Russell shrugged. 'I'd like to think not, but when you consider the cost implications…'

That would no doubt be a huge factor. It takes months just to get through basic training, during which time the troops have to be housed and fed. If that could be cut to a few weeks, the savings would be immense. No right-minded politician would turn their nose up at that.

'Don't dwell on it too much,' Russell added. 'Just go there and do your job. I'll see you at seven.'

The captain split off to return to his office while Gray went to pass on the news to the rest of his patrol. He found them preparing to head for the DFAC.

'Good news and bad news,' Gray told them.

'Good news first,' Smart said.

'Our replacements will be here in three days. The boss is sorting a few days off.'

'About time,' Sonny sighed. 'Please tell me the bad news is that the chef ran out of liver.'

'You wish,' Gray said. 'We're going out again tonight.'

'That's it?' Smart asked.

'With Balmer,' Gray told him, earning groans all round. 'We're going to pick up the Dagher woman.'

'They found her? Excellent!' Sonny produced a deck of cards from his footlocker and offered them to Gray. 'Cut.'

'We've no time for card games.'

'No, it's to see who gets to slot her. The bastards who killed Josh's brick must have been given her virus. It's only fair that one of us does it.'

189

'Not gonna happen. They want her back alive.'

'Yeah well… things happen in the heat of battle,' Levine pointed out.

'Not this time,' Gray said. 'They'll have eyes on us throughout. Durden basically told me that if we don't get her out alive, we might as well not come back. That came from the very top.'

'Someone wants her virus,' Smart said.

'My thoughts exactly,' Gray agreed. 'Maybe the PM wants to even things up by giving it to us, too.'

'Why bother?' Sonny asked. 'There's plenty of performance-enhancing drugs around, but they're not routinely given to troops. Why start now?'

'He's right,' Levine added. 'There'd be a political shitstorm if word got out that we were injecting our own men with this thing.'

'Then maybe they want it for something else,' Gray conceded, 'but all I know is they don't want her in a body bag.'

'How did they find her?' Smart wanted to know.

'He wouldn't say.'

'Why not?'

'Classified,' Gray said sarcastically.

Chapter 26

No-one spoke as they flew south. Enough had been said during the hour-long briefing.

It hadn't been a cordial gathering by any means. The target building consisted of one storey and six rooms, so there was no need for all eight men to go in, especially as they would have a real-time infra-red feed from overhead and could pinpoint the locations of the enemy. Both Gray and Balmer wanted to spearhead the assault while the other team remained on the fringes to provide cover, with Gray arguing that in Sonny they had the best available—he was a CQB instructor at Hereford. Balmer had countered that his team had more missions under their belt. Not even the intervention of Bridges and Russell could break the deadlock, and in the end they'd drawn straws to see who would go in for Dagher.

Gray had won, though Balmer had been quick to sour his victory.

'If this goes to shit, it's your ass on the line,' he'd said.

With just minutes before they touched down, the weight of the responsibility was sitting heavily on Gray's shoulders. He told himself that all he could do was perform his duties as he had many times before, with professionalism. If the gods of war decided to deal him a shitty hand, so be it.

'Two minutes,' the crew chief said.

Gray checked his magazine for the umpteenth time, then stood and walked to the rear of the chopper. Through the green tint of the NVGs, he watched the ramp drop, revealing a dark canvas dotted with stars. The moment the bird hit the ground, he was out running. He threw himself to the dirt twenty yards from the helicopter and pointed his weapon into the night. Seconds later, the chopper took off once more, and Gray waited for silence to descend before performing a radio check. The other seven members of the team acknowledged that they were good to go.

'Balmer, you take point. Sonny, you're tail-end Charlie.'

It was forty minutes before the village came into view. They'd approached from the north, then tacked east to get a better angle on the building that Dagher was known to be in. There was now only one house between them and the target.

They crouched down four hundred yards from the nearest dwelling. Gray took out his poncho and took a knee next to Balmer. He put the waterproof coat over their heads and took out the tablet Durden had given them. After powering it on and waiting for it to load, Gray clicked on the icon that connected them to the satellite feed beamed from over a thousand miles above. There were five heat signatures coming from the building where Dagher was thought to be, as was the case earlier that day. Three of them looked to be sleeping, while one was in a sitting position and the last was walking slowly outside in the garden. Gray zoomed out a little to take in the surrounding area.

'Looks quiet,' Balmer said.

It did, but Gray knew how quickly situations could change. 'Okay, keep me updated on movements. We'll go in three minutes.'

'Don't fuck it up.'

It was as close to a 'good luck' as Gray was going to get. He crawled out from under the poncho and gestured for his team to gather around.

'We go in three,' Gray told them. Sonny, Smart and Levine all nodded. They were ready, having gone over the assault a dozen times before boarding the chopper. Each knew his task, and Gray gave them a final update before they set off.

'Good to go,' Balmer said in Gray's ear. He would feed live updates throughout the mission which would be crucial if they were to avoid turning this into a firefight.

Gray tapped his mic twice in acknowledgement, then stood and walked towards the village.

'Still clear,' Balmer said when Gray was a hundred yards from the nearest building. As rehearsed, Smart and Levine split off, the two pairs of men going either side of the first house. Gray and Sonny would take out the guard in the front garden, while the others would assault the building from the rear.

'Got you on visual,' Balmer said. 'Clear to the target.'

Gray moved slowly across the street with Sonny in close attendance. They stopped against the wall, three yards from the wrought-iron gate that gave access to the house. They would give Len and Carl two minutes to get in position and lay their explosives. The plan was for them to set a framed charge on the rear wall, and on Gray's signal they would blow it and rush in through the back doors. Gray watched the seconds tick down, then pressed his throat mic to signal Balmer that he was ready to go.

'Exterior guard is behind the wall, two yards to your south, three yards from the perimeter.'

Gray indicated the position of the guard to Sonny who nodded before slowly pulling out his suppressed pistol.

'He's maintaining position,' Balmer told Gray, who acknowledged the report.

The wall was nine feet tall, and Gray had to cup his hands so that Sonny could climb up and take the shot. Even with the silencer, the round sounded like a clap of thunder as it left the handgun.

'X-Ray one down,' Sonny announced as Gray heard the body crumple to the ground.

He let Sonny down and they sprinted to the gate. Sonny shot out the lock and Gray pulled the iron rail aside.

'Clear,' Gray heard. He clicked his mic three times to let Smart know there were ten seconds until the strike began. He used that time to creep up to the front door, counting as he went. On three, he aimed at the lock. On one, he fired.

Sonny pushed past Gray and kicked the door open, rushing inside and sweeping the house with his rifle. They knew from the satellite feed where the occupants were, though they couldn't tell which was Dagher. They would have to go room to room to determine who lived and who died.

Gray heard a loud *crump!* as Smart's explosive charge blew a hole on the back wall. That, and the door being kicked in, would be enough to wake the residents.

Gray stood beside the first door on the left, where the tablet had informed them a figure had been sleeping. He pulled a stun grenade from his webbing and removed the pin.

'Bravo One,' Balmer said, indicating the two-man team of Gray and Sonny, 'the occupant of the room is up and active.'

'Where?'

'Directly behind you.'

Gray's first instinct was to fire through the wall, but there were two problems; the structure was solid brick, meaning his rounds wouldn't penetrate, and there was no telling who it was. It could be the other armed guard... or Dagher.

Gray whispered the person's location to Sonny, then stepped back and let his companion kick in the door. Gray tossed the grenade inside and got out of the way of the blast that came two seconds later. As soon as it blew, Sonny was inside, and before Gray could join him, two shots rang out.

'X-Ray two down,' Sonny informed all those listening in.

'Cover them,' Gray told Sonny, pointing to the next room that was known to be occupied. Two heat signatures had been seen here, suggesting it was a husband and wife. They would be allowed to live as long as they stayed where they were, but if they tried to intervene it would be a fatal decision.

Gray ran to the only other room where the satellite had picked up body heat. He was joined by Smart and Levine.

'Sit rep on X-Ray five,' Gray asked Balmer.

'Still motionless on the bed. Looks like she's got her hands up.'

By a process of elimination, it had to be Dagher. But why was she just lying there? She must have heard the commotion by now. Perhaps it was a trap.

Gray kicked the door in and saw her staring at the ceiling, her arms above her head, palms up and empty.

'Get up!'

She swung her legs off the bed and stood, her hands still in the air.

'Turn around!'

She did as Gray barked and he held the muzzle of his gun to her head as he patted her down. She was clean. No explosive vest under her clothes, and no weapon of any description. Gray was silently willing her to make a move, to give him an excuse to blow her away, but Dagher was following his commands to the letter.

Gray grabbed her by the hair and pushed her towards the door, just as the sound of an AK-47 reached his ears. It was quickly followed by the familiar clack of a suppressed Browning Hi-Power. Gray shoved Dagher to the side and peered out the door in time to see Sonny pacing towards him.

'They fired through the door,' Sonny explained, with no need to add what the result of that had been.

'You've got company,' Balmer told them. 'Five... no, six heading your way from the east. Hold on... two more from the west. They're currently two houses over and closing fast.'

'Shit's about to get real,' Gray told Smart, who'd also heard the news. 'You and Sonny go right, I'll take the left.' He pushed Dagher towards Levine. 'Cuff her and keep her safe.'

The three men ran to the gate just as the first of the armed Taliban reached the house. He was cut down immediately by Smart, which brought a fierce response from his fellow countrymen. Rounds slammed into the wall Gray was taking cover behind, sending razor-like shards flying through the air. Gray tossed a grenade out into the street and the moment it exploded he added a few bursts from his rifle. Another Afghan fell, three bloody holes in his chest, but his friends continued to advance

'Bravo One, you need to punch a way out of there. You've got another three heading your way.'

'Working on it,' Gray told Balmer as one of Sonny's grenades took out two more Taliban. Gray ejected his empty mag and slapped a new one home, then chambered a round in his underslung M203 grenade launcher and fired at the car two Afghans were using as cover. The vehicle jumped in the air as the explosive hit the petrol tank, reducing the enemy number to seven. That could change at any moment, though. Reinforcements would be called in to protect such a high-value prize like Dagher, and the longer Gray and his team remained in place, the less chance there was of getting her out alive.

'Alpha One, tell the guys in the sky to hit anyone outside the wall. We can't bring the target out through this.' Gray fired another burst, his rounds striking a wall rather than flesh.

'Roger that. Get back in the house and find cover. This could get noisy.'

Gray didn't have to tell the others. The trio ran back inside the building and told Levine and Dagher to hit the floor.

Less than a minute later, the battle was over. Thousands of 20mm rounds spat down from the M61 Vulcan rotary cannon on board the orbiting AC-130, tearing up the street and anyone in it. It was another minute before the aerial bombardment ended, and Gray was given the all-clear.

'Let's go.'

Gray took the lead as they left the house for a second time, and the devastation was hard to comprehend—even for a seasoned soldier like Gray. Balmer's warning had been spot on, as a couple of hundred bullets found their way into the garden. The wall Gray had been using as cover was almost completely destroyed. Two trees that earlier stood proud had been reduced to jagged stumps. Out in the street, it was carnage. Gray couldn't make out how many people had been caught in the thunderous fire, but there were body parts everywhere.

Sonny looked up at the night sky as they trotted back to the LUP. 'Glad those guys are on our side,' he muttered.

'Bravo One, Alpha Two is at your twelve o'clock, one hundred yards.'

'Acknowledged.'

As planned, two of Balmer's team, along with Levine and Sonny, would remain in the vicinity until the evacuation was complete, then make their own way back to the rendezvous point to pick up their transport to base. The priority was to get Dagher back safely, and they couldn't guarantee that if they all got on the incoming chopper. Someone had to stay behind and keep any remaining Taliban occupied until the bird was out of range.

Balmer had already called the bird in, and it landed a kilometre from the village. Dagher didn't mutter a single word as she was quick-marched onto the helicopter. He noticed that she avoided eye contact, too. Whether that was through guilt, fear, or both, he didn't particularly care.

Balmer sat directly opposite Dagher, and Gray took a seat next to him. Smart and Lomax flanked the prisoner.

The chopper leapt into the air, and Dagher turned her head to watch the desert floor disappear in the darkness.

'Can you please close the door?' she asked. 'It's cold.'

'Maybe.' Balmer said. 'First I have to decide if we're gonna throw you out.'

Chapter 27

It was what Miriam Dagher feared most. She'd been steeling herself for a bullet between the eyes the moment the soldier had entered the room, but it hadn't come. She'd thought that perhaps they were going to bring her out safely, just as her CIA handler had told her they would, but now—shivering in a helicopter with threatening eyes staring at her—she wasn't so certain.

'What kind of person creates a virus to kill British and American soldiers?' Gray asked. 'I just want to know before I give my friend here his wish.'

Tell them nothing.

The words from her handler rang loud in her ears, but it was easy to agree to them in the comfort of a warm office in Virginia. Here, on a cold, noisy helicopter speeding over the Afghan desert and facing the prospect of a long drop, self-preservation was her only concern.

'I… can't tell you about it. It's classified.'

She saw the look of confusion on the two men's faces, but didn't want to elaborate. She'd been told that they would be instructed not to interrogate her, and she hoped that they followed those orders.

It wasn't to be.

'That word's cropped up a lot during this mission,' Gray said, 'and frankly, it's beginning to piss me off. How can being party to the deaths of our friends and colleagues be classified?'

Miriam wanted to tell them everything, to assure them that they had her all wrong, but she knew that if she did, she'd be risking her entire future. Then again, that future relied on her getting back to base in one piece, not smeared across the desert floor.

'How do you wanna do this?' Gray asked Balmer. 'We can't say she overpowered us.'

'We could snip her cuffs off and say she jumped,' the American suggested.

Gray shrugged. 'Sounds good to me.' He got up and took out his knife, a seven-inch beast with a serrated edge, then made a move for Miriam's seatbelt.

'No!' she cried. 'Stop!'

'Too late, lady, you had your chance.'

Tears began to roll down Miriam's face. 'Please! I'll tell you everything!'

He stopped fiddling with the clasp, paused, then sat back down again.

'I want to know *everything*.'

* * *

The bird circled, then dropped quickly to the ground. Once it hit, Gray removed her seatbelt and pulled her to her feet.

'I'm going to be rough with you,' he said. 'We have to keep up the pretence.'

He pushed her towards the ramp, where two men were waiting. Once they were on the ground, he shoved her towards one of them, then took out his pistol. He ejected a bullet and tossed it to her new guardian. 'Do me a favour,' Gray said. 'Once you're done interrogating her, put that through her skull.

Chapter 28

Abdul al-Hussain looked at the phone on the table next to him. He was sitting in the garden sipping tea, waiting to hear news about the attack on the base the Americans called Vincent. He'd sent two hundred and fifty men to wipe out the invaders, and it shouldn't be too long before he received news of their victory.

It would be the first of many, he was sure. The virus Dagher had given him was truly a gift from Allah himself, and he already had enough to build an unstoppable army. By the end of the year he would have over fifty thousand skilled soldiers at his disposal, enough to drive the Americans and British out of Afghanistan forever. He wouldn't stop there. Once the Westerners were gone, Kabul would be his next objective. The American puppet masquerading as president would be banished, and the Taliban would rule once more. Until now it had always been his ambition, but in light of recent events it was no longer just a dream.

His son, Jamal, brought him another tea and a plate of food, treading carefully in the darkness so as not to spill any.

'You should be in bed,' al-Hussain told the boy. It was after two in the morning, and normally al-Hussain would have been tucked up, too, if his mind were not racing.

'I'm not tired.'

'Then I'm not working you hard enough.' Al-Hussain smiled. 'I will find something for you to do in the morning. Perhaps eight hours digging a drainage ditch will help you sleep.'

Jamal turned his face to hide his displeasure, but al-Hussain caught it anyway.

'It's not that. I just... I had a feeling something bad was going to happen.'

Al-Hussain pulled him closer. 'Bad things happen all the time,' he told his son. 'It is how we react and deal with it that counts. I have seen so many tragedies in my time, yet I am stronger for it. Besides,' he said, ruffling the child's hair, 'you are too young to worry about anything other than your studies.'

The phone on the table rang, and al-Hussain snatched it up.

'Bed!' he mouthed to Jamal, who slinked away. Once the boy was walking away, al-Hussain answered but didn't speak. There was no need. Only a handful of people had the number, and he didn't need to introduce himself to any of them.

'Samir's house was attacked by the Americans.' It was Badrawi, one of the men from the village.

'What about our guest?' al-Hussain asked.

'They took her.'

Al-Hussain remained silent for a moment, then ended the call. There was nothing else to be said, and the longer he was on the line, the higher the chance of his location being detected. People will have died to protect her, he knew that, but he would find out the details later. What was done was done, and he couldn't change it.

Dagher's loss was a bitter blow to his plans, but it wasn't a complete tragedy. He still had a vast supply of her virus, and steps were already being taken to find enough recruits to inject it in to. Perhaps he could find another virologist to take up her work, though that wasn't a priority. She had seen the training camp run by his friend Kamal, so that would have to be moved immediately. The Americans would no doubt try to get information out of the woman, and at her age, it shouldn't take long.

He would also have to find out who gave the Americans the woman's location. Few knew where she had been staying, so it would limit his search. Someone had given her up, probably in return for a handful of American dollars—an act that would prove costly.

A thought suddenly struck him; why give up the woman and not him? Abdul al-Hussain considered himself a much bigger prize than Miriam Dagher. If one of his men was working with the Americans, why not give them a Taliban leader? Why the woman?

The thought bounced around his head for a few minutes, but he came up with no answers. Eventually he decided that it couldn't be someone who knew his movements—few did, and their loyalty was unquestionable. It must be someone lower in the ranks who got a sniff of Dagher's whereabouts and was tempted by the lure of riches. Well, he would smoke them out and show them the price of disloyalty.

Al-Hussain dialled a number and spoke as soon as it was answered. 'We have a problem. You must move the training camp immediately.'

'What happened?' Kamal asked sleepily.

'I'll explain later. Get moving, I'll contact you in two days.'

Al-Hussain ended the call and put the phone back on the table next to the plate of food Jamal had brought him. Jamal, with his portents of doom. Had he foreseen Dagher's capture, or was there more to come? An involuntary shiver shook his body, and al-Hussain picked up the glass of hot tea and cupped it in his hands.

Something told him he would find out soon.

Chapter 29

Gray glanced back and watched Durden lead Dagher away.

'What's going to happen to her?' he asked his captain.

'Don't know, don't care. We've got bigger fish to fry. FOB Vincent was hit fifteen minutes ago.'

Gray stopped and looked at Russell. 'Again? How many?'

'A couple of hundred at least. The 654th have no support. And to make matters worse, there are roughly fifty civilians at the base. I need you and your team to gear up and get over there now.'

'What about Jeff's brick?' Gray asked.

'Already en route, as are the rest of Balmer's ODA. A chopper's fuelled and ready to go. You've got three minutes.'

'Okay. Let 'em know we're coming.'

Gray dashed over to Sonny, Smart and Levine, who were waiting for him. He told them to follow him and filled them in as they jogged to the armoury. Two minutes later, with their ammo replenished, they ran to the HH-60 Pave Hawk that was already winding up. Balmer and his men joined them a minute later, and the bird leapt into the sky as they strapped themselves in.

The pilot pushed the helicopter to the max, driving every ounce of power out of the engines. The trip had taken twenty minutes in a Chinook on their first visit two weeks earlier, but this time the camp was visible on the horizon in twelve.

While Balmer contacted his team on the ground, Gray got on the radio to Jeff Campbell and asked for a sit-rep.

'We're outside the north corner, engaged with thirty-plus. The wall has been breached to the south and west, and there's at least a hundred of them inside the base. Get down here sharpish.'

'Roger that. We'll form up on you.' Gray switched to the intercom to speak to the pilot. 'I need you to put us down two hundred yards north of the camp.'

'Negative. It's too hot.'

'That wasn't a request, just fucking do it! We'll clear the immediate area.' Gray unstrapped himself and moved over to within earshot of the gunner mounted on the right of the aircraft. 'When I give the signal, my mate's gonna pop smoke. When you see it, blast everything within ten yards, nothing more. We don't want a blue on blue.'

Gray took his seat once more and contacted Campbell again. 'Can you pop smoke on the X-rays?'

'Sure, gimme five seconds.'

'Make it twenty, we need to get in position.'

'Roger that.'

Gray passed on instructions to the pilot and gunner, then put on his NVGs and readied his own weapon. The bird flew down the east wall of the base at an altitude of a thousand feet, AK-47 rounds pinging harmlessly off the undercarriage. When they reached the north-east corner, the pilot turned and dipped the nose and the Pave Hawk dropped like a stone. From his window, Gray could see smoke billowing from just outside the camp.

'There's your target!'

The gunner's GAU-18/A .50 calibre pounded the area, geysers of sand leaping into the air with each round. Gray saw at least fifteen Taliban go down—the rest ran for their lives.

'Put us down!' Gray told the pilot. And with the immediate threat gone, he did as asked.

It was a bumpy landing—Gray was almost thrown out of the helicopter when it hit the ground. He got his balance and ran in a crouch to avoid the rotors overhead, throwing himself to the ground.

'At your six, a hundred yards,' Gray told Campbell.

'Roger that. Go west, see if you can get inside. We're going after the stragglers.'

Gray saw Campbell and his three men set off to the left in pursuit of the fleeing Taliban, and he and Balmer took their men right. They ran for three hundred yards before coming to the corner, where debris that had once been the watch tower lay smouldering. Gray stuck his head around the corner and saw the action unfolding four hundred yards away. At least thirty Taliban were engaged with the troops manning the wall, and most of the fire was incoming. The men of the 654th were outnumbered two-to-one, and they had a long perimeter to defend.

'Balmer, we go in here,' Gray said. He stood with his back to the ten-foot wall and cradled his hands so that the American could climb up. Once Balmer was over and providing cover, Gray helped the other six men over the wall. Lomax and Smart then leaned over it to pull Gray up.

The scene was utter chaos. Mini firefights had broken out everywhere, several fires were raging and bodies were strewn across the ground. The Taliban were so entrenched in the American lines that air support was out of the question.

Gray prioritised the safety of the civilians as their first objective, but they would have to fight their way to them. He pointed out the two closest skirmishes and assigned one to Balmer and his men. He took Smart, Sonny and Levine to help three Americans who were pinned down by a dozen Taliban.

They attacked from the left flank, opening up when they were fifty yards from the enemy. Four fell instantly, and the rest diverted their fire towards Gray's team who took cover and answered with accurate fire. Two more were hit, but the rest went to ground, scrambling behind piles of timber. Gray and his men kept them pinned down, allowing the three men from the 654th to regroup. They managed to get behind the Afghans and take out another two. Faced with assault from three sides, the remaining Taliban quartet didn't stand a chance, but they put up a spirited fight to the end. It was only a couple of grenades that silenced them once and for all.

There was no time to dwell on the victory, though. Gray left the American trio to their own devices and went in search of the next engagement. He found it a hundred yards away, where fifteen Taliban were shooting up some wooden buildings he knew to be the civilian quarters. The men from the infantry were dotted around and inside the hut, mustering what defence they could, but Gray saw three of them gunned down in quick succession.

Gray told Smart and Sonny to split off and get a better angle on the bad guys, while he and Levine would draw their attention. Gray crouched behind a huge bag of gravel and waited until the other two were in position, then opened fire. He hit his target, and Levine also registered a kill. But it brought a hail of bullets their way, forcing them to take cover. Gray then heard Sonny and Smart open up—giving him an opportunity to stick his head out and take down another Afghan.

The three-pronged attack was probably not what the Taliban were expecting, but to their credit they maintained their discipline. They didn't waste rounds, nor look flustered in any way. For Gray, it was like watching a training exercise back in Hereford.

But they weren't invincible.

Gray switched out magazines and fired three bursts at the enemy, hoping to draw their fire and let his teammates get in closer. It worked, but Smart and Sonny were only able to move a few feet before bullets started flying their way. Gray took the opportunity to sprint behind a bulldozer, with Levine close behind him. It gave him a better angle on one of the Taliban, and he made his shots count. He fired another few bursts at another target, then hit the catch to release the empty magazine just as bullets pinged off the bulldozer next to his head.

'Fuck!' Levine shouted. 'I'm hit!'

Gray turned to face the threat and saw a young boy, no more than sixteen, running towards him. The kid raised his AK-47 and squeezed the trigger as Gray waited for the punch that would signal a hit.

None came.

The boy dropped his empty weapon and pulled out a knife, then hurtled towards Gray, who was fumbling in his webbing for a fresh magazine. He managed to get it out, but the kid was on him before he had a chance to slam it home. Gray stood and threw his rifle at the boy's face, but the youngster easily deflected it and rushed at him, thrusting the knife towards Gray's stomach. Gray parried the strike and caught the boy with a vicious right hand to the head, but the boy shook it off and came again, slashing wildly as Gray backed off. With the knife swishing closer and closer to his face, Gray took another step backwards and caught his heel on a timber beam. He tripped, landing heavily on his back. The Taliban youngster leapt on him; the blade high and arcing towards Gray's face. Gray grabbed the knife arm near the wrist, confident that he had power advantage, but the kid seemed possessed. Gray didn't know if it was the virus, or the boy's natural survival instincts, but he seemed to have the strength of three men. Gray strained every sinew to keep the knife away from his face, but it inched closer with every breath he took. He could almost feel the cold blade as it searched for his left cheek, and for the first time in his life, he feared his moment had come. This wasn't how he planned to go—defeated in one-to-one combat by a child. Brute strength alone wasn't going to win this, but Gray had been around the block a few times. He coughed up a ball of phlegm and spat in his attacker's eyes, and the moment the young Afghan jerked his head back, Gray twisted and threw the boy to the side. Gray rolled away, out of reach of the blade, then whipped out his pistol and fired twice. The bullets found their mark, but Gray didn't have time to reflect on his personal victory. He picked up his rifle and inserted a fresh magazine, then jogged over to Levine who was still engaging the Taliban.

'You okay?'

'Yeah,' Levine told him. 'Got hit in the leg. It's just a scratch.'

Gray fired at a head that had poked out from behind a pile of timber, but his snapshot missed. 'Good. Let's finish these guys off.' There were only four remaining, the rest having been picked off by the 654th as well as Sonny and

Smart. The infantry had managed to force their way closer, and the Taliban were in a hopeless situation. That didn't seem to faze them though, as they fought resolutely for the next three minutes. But the odds were never in their favour. Sonny took out the last of them, but the fighting continued around the camp.

Gray ordered the 654th to set up a defensive perimeter around the civilians, while he checked out the skirmishes taking place all around him. There were plenty to choose from, and the Taliban seemed to have the upper hand in most of them. They needed more boots on the ground, and fast. He radioed the base and asked when they could expect some help, but the news wasn't good. Two more choppers were being fuelled to bring in a platoon from the Australian commandos, but it would be at least twenty minutes before the Chinooks arrived.

Air support was out too. With the perimeter breached and everyone fighting at close quarters, there were likely to be as many coalition casualties as Taliban.

They were going to have to clear them out themselves.

'Balmer, what's your situation?'

'Engaged with three near the north-east corner, but they're dug in.'

'Get it done, then form up on me. I'm at the Caterpillar by the accommodation block. We need to co-ordinate our attack.' Gray radioed Sonny and Jeff Campbell and gave them the same instructions.

With the civilians relatively safe, it was time to clean up— the best way to do that was as one large unit instead of small teams dotted all over the battlefield. Four-man patrols were ideal for covert incursions behind enemy lines; it was what the SAS were best known for. It wasn't the only song in their repertoire, though. First and foremost they were soldiers, not averse to a good-old, straightforward firefight.

The base was too big to move line abreast and clear it from north to south; they would be spread out too thinly. Instead, Gray decided to head to the hole in the west wall, deal with anyone still trying to get in, then get the 654th to set up defences in case the Taliban committed more men to the assault. After that, they would join each engagement, using overwhelming fire to their advantage.

Balmer and his men joined Gray and Levine moments later. He shared his plan, and Balmer simply nodded before leading the way.

A tented village stood between them and the west wall, slowing their progress as they had to check around each corner before moving to the next row. Sonny was on point, and when he reached the end of the second tent he checked the alley way and saw an enemy combatant on the run. Sonny already had his rifle up and got the drop on him, and after a few seconds indicated to the others that the coast was clear.

Gray noticed a lack of gunfire coming from the direction they were heading, and when they reached their destination he saw why. The only infantry they could see were lying still on the ground, their battles fought and lost.

Gray looked through the hole and out into the night. There was no sign of anyone, which suggested that all of the protagonists were already inside the base. No point wasting resources by leaving someone to guard the ersatz entrance. Instead, he followed his ears and indicated the direction the closest noise was coming from. All fifteen men followed Gray, who ran around the back of a coffee house until he reached the corner. Poking his head out, he saw a handful of

Taliban fifty yards away. They had their backs to him, firing at two men from the 654th who were trying to pull an injured trooper to cover. One of the infantrymen took a bullet to the leg and the other was killed instantly. The Taliban immediately swarmed the two wounded men, shouldering their rifles and drawing their *pesh-kabz*—Afghan knives that were eighteen inches long. It was clear how they intended to finish the vulnerable men off.

Gray moved forward and to the right, allowing Sonny to follow him and get a bead on the Afghans—they opened up just as the first of the Taliban raised his weapon. All five fell, and Gray ordered Smart—the patrol medic—to help him deal with the casualties. Smart gave them a once over. They would survive, but only if they got to a hospital in the next thirty minutes.

A huge explosion lit up the night, and a second later the ground beneath Gray's feet juddered violently. It had come from the south of the camp, and from memory Gray knew it had to be the fuel dump where thousands of gallons of gasoline had been stored. He watched a colossal black cloud mushroom into the sky, blind to the swarm of Taliban emerging from behind a burning building until they were firing. With no immediate cover available, he threw himself to the ground and replied, his efforts soon joined by those of the men with him. Gray rolled to the side and took out another enemy combatant with a burst to the chest, then jumped to his feet and got between the Taliban and the casualties.

'Get them out of here!' Gray screamed at Smart, who used the cover fire to pull one of the injured men behind the hut. Lomax used one hand to drag the other while firing his rifle at the enemy. The hut's flimsy build offered no protection from the incoming rounds, so they lifted the casualties onto their shoulders and retreated towards the centre of the base.

The remaining seven men of the SAS continued to lay down suppressing fire while Balmer's team retreated twenty yards. Then they swapped disciplines; the Delta Force members allowing Gray and his men to pull back. Once they were all among the tents, Gray told Balmer to fall back to the accommodation block. They would set up their defences there and try to hold out until the Aussies arrived.

As they ran to the RV point, bullets whistled past Gray's ear. The Taliban were fearless, following the more experienced soldiers, keen to take the fight to them. Gray thought that perhaps they didn't know who they were up against, but it was more likely that they simply didn't care. He turned and let off a couple of bursts to slow their progress, but it only bought a few seconds of respite.

As they turned a corner, Gray spotted the body of a young American soldier. Instinctively, he picked up the man's rifle and took the magazines that were sticking out of his pockets. They would need all the ammunition they could get their hands on.

They reached the area where the civilians had been gathered. Gray saw that only half a dozen men remained from the 654th. The sounds of battle that earlier reverberated around the base had now faded, which suggested they were the last coalition forces alive. Sixteen members of the special forces and a handful of infantry against an unknown number of chemically-enhanced Taliban.

These were the moments Gray had trained long and hard for.

'Get them inside,' Gray told Smart and Lomax, who carried the injured to the nearest hut. Gray joined Sonny and Levine who were crouching behind the body of the yellow Caterpillar. He got on the radio to update Kandahar on the situation and when he asked about reinforcements Gray was told that they were twelve minutes out. As bullets started to fly, Gray just hoped the Taliban didn't have any heavy weaponry, otherwise that would be ten minutes too late. He asked for a medevac to be put on stand-by, fearing the casualties could soon mount up.

They came in a swarm. The ones chasing Gray arrived on scene first, but moments later it seemed as if every Taliban in the region wanted a piece of them. That also made it a target-rich environment and so Gray helped himself to a few kills right off the bat. Those that fell, though, were quickly replaced. Gray estimated that they were up against at least eighty, and with those numbers and an ounce of tactical knowledge, they could easily flank his men. There was no alternative but to go on the offensive before the enemy managed to evaluate the situation and take advantage of their superior resources. Gray was at the point of the defensive V. He got on the radio and told Balmer to work on their left flank and Campbell to attack the right. If they could concentrate their fire on the outer edges of the enemy ranks, it should deter them from trying to get in behind.

The tactic worked like a charm. Balmer and Campbell bombarded the Taliban flanks with grenades from their underslung M203s, and the enemy fighters edged away from the onslaught so that they were concentrated in front of the V formation—like a shoal of mackerel forming a ball to protect themselves from predatory sharks. All they did was make it easier for the coalition forces.

Gray plucked a grenade from his webbing and ripped out the pin. The enemy were fifty yards away, which was much farther than he'd ever thrown one. His personal best in training was thirty-seven yards, but with the dry ground he reckoned he could get ten yards of bounce out of it. He got to a standing position and hurled it with all his strength at the closest Taliban before shouting a warning to his own men and throwing himself back behind cover. His aim was slightly off, but the grenade skimmed off the parched ground and landed between two enemy fighters. The explosion, five seconds after it left his hands, ripped them apart.

Those with M203s took his lead and rained munitions down on the Taliban, who had nothing similar in their arsenal to respond with. Bodies and body parts flew into the air as round after round fell among them. The survivors scattered, a dozen fleeing figures acting as target practice for the marksmen of the SAS and Delta Force. The last of the Taliban managed to find a hiding place behind a stack of corrugated iron sheets, but his brief stand was ultimately futile. When he ran out of ammunition, he bravely drew his knife and ran at his enemies only to be taken down by the bullets from four men simultaneously.

The sounds of battle dissipated, replaced by the screams of the wounded and the crackling of burning wood from several raging fires. Gray told everyone to stay frosty until they were sure the last of the enemy had been dealt with. They waited in position for a couple of minutes, until the rapid chop of helicopter rotors grew louder.

An incoming radio transmission asked what the situation was and Gray proceeded to update the captain from the Australian commandos. He suggested they land by the breach in the west wall and make their way in from there.

'Talk about a slaughter,' Balmer said as he walked over to Gray.

It was, and both sides had suffered huge losses. Campbell and Smart were already organising medical assistance for the wounded, while the rest of the men were checking to make sure none of the Taliban were able to re-join the fight.

'The scary part is, there's more of this to come,' Gray said. 'Dagher said there was enough for about ten thousand doses.'

'They'll have to beef up security at every base from now on,' Balmer agreed. 'And you and I can kiss any R & R goodbye.'

The Australians arrived in the camp, and Gray and Balmer sought out their commander—a captain named Wilson. They told him that medevac had been called in, and transport had been arranged for the civilians that were safely secured in their barracks. In turn, Wilson informed them that men from the 667th were en route to shore things up, and that once they arrived, the special forces teams could stand down.

Gray was glad to hear it. He went around to check on his men, stopping first at Carl Levine who was sitting on a box.

'How's the leg?'

'Hurts like a bitch,' Levine told him. He rolled up his trouser to show off his wound. The bleeding had stopped, but it would leave a nasty scar; a lifetime reminder of his exploits in the Afghan desert.

'I'll get Len to look at it when we're on the chopper.'

On checking on the rest of the team, Gray found that no-one else had suffered as much as a scratch—a testament to their skill and training but also down to a huge slice of luck.

They couldn't expect to be as fortunate the next time they were called into action against such a disciplined enemy.

Twenty minutes later, three Chinooks arrived and the civilians were led out of their huts and straight on board. The first two choppers departed, then Gray and Balmer led their men aboard the third.

'I bet Sentinel knew about this attack,' the American said as they took their seats.

'He had to,' Gray agreed. 'First thing I'm gonna do when I get back is ask Durden what the fuck he's playing at.'

Chapter 30

Lance Durden wished the CIA would get with the times and come up with some decent phone tracking software. The one he'd uploaded to Sentinel's cell was the best they had to offer, but it left him playing catch-up. By the time Sentinel had spoken to Abdul al-Hussain, the file of that call uploaded to Langley, queued for action and then analysed, the conversation had long ended. What he wouldn't give for the ability to identify the other phone and pinpoint its location.

Fortunately, the meeting they'd arranged was hours in the future, enabling Durden time to get assets in place. He'd chosen two women for the job, simply because they were less likely to arouse suspicion. Both were brown-eyed soldiers from the 1-24 Signal Battalion, 4th Infantry Division; one a lieutenant, the other a corporal—both picked because they spoke Pashto. Dressed head-to-toe in black burkas, they had been dispatched to the market near the café where Sentinel would meet his boss. They'd spent their time shopping and were waiting for their targets to arrive when he received word that Sentinel was there. All he had to do now was wait for al-Hussain and his assets could fulfil their mission.

* * *

Lieutenant Gloria Gayle was as nervous as she'd ever been. When she'd first heard she was shipping to Afghanistan, there had been butterflies, but now the sensation in her stomach was more akin to tremors. As a soldier, she'd been prepared to fight for her country should the need arise. She hadn't been expected to be seconded to the CIA for an undercover mission.

Undercover being the operative word; the burka was suffocating. How women could wear it day in, day out, she would never understand. The tiny lace window limited her vision, swamping her in a feeling of vulnerability and the padding around her body made her feel like she was auditioning to be a Thanksgiving centrepiece. She had her sidearm should she need it, and five clicks on the radio attached to her hip would summon the cavalry. But Gayle still felt oddly naked—despite being dressed head-to-toe—as she walked the streets of the small town.

In contrast, Corporal Karen Jones seemed to be in her element. She'd been the epitome of composure since they got into the truck at the base. And while it was Gayle's job to guide and reassure her subordinate in stressful situations, it proved to be the other way around. Gayle drew confidence from Jones, determined not to be upstaged by someone from the lower ranks. That still didn't make her totally comfortable masquerading as a local in a hostile environment.

'We need apricots,' Jones said in Pashto, the only language they were to use on the mission.

'Here,' Gayle said, pointing.

They ambled over to a market stall and checked out the wares, to see if the fruit was ripe. Gayle let the corporal do the talking as she spoke the language like a native; another reason she was glad Jones had been chosen alongside her. They settled on a kilo of apricots, along with some potatoes, eggplant and tomatoes. Jones paid for them while Gayle kept one eye on the café that Sentinel had entered a few minutes earlier. Although they didn't have a recent photograph of Abdul al-Hussain, they'd been told to expect a man in his early sixties who would likely be accompanied by a small—probably armed—entourage.

Gayle hadn't seen anyone like that, but there were still a couple of minutes until the meeting was supposed to take place. After Jones had paid for their groceries they walked to the next stall. Gayle was a big fan of Asian cooking, and the selection of spices and herbs on show almost made her forget her mission. The heady aroma was to die for, and she envisaged the wonderous meals she could concoct with the wide variety of delicious options in front of her.

'Choose quickly,' Jones said, bringing Gayle back to reality. 'We have to go.'

Gayle pointed to a spice, and Jones purchased a small amount. As they walked away from the stall and towards the cafe, Gayle noticed a black SUV pulling up. The rear doors opened and two men with AK-47s stepped out. After looking around, one of them muttered something and stood back. Gayle watched an elderly but spritely figure emerge from the vehicle and knew it must be the man they were waiting for.

The mission had been nerve-wracking to this point, but this was the moment that really counted. Gayle knew that if she screwed this up, it would cost her dearly. Not just her, but Jones, too. They would undoubtedly lose their lives, as well as the chance to snare such a valuable prize as Abdul al-Hussain.

Composing herself, Gayle adjusted her grip on the bag she was holding. A slit had been cut in the side, and up to now she had been holding it in such a way that the contents were safe. Along with Jones, she approached the rear of the vehicle. Timing would be crucial, and although she'd practiced this a few times already, there was no telling if the contents of the shopping bag would behave as she wanted them to. There was little she could do about that. If the opportunity didn't present itself, her orders were to back off rather than push a bad position—there would be other chances to capture the warlord.

Gayle didn't want to consider that option. It would represent failure, and that wasn't a label she was prepared to have pinned to her. She might be nervous, but she told herself that was normal. It certainly wasn't an excuse to quit.

She inhaled slowly through her nostrils, then let it breeze out even slower between her lips.

They crossed the road, aiming for the vehicle's rear corner, with Jones to Gayle's right. Gayle could see the driver's reflection in the side mirror, and he seemed to be staring at her. She could feel his eyes burning into her flesh, but she kept going, just an innocent woman waddling along with her shopping. To stop now would be to admit her guilt. She was five yards from the SUV—she had to make a decision; go or no-go.

Gayle decided to risk it. Worst case, she wouldn't be able to attach the device. If that was the case, she'd regret it, but still be alive.

Two yards from the SUV, she let go of the side of the bag. Fruit immediately spilled to the ground, and Jones let out a cry of frustration. Gayle had her eyes on the vehicle's mirror, and she saw the driver grin maliciously at her misfortune, then to her great relief, he turned away.

Gayle got down on her hands and knees and started to gather her purchases, some of which had thankfully rolled underneath the SUV. It gave her the perfect opportunity to slip the small tracker from her waistband and attach it to the underside of the chassis. Satisfied that it was firmly in place she picked up a couple of potatoes and put them into a spare bag she'd brought along.

Once all of the produce had been recovered, Gayle and Jones walked past the driver's open window, with Jones remonstrating with Gayle for being so clumsy. They were a few yards past the vehicle when the door snatched open.

'You! Wait!'

The blood in Gayle's veins turned to ice—her first thought was the sidearm in the holster under her left arm. Was there time to draw, turn, aim and fire? In these clothes probably not, but what choice did she have?

'Hey!'

Before Gayle could make a decision, Jones stopped then slowly turned to face the driver. Gayle put her shopping down, as if glad of the chance to shed the weight temporarily. Her right arm slipped inside the slit cut in her clothing, reaching for the service pistol she'd never once fired in combat. Her hand tightened around the grip as she flicked off the restraining clasp with her thumb. She would have to remove the safety and draw in one movement—something she'd never practised.

'You dropped this.'

Gayle heard Jones thank the man, and realised she'd been holding her breath. She let it out with a sigh, then released her grip on the weapon. Looking back, she saw the driver hand Jones an apricot. Jones thanked him and opened her bag so that he could drop it in, then turned back to Gayle and admonished her for not picking up all the fruit she'd dropped. Gayle made conciliatory noises, then picked up her own shopping. They walked away from the vehicle; Gayle's legs quivering from the fright. Once they were around the corner, Gayle felt her shoulders relax. The car that had dropped them off was waiting, and they put their shopping in the trunk and climbed into the back seat.

'Just a walk in the park,' Jones said.

Gayle managed a laugh as the adrenaline from the mission coursed through her. 'Yeah, Jurassic Park... at midnight... three days into the feeders' strike!'

The driver, an interpreter seconded from the Afghan National Army, steered the car towards the base while Gayle called in to confirm the mission's success.

* * *

The radio next to Durden's computer screen squawked into life, and Lieutenant Gayle's voice fizzled through loudly, confirming the tracker was in place. Durden checked the screen in front of him and saw the green blinking light overlaid on a digital map, right next to the meeting point.

Gotcha!

Despite a desire to send in a battalion to wipe al-Hussain from the planet, Durden forced himself to be patient. A busy marketplace wasn't the right environment. For one, there were too many escape routes, and even if he covered them all off, there was still a risk that civilians could get caught up in the fight. With the tracker where he wanted it, he could allow himself the luxury of choosing the time and place. It would have to be soon, though; the tracker had a finite battery life.

With the head cut off the snake, the war in Afghanistan would soon be over; allowing US interests to step in and make a fortune from the rebuilding process. Not that it would mean an end to his time in the Middle East. There would be other wars to fight; Libya, Syria, Yemen all ripe for sowing the seeds of discontent.

The door to his office burst open and two pissed-off soldiers marched in.

'Ah, Gentlemen. Perfect timing. How do you like the idea of paying Abdul al-Hussain a visit?'

'Based on Sentinel's intel?' Tom Gray asked. 'No thanks. If he was genuine, he'd have given you advanced warning about the attack on Vincent. The guy's playing you.'

'I know,' Durden told him. 'And he just led us right to the main man himself. I'll know where al-Hussain lives in the next twenty-four hours. Once it's confirmed, he's all yours.'

Their brows unfurrowed. Gray, however, was still sceptical.

'So how did you find him?'

Durden explained how he'd downloaded software onto Sentinel's phone and told them about the mission that had just successfully concluded. He didn't add that he'd suspected Sentinel from the beginning, not after having sent these men on missions based on his word. He also couldn't tell them that the satellite used to watch over Dagher had been available to him all along, otherwise they would have seen that most of the missions based on Sentinel's intel were bogus. If they hadn't taken on the missions, Sentinel would have known he wasn't trusted, and they would be no closer to finding the elusive al-Hussain.

'If he's still there, we can go in now,' Gray said.

Although he admired the man's attitude, Durden could see that Gray was spent. They both were. After two firefights in the last six hours, he couldn't blame them.

'No. The risk of collateral damage is too high. And if he manages to escape he'll know we were on to him and we might not get another chance. Let him continue to think he's safe and we'll strike when he least expects it. Besides, I need you guys fresh when you take him out. You look wrecked, and that'll lead to mistakes.'

'We're fine,' Gray assured him.

'You may think so, but I'm not prepared to risk it. Get some sleep.'

'He's right,' Balmer said to Gray. 'He's probably got lookouts all around the town. One sniff of us and he'll go to ground.' He turned to Durden. 'What about Sentinel? Do we get him, too?'

'Just as soon as al-Hussain is out of the way. I already have an address for him, so you can pick him up as soon as you've got the main target.'

'What's the objective?' Gray asked. 'Dead or alive?'

'For al-Hussain? Alive would be nice, but you'll be the guys on the ground. Not my job to second guess you.'

'But it was with Dagher,' Balmer pointed out.

Durden shook his head. 'Yes, but that was an exception. Way above my pay grade. This time, it's up to you.'

'Will there be eyes on?'

'No. Just you guys and a Pave Hawk if you need it.'

The two men exchanged a look. 'Okay. Let us know as soon as you have his location.'

Durden expected them to be parting words, but Gray fixed his gaze on the wall to Durden's right. He looked like he had something to get off his chest.

Durden followed the soldier's eyes and saw the photograph of Miriam Dagher that was still pinned to the board. 'What is it?'

'Nothing,' Gray said. 'I was just thinking about the people who have died because of her.'

Durden wasn't so sure. Gray seemed conflicted, like he was holding something back. Before he could press the soldier further though, the two men abruptly turned and left.

Perhaps Gray was just curious as to why they wanted her out alive.

Durden was wondering the same thing.

Chapter 31

A plume of dust on the horizon signalled the imminent arrival of a vehicle.

'This has to be him,' Gray muttered.

It was about time, too. They'd been lying up on the hillside a mile from the farmhouse for almost two straight days. Durden's prediction that he'd have the location of al-Hussain's residence within twenty-four hours had been on the optimistic side, and it had been three days before he'd given the go-ahead to pick up the warlord. That was only after the house had been photographed from every angle by airborne assets and the occupants categorised. Once it was confirmed that al-Hussain lived there and wasn't just visiting, Gray and Balmer had been given the green light.

It had been half an hour too late.

While they were heading for the chopper, a drone had seen al-Hussain's black SUV and another vehicle leave the house, and instead of immediately calling them back, Durden had left the decision to Gray. He'd decided to take advantage of the situation and use the time to recce the layout of the house and surrounding areas. The first thing he'd done was have a two-man team watch over the only road that led to the farm to give advance warning of al-Hussain's return. He'd then gone with Balmer to check out the house.

229

MQ-1 Predator drones had been watching the place since al-Hussain first turned up, and in addition to the warlord, they had seen two children, two women and five armed men. With al-Hussain and his bodyguards gone, they looked like any other family going about their daily business. They tended the crops and fed and watered the livestock as if being descended upon by the world's finest elite soldiers was the last thing on their minds.

'I think we should take him out before he gets back to the house,' Balmer whispered, even though they were hundreds of yards from the nearest set of ears.

Gray had been thinking the same thing. Al-Hussain and his men were all viable targets, but Gray didn't like the idea of killing him in front of his family. There was nothing to gain apart from evolving the hate towards Westerners and perpetuating that vicious cycle. The alternative was to kill everyone there, but Gray wasn't in the business of taking the lives of women and children. He was glad to hear that Balmer felt the same way.

'Agreed. Let's scope out a suitable ambush point.'

They formulated a plan. The location was almost a mile from the farm, nestled in a shallow valley. Claymore mines had been set in two places. One was buried beneath the track that led to al-Hussain's home, while the other was nestled among a pile of rocks facing the road. They were working on the assumption that al-Hussain would be in the black SUV, and they wanted the other vehicle and its occupants out of the fight as soon as possible. The warlord himself was to be taken alive.

In addition to the Claymores, Gray had positioned two snipers so that they could take out either driver. Jeff Campbell would focus on the lead car, while Liebowitz from

Delta Force had the job of disabling the vehicle at the rear. The rest of the men were close enough to deal with anyone who managed to survive the initial assault.

It was another ten minutes before the vehicles were clearly visible. They were still a couple of miles away, but through his binoculars Gray could make out the black SUV behind the Toyota truck. He passed this information on to the team and received clicks in acknowledgement.

Gray had control of the clacker that would detonate the Claymore facing the road. It was all a matter of timing. And while the explosive had a lethal range of fifty metres, he wanted the vehicle to be closer than that. Thirty would be optimum, certainly close enough to incapacitate the driver. Balmer was in charge of the second Claymore, situated a hundred yards down the road.

When the small convoy eventually drew closer, Gray judged the speed of the lead vehicle at about thirty miles an hour, limited by the rough terrain. That would make his task much easier. He watched the Toyota drive over the first Claymore, with the SUV about ten yards behind it. Gray had already chosen a spot to detonate the anti-personnel mine, and the moment the truck reached that point he squeezed the clacker.

The explosion rocked the valley. A cloud of debris enveloped the Toyota, but it seemed to have little effect on the vehicle. It continued down the road as if the blast had been nothing but a minor inconvenience, and Gray was worried that he might have detonated the mine too soon. But his fears were allayed when it veered off the road and nose-dived into a gully. The rear end of the truck was protruding into the road, blocking it. The Toyota was hit by a vicious volley of fire, and the two men in the rear were dead before they could even consider mounting a defence.

The driver of the SUV threw it into reverse and dashed backwards, only to be stopped by a second explosion that ripped a hole in the road. He slammed on his brakes, but before he could put the vehicle in first, a round from Liebowitz's rifle took off the top of his head, leaving a blood-stained mess on the side window. The remaining bodyguard opened the driver's door and kicked the body out, but before he could get settled behind the wheel, he too succumbed to Liebowitz's marksmanship.

Silence fell over the scene, with just one man remaining in the back seat of the SUV. Gray could see him sitting motionless.

'Have you got the shot?' Gray asked Liebowitz. He heard three clicks in his ear, confirming that the Delta Force sniper had al-Hussain in his sights.

The figure in the vehicle leaned over and picked something up from the front seat. Gray could see that it was an AK.

'Take it.'

* * *

Abdul al-Hussain knew that one day he would die. It came to everyone, and it was only with the blessings of Allah that he had been able to reach such a ripe age. He didn't expect it to happen like this, though—trapped like a rat in a cage. It had to be Western troops, but there was no time to wonder how they'd found him. If someone had given his location to the Americans, he would never learn who it was.

Even in the afterlife, he would not be able to face his betrayer; Allah wouldn't allow such a treasonous snake into Heaven.

All that remained for him was to choose his way of transitioning to Allah's kingdom. They would no doubt want him alive so that they could interrogate him, but there was no way he would talk. They would turn to torture for the information in his head, and though he was no stranger to pain, there were other methods such as psychotropic drugs that might loosen his tongue. He couldn't allow that. If they found out where the training camps were located, or the stores of virus Dagher had prepared for him...

He lightly shook his head and muttered a prayer. There was only one way out now. And that was with a rifle in his hand and God in his heart.

He leaned over to the front seat and picked up the AK-47, then sat back and cradled it to his chest, reassured by the familiar weight. It had been a long time since he'd fired one, but his finger wrapped itself around the trigger while his thumb instinctively nudged the fire selector from safety to fully automatic. No point going to semi-automatic, as there was no need to conserve his ammunition; he'd be dead well before the magazine was empty. Better to get out and spray as many bullets as he could, in the hope that one of them might find its mark.

His head was suddenly filled with images of his family. What would become of them? His wife, he knew, would not remarry, and his children would grow up with such a hatred of his killers that their destinies were already assured. He felt no anguish at the thought of never seeing them again, just a warm glow in his chest as if Allah was calling him.

Al-Hussain put his left hand on the door lever, but that was as far as he got. The side window shattered and he was punched back into his seat. He tried to bring up his weapon, but his right arm refused to obey him, and his eyes went to the source of the burning pain. His shoulder was wrecked; blood seeping out of a gaping hole that revealed flesh and bone.

Movement caught his eye, and al-Hussain saw three figures with weapons raised advancing on the SUV. He transferred the rifle to his left hand, but before he could take aim, another bullet pierced into him. His left collarbone exploded, and his arm dangled hopelessly by his side. Stunned by his injuries, he was helpless as the door yanked open and he was pulled out of the vehicle by his hair. He landed heavily on the ground, lightning bolts of pain shooting through his body.

* * *

'Prep him and move him out!' Gray shouted.

After a quick body search, tape was put over al-Hussain's mouth and two men grabbed a leg each, while another two took hold of his arms. Ignoring his muffled screams, they carried him up a small hill, then double-timed it to the RV point two kilometres away, where they'd left their motorbikes.

The men carrying al-Hussain dumped him on the floor and took a well-earned breather. Gray and Balmer dragged the prisoner to a rock and leaned him against it, then Gray ripped the tape from his mouth, taking large strands of his beard with it.

'You should kill me now,' al-Hussain managed to mumble through gritted teeth. 'You could keep me for thirty years in your prison and I will never talk.'

'You'll talk,' Balmer said, standing over him. 'As for prison, you won't be seeing one. You're going to die right here, on this spot.'

'Then I have no reason to tell you anything. My fate is already sealed.'

'Not quite… you still get to decide which body parts you take with you.'

Al-Hussain remained defiant. 'You can do what you like to this body. My spirit will remain whole.'

'I intend to break that, too,' Gray told him. 'Your men ambushed a patrol near Ghorak three weeks ago. Two of my men were killed, two are missing. Where are they?'

'What do you think? Having tea with my sisters?'

'I know they're dead,' Gray growled. 'I just want their bodies.'

Al-Hussain tried to shrug, but the action made him wince. 'I don't know where they are. They were the spoils of war. You would have to ask my men.'

'Then tell me where your men are.'

'Dead,' al-Hussain said. 'They died a few days ago, at your base called Vincent.'

'I told you this was a waste of time,' Balmer said. 'We all know what these guys do to the people they capture. Let's just do the same to him and go home.'

'Yes, listen to your big friend,' al-Hussain told Gray. 'Finish me. But know this: a storm is coming, the likes of which you've never seen. In the next few weeks ten thousand of the finest warriors you can imagine will descend on your bases, and you will be powerless to stop them.'

Despite being moments from a grisly death, Abdul al-Hussain wore the grin of a victor.

Gray was more than happy to wipe it from his face.

'Sorry to piss on your bonfire, Abdul, but Dagher played you. She works for the CIA.'

Al-Hussain was momentarily stunned by the revelation, but he soon recognised it as a taunting ploy to spoil his last moments on earth. 'That is a lie. I saw the effect it had on a nobody, a skittish boy. It transformed him.'

'Yeah, we saw it, too,' Gray said. 'The ones we came up against fought really well, didn't they, John?'

Balmer nodded. 'Toughest fights I've ever had,' he agreed.

'Only, it doesn't last very long,' Gray added.

'She told me it would last a lifetime,' al-Hussain said.

'A lifetime? Well, she was right about that. We had a little chat with her after we picked her up… and she told us everything.'

* * *

Miriam Dagher looked like she was about to lose it. She swallowed a ball of mucus and fought to catch her breath, unable to wipe her face because of the plastic cuffs binding her wrists behind her back.

'Come on lady, we haven't got all day. Ten seconds, then it's adios.'

'Yeah,' Balmer added. 'Tell us why you created this virus to help the Taliban, otherwise we're gonna throw you out and leave you for the buzzards.'

'I didn't,' Miriam finally managed. 'It was created to be used against them.'

The two soldiers looked at each other, then Gray spoke. 'I saw the news reports. You were developing something to do with childbirth.'

'That was the cover story they fabricated,' Miriam told him, her head dropping.

'Fabricated? And who's *they*?'

'*They* are the CIA.'

Another glance was shared between the two men. 'Then you'd better tell us the whole story, because this little venture cost the lives of some good men, and many of them were our friends.'

Miriam took a deep breath and then exhaled it really slowly. 'Okay, but you have to swear not to share this with anyone, not even family. It could cost you your lives.'

'Just tell us,' Gray growled.

Miriam tried to compose herself. 'What I'm about to tell you could cost me dearly,' she said. 'I was approached two years ago in a coffee shop in Washington. His name was Henry McCall, and he told me he'd seen my research papers on the virus I'd worked on... the one to help alleviate pain during childbirth. I explained that it had been shelved due to negative side effects, but he said he still wanted to have a chat with me about it. He gave me a card and told me to call him. The address on it was Langley.

'I gave it a couple of days, wondering what he could possibly want with me. But eventually I called him. He arranged a car to pick me up and drive me to Virginia, but I said I would have to clear it with my boss. He said there was no need; time off had already been arranged. Minutes later I received an email from Professor James at the university where I worked, telling me I'd been granted a few days' leave. The car picked me up from my home an hour later. It was the first and only time I visited CIA headquarters. McCall took me to his office and sat me down, then asked about the virus. I told him it was a dead project. It produced the results we were looking for — in mice, at least — but the side effects couldn't be overcome. That's when he said it was those side effects that he was interested in. He wanted to know what they were and if they could be... enhanced.'

Gray stared at her. He was tempted to interrupt, but didn't want to disturb her flow.

'I told him what the issue was. In small enough doses, it provides the instant pain relief we were hoping for, along with heightened senses and cognitive enhancements, but the virus has an incubation period of about six to seven weeks. That's when the trouble starts. Once that incubation period has ended there is a rapid expansion of the viral cells throughout the body until there are enough to stimulate the constant release of norepinephrine. This causes acute hypertension, rapid heartbeat, chest pains, nausea, dizziness and headaches. This isn't fatal in itself as norepinephrine is normally broken down by the enzyme Monoamine oxidase, which is found bound to the outer membrane of mitochondria in most cell types in the body–'

'Enough with the science lesson,' Gray said. 'What does it all mean?'.

Dagher nodded quickly. 'Sorry. The result is a heart rate that leaps into the 300s, and as the heart doesn't have time to fill before it pumps, blood flow around the body is severely compromised. Within minutes, the brain is starved of oxygen and the victim suffers brain hypoxia, rendering them unconscious. If anyone manages to get to a competent medical facility within a few hours, they'll be likely to live out the rest of their lives drooling into their soup. The fortunate ones will die as the brain shuts down and bodily functions quit.'

'So…whoever is injected with this stuff is gonna die within two months?'

'That's right. I gave al-Hussain a couple of demonstrations and he was so pleased he demanded enough for ten thousand subjects.' Miriam looked down at her hands. 'When the idea was sold to me, I thought about the deaths that would occur as a result of my actions. I voiced my concerns to McCall. He told me that the Taliban would be defeated one way or another. This was an opportunity to end the war before more coalition forces were killed. I didn't once think that our own people would be hurt, too. The men who escorted me from the airport… I was told that they would surrender and let them take me. I never imagined they'd risk their lives to protect me.'

'That's what private security teams do,' Gray said. 'No-one's gonna pay a grand a day for someone who'll put their hands up when things turn shitty. Their job is to keep you safe.'

'And if they were paid to protect you and then told to give you up at the first sign of trouble, that would raise questions,' Balmer added. 'My guess is, they weren't given those instructions.'

'Believe me,' Miriam told them, 'I didn't want it to happen that way. My job was to get some of the virus to al-Hussain, give him a demonstration, then manufacture as much as I could over the next four weeks.'

'Then what?' Balmer asked.

'Then? Activate the tracker that was implanted in my body so that you could rescue me.'

'*That's* how they knew where to find her,' Gray told Balmer.

'And now we know why they didn't want us talking to her.'

'Remember,' Miriam said, looking at all four of the soldiers around her, 'you can't breathe a word of this to anyone. If this gets out, the CIA will come looking for loose threads. That's from McCall's mouth.'

'So, what's your plan?' Gray asked. 'It's not like you can just go back to work and forget the whole thing ever happened. Your photo has been all over the TV and newspapers. Someone will recognise you.'

'That's been taken care of. As I said, I met McCall two years ago. And within that time they've done a lot to prepare for my return. Any photos of me before 2002 have been destroyed, including the ones for my driver's licence, social security and passports. I gained about ninety pounds to do this, and I'm going to take a year out to shed the weight again. After that, a little plastic surgery—nothing too extensive, just a little reshaping of the face—and I'll have a new ID set up and ready to use. I'll be working for the CIA from now on, in some Midwest backwater.'

'And if someone does recognise you?'

'It's unlikely,' Miriam told Balmer. 'News will leak that I took my own life while in custody, and that'll be the end of the matter. In a year or so, with my new look, no-one will give me a second glance.'

'If you make it that far,' Balmer said. 'Knowing the CIA, they'll make you disappear permanently. Loose ends well and truly tied.'

Miriam suddenly looked panicked. 'McCall had played heavily on my patriotism, telling me how I'd be doing my country a great service. I never once considered the possibility that they'd find me a liability once the mission was complete.' She managed to rub her cheek on her shoulder to wipe away a few tears. 'I never wanted to take on the mission. I told them I wasn't the right material. But McCall insisted that I was perfect for the role. I was single, no kids, the right ethnic background. And I'd worked on the virus from the beginning. There was simply no-one else capable of doing the job. It had been carrot and stick from then on. Without me, hundreds—maybe thousands—of Americans would lose their lives in a war that I could have cut short. In return, I would be looked after financially for the rest of my life.'

'Sergeant,' the crew chief said to Gray, 'Captain Russell will meet you when we land. We're four minutes out.'

Gray acknowledged him curtly, then turned back to Dagher. 'I kinda wish you hadn't told me,' he said.

'What?' Lomax snapped. 'You didn't wanna know who was responsible for Josh's death? For all their deaths? I'm sure as hell glad she told us.'

'And what are you gonna do about it?' Smart asked him. 'Confront Durden? And say what? We disobeyed orders and forced her to tell us everything? At best we'd be kicked out of the army. Worst case, they consider us a threat to national security—and we both know that wouldn't end well.'

'He's got a point,' Balmer said. 'Each time I meet Durden I'll have to pretend I don't know anything, even though he sent us out there knowing the threat against us was made in the US of A.'

'Agreed,' Gray said. 'This conversation never took place.'

His words seemed to lift an immediate weight from Dagher's shoulders, but Gray doubted she'd ever get over

241

the loss of life. McCall had probably tried to rationalise it, telling her that people died every day in war. She might be taking lives to save others, but that didn't mean she'd sleep well at night.

Lights from the base twinkled as they flew over it.

'I'm sorry for the loss of your friends,' Dagher said. 'If I could have done it any other way, believe me, I would have.'

'You could have altered the virus so that it killed them within a week,' Balmer replied.

'True, but then I would have been able to administer it to just a handful of people, and al-Hussain would have killed me. We would have achieved nothing. As it stands, the Taliban will be decimated in the next few weeks. By the time they realise what's going on, it'll be too late to do anything about it.'

'Won't it raise questions when thousands of men suddenly die from the same symptoms?'

'I asked McCall the same thing... he assured me that it wouldn't be an issue. He said it would be put down to being manufactured in crude conditions, and as I'll have been pronounced dead by that time, I can't be questioned about it.'

* * *

Al-Hussain's mask slipped a little. 'Lies! Desperate lies because you know you have lost!'

'Far from it,' Gray told him. 'You've handed us victory on a plate. The first of your men should have their heart attacks in the next few days. I just wish you could be around to see it.'

'I refuse to believe it!'

'Refuse all you want… makes no difference to me. But you might want to ask yourself how we managed to find Dagher.'

'Someone betrayed me,' al-Hussain said.

'Wrong again. She had a tracker sewn into her body. She was just waiting for the right time to activate it—and that was when she'd made enough of the virus to kill the next generation of Taliban. Your men will be administering it as we speak.'

Gray watched al-Hussain's demeanour change completely. The arrogance was gone, and he looked like a broken man. Gray almost felt sorry for him.

Almost.

This man was responsible for the deaths of his friends, and a lot more people besides.

'Fetch the tool kit,' Gray told Balmer.

As the American walked off to get the instruments of al-Hussain's death, Gray knelt down next to the warlord.

'When you get to Heaven, tell Allah that he's gonna need a lot more virgins, because it's gonna get busy up there.'

Chapter 32

They flew back to the base in silence, each consumed with their own thoughts. Gray suspected that, like himself, none felt any remorse over the grizzly demise of the Taliban warlord. Al-Hussain was an enemy combatant, plain and simple—and Gray was trained to kill them. That al-Hussain had been captured and was injured made no difference. International law stated that his wounds should have been treated before he was transported to a prison, but as far as Gray was concerned, he would only obey such rules when the other side did.

He tried to turn his thoughts to happier subjects, but couldn't shake the image of Josh Miller's face. Death was part and parcel of the job, and no member of the SAS feared it. Though that didn't make it any easier when a friend was taken too soon. It was Josh's wife that he felt for most, and that in turn led him to considering his own situation.

Soldiering was everything to Tom Gray. He'd spent his entire adult life—twelve years—in uniform, and though he had a plan for when he left the SAS, he wasn't at a point where he was counting down the days. Transitioning to civilian life would be a big step, as it was for many career soldiers. It would help to have someone like Dina by his side.

The pilot announced two minutes to touchdown, and the men in the cabin readied their gear.

'Food, shower, bed, in that order,' Sonny said to no-one in particular.

'Sounds like a plan, Tiny,' Balmer laughed.

'Normally I'd agree,' Gray said, 'but I want to see Durden. We've still got to deal with Sentinel, and I want to do it before he gets wind of al-Hussain's death and bolts.'

'Count me in,' the American said. 'Food can wait.'

The moment the chopper hit the ground Gray and Balmer handed off their kit and made their way to Durden's office. They caught him just as he was about to leave for the day.

'Gentlemen, I heard you got him.'

'Yeah,' Gray said, 'but he didn't make it. Took a couple of rounds in the firefight. We tried patching him up, but he'd lost too much blood. We buried him in the desert.'

It was a lie they'd come up with while waiting for their transport home, and both teams were comfortable with it. The truth was they'd left him where he lay, knowing the carrion birds would pick his bones clean within hours.

Durden looked at both men in turn, then nodded his acceptance of their story.

'Pity. He would have had some useful information.'

'Didn't strike me as the talkative kind,' Balmer said.

Sure could scream, though, Gray thought to himself. 'Now that he's gone, we want Sentinel,' he said to Durden.

'I already have a plan for him,' Durden said.

Gray couldn't believe what he was hearing. Maybe it was the fatigue, or the wearing off of adrenaline after the fight, but he had a firm desire to rip Durden's head off. 'You said he was ours,' he growled. 'That was the deal.'

Durden smiled, the first time Gray had ever seen him do so. 'I think you'll like what I have in mind.'

* * *

After a quick visit to see Captain Russell for a debrief, Gray's next stop was the DFAC. His team had been making up for two days with just dry rations, the empty plates on the table having been licked clean. Gray helped himself to a large serving of cottage pie and chips before joining them.

'Have I got time for a kip before we go and get this Sentinel guy?' Smart asked.

'Yeah, please tell me he's got time to get his beauty sleep,' Sonny added. 'I can't bear to look at his ugly mug anymore.'

'Says the man who lives on *short* naps,' Smart retorted as he threw a buttered roll at Sonny's head.

'Relax,' Gray told them, 'you can sleep as long as you like. Sentinel has been taken care of.'

When they began to protest, he shared Durden's plan with them—they liked it as much as Gray and Balmer had.

With dinner out of the way, Gray and his men walked back to their accommodation. Inside, they found that the mail had been delivered in their absence. On Gray's bunk sat a letter and a small parcel—both from his wife, Dina. He opened the letter first.

My darling Tom,

I miss you so much, as always. It's lonely at night, even though Mum pops round every day. She's still working at the supermarket, and Dad's just got a promotion. They're going to Greece for their holidays in a couple of weeks.

The weather here is fine. Lots of hot days, then a thunderstorm to clear the air, then sunshine again. I'm getting a nice tan. I bet you are, too!

There's something I have to tell you. I didn't want to put it in a letter, but if I keep it to myself, it's going to drive me crazy. It's something I wanted to tell you in person when you got home, something that's going to change our lives forever, and if I wait, you won't know to be extra careful. You have to be, because you're going to be a daddy!!

I don't know the sex yet (it's only week ten) but we can find that out the next time you get leave.

I love you, darling. Please come home soon.

Always & Forever,

Dina (and the little one!) xxx

Gray was stunned, though he smiled when he thought back to the last night he and Dina spent together just before he had been shipped back out to Afghanistan. He re-read the letter twice as a fire ignited in his chest. All he wanted at that moment was to get on a plane and see his wife. But compassionate leave was for funerals or serious illnesses to loved ones, not pregnancy. Besides he didn't want to leave his team short-handed, not when Dina was only a quarter of the way. Even if she was a week overdue, he doubted he could swing a few days off.

Not that it would come to that. He'd planned for some time to quit the army once Dina became pregnant, and now that it was a reality, he was having no second thoughts.

It would be hard to say goodbye to the lads. They'd been his family for as long as he could remember—he considered them all brothers. It wasn't as if he'd never see them again,

Alan McDermott

but once out, he envisaged a quieter life. No more spending the nights under the stars in a foreign land, waiting for the bullets to start flying. His plan was to recruit only the best ex-soldiers for his new business, and he couldn't think of a finer bunch than the men under his command. To a man, they were dependable and excelled at what they did.

'What's up?' Smart asked, breaking into Gray's thoughts. 'Bad news?'

'Depends who's asking. Bad news for Sonny, good news for you.'

'I don't get you.'

'I'm quitting,' Gray said to Smart, 'and you're next in line to take over the team.'

'What? Why?'

'It's the lottery,' Sonny said. 'I bet he's won the lottery!'

'Kind of,' Gray smiled. 'Dina's pregnant.'

Roars of congratulations broke out, along with a hefty dose of back-slapping.

'So, any idea who the father is?' Sonny asked.

'Me, you dick,' Gray said, pushing Sonny onto his bunk.

'Hey, I'm just asking. You've been here for a while, and she just found out. You do the math.'

'Ignore him,' Smart said to Gray, 'he's just winding you up. So, when are you leaving?'

'I'll ask Russell to start the paperwork tonight. It should all be sorted by the time we rotate back to the big H.'

He hoped so, at least. Finishing this tour would be hard enough; he didn't need the added pressure of deploying to another war-torn hotspot.

'Well, I say good luck to you,' Smart told Gray. 'In fact, the sooner you get things up and running, the better. Pencil me in for your first contract.' He gestured towards Sonny. 'Not sure how much longer I can put up with this little shit.'

Gray knew it was just banter. Smart and Sonny were so close they could be twins, their physiques notwithstanding. If he got his business up and running and Len started working for him, it was a safe bet that Sonny wouldn't be far behind.

'The moment you get out, come and see me. I'll put you at the top of the list.'

Gray opened the package. It was Dina's fortnightly supply of chocolate bars, magazines and a selection of video tapes of his favourite shows that she'd recorded from the television.

'Enjoy those while you can,' Sonny warned Gray, as he studied one of the tapes. 'Once the kid comes along, you can kiss your free time goodbye.'

'Gotta agree with the runt this time,' Smart said. 'Your life's really gonna change, but mostly for the better. By the time the kid's two, you'll have forgotten the sleepless nights and shitty nappies. If it's a boy, are you gonna push him towards the army?'

'Never thought about it,' Gray admitted, though he instantly disliked the idea. He knew first-hand how dangerous soldiering was, and the thought of his child being in harm's way didn't sit well. That was a long way off, though. Plenty of time to steer his son or daughter towards a different path. 'I'll deal with that when I come to it. Let's get the kid through kindergarten first.'

Gray picked up his towel and wash bag, then headed towards the showers, his head filled with the future.

Chapter 33

Farhad Nagi's hands shook as he tried to stuff his belongings into the bag.

It had been less than two days since Abdul al-Hussain had been reported missing by his wife. The men who had gone to his farm to investigate had found two wrecked vehicles and the dead bodyguards, but there had been no sign of the man himself. Bullet casings found at the scene pointed to the British and Americans—and if they had the warlord, they would be coming after his men, too.

How they had found al-Hussain was a mystery, but Nagi suspected the CIA man he'd been dealing with in his role as Sentinel had something to do with it. All of his talk of visas and plane tickets to America had been lies, not that Nagi would have used them. His devotion was to Abdul al-Hussain and the Taliban. The man who called himself Durden had tricked Nagi, and with the great man gone, his usefulness was at an end.

They would come for him next.

He had to get out of town, and quickly. He had a sister who lived in the north, but staying with her would be risky. He didn't know how far the CIA tentacles stretched, so it would be better to go where he knew no-one—and no-one knew him. He'd considered going to stay at the training camp run by al-Hussain's one-handed friend Ali Kamal, but if the Americans had made Abdul talk, that would be one of their first targets.

Nagi froze as the door to his house shook under a barrage of fist-thumping. He cursed himself for not running the moment he learned of al-Hussain's capture. Abandoning his belongings, Nagi ran to the back door and flung it open, only to find his way blocked by an imposing figure.

'Going somewhere?' Ali Kamal asked.

'Oh, praise Allah, I thought you were the Americans.' Nagi stood aside to let Kamal enter his home. He was followed in by two large men.

'And why would you be expecting a visit from our enemy?' Kamal asked as he looked around the room. His eyes came to rest on the partially-packed bag.

'After Abdul was taken by them, I assumed they would come for the rest of us. He is a great man, but he is old. And there is no telling what means they are using on him. If they manage to make him talk, none of us will be safe.'

'We are quite safe,' Kamal assured him. 'Our leader is dead. He won't be talking to anyone.'

Nagi was stunned. 'Dead?'

'He was hacked to pieces and his body left for the buzzards. We recovered it and gave him a proper burial.'

'But… how did you find him?'

'A note was delivered to his widow early this morning,' Kamal said. 'It made interesting reading. She contacted me straight away.'

'A note? Who was it from?'

'That, I do not know. But it gave the name of the man who betrayed Abdul.'

'That is great news!' Nagi beamed. 'Who was it?'

Kamal wandered over to a dressing table. It stood on four spindly legs, atop an ornate rug. He turned and faced Nagi.

'You,' he said.

'What? Are you serious? I loved Abdul like a father!'

Kamal indicated for the two men to move the dresser. They picked it up and shifted it out of the way, then Kamal crouched down and lifted the rug. 'Then explain this,' he said.

Nagi walked over and saw that a shallow hole had been dug in the compacted dirt floor. Inside the scraping lay an envelope and a cell phone.

Nagi pointed at them, perplexed. 'Those are not mine!' He went to pick them up. But Kamal's henchmen grabbed him by the arms and held him back.

Kamal reached down and took the items from the hole. He turned the phone on and checked through the messages, nodding solemnly. Then he took two documents from the envelope.

'A US visa and a plane ticket to Washington, DC. Both are in your name. Now why would you need these?'

Nagi was lost for words. He had no idea how the papers had found their way into his home, but they certainly weren't his. He'd never asked for them, and had no intention of leaving Afghanistan. He could only think of one explanation.

'The American, Durden. He is framing me.'

'And he sneaked into your home, planted these items, and then sent a note to Abdul's widow? What possible reason could he have for doing that? Why not just kill you if he wants you out of the way?'

Nagi struggled to answer. He had to say something, though, because the evidence—even if manufactured—was stacked against him.

'Perhaps they want us to fight among ourselves,' was all he could come up with.

'An interesting notion,' Kamal said, 'but I'm afraid I don't believe you.'

He nodded for his men to release their grip, then handed the phone to Nagi who looked at the screen. It was open on a text message. He read it silently.

Farhad. Thank you for all you have done. In return for giving us al-Hussain, I will have your visa and ticket sent to you in the next hour. Enjoy your new life in America. LD.

Underneath, there had been a reply from the phone he was holding:

Thank you. It was my pleasure. God bless America.

Nagi knew he was being set up, but he would have a hard job convincing Kamal of the truth.

'I swear by all that is holy, I did not send that reply. I have never seen this phone before in my life.'

'Your lies are becoming tiresome,' Kamal said. He turned to his men. 'Take him outside. I want everyone to witness what happens when you betray your people.'

Nagi began screaming in protestation, but his words fell on deaf ears. He was dragged out into the bright sunshine, and continued his denials until his dying breath.

Chapter 34

'What do you think this is about?' Sonny asked Gray as the plane began to taxi to the runway.

Gray hadn't had much time to form any kind of opinion. An hour earlier he'd received instructions to report to Captain Russell who had told him to inform his brick that they were shipping out on the next Hercules. Gray had asked where to, and the response had been Hereford. A military transport would take them to Kuwait where they would catch a civilian BA flight to Birmingham International and make their own way to the base from there. When he'd pressed for a reason for the hurried return to England, Russell told him he knew as much as he did. 'The orders have come from so high up that I've had a nosebleed just reading them,' he was told.

It had to be serious, though—they were in some kind of trouble.

'They know about our conversation with Dagher,' Gray told Sonny. 'That's all I can think of.'

'So what if they do? We've all signed the Official Secrets Act, so it's not like we're going to tell anyone.'

'With things this serious, a signature on a piece of paper isn't going to convince them that we won't go to the media.'

'Tom's right,' Smart said. 'If this gets out, a lot of powerful people will be in some deep shit. They'll want us silenced as soon as possible.'

'Permanently?' Sonny asked.

'I doubt they'd go that far,' Gray said, though even as the words left his lips, he wasn't sure he believed himself. The way the virus had been deployed was tantamount to chemical warfare. It was one thing for it to be stolen and misused by the enemy, but for the British and American governments to willingly unleash it... well, that simply couldn't be allowed into the public domain. 'Keep your eyes and ears open, just to be on the safe side.'

Gray's conversation with Russell hadn't been all bad news. Gray had been put forward for a Distinguished Gallantry Cross—second only to the Victoria Cross—for his actions at FOB Vincent, and the three men he was travelling with had been nominated for the Military Medal. Whether they actually received them now remained to be seen.

Half of the journey home would be spent on a commercial flight, which meant they hadn't been able to bring their weapons along. Gray felt particularly naked without as much as a sidearm to protect himself.

His fears proved to be unfounded.

The transition from military to civilian aircraft in Kuwait went without a hitch; no wet team waiting to smoke them. Nor did the government think it necessary to plant a bomb on the British Airways flight.

After touching down in Birmingham Gray decided they should hire a car rather than take the coach to Hereford. He wanted to be in control of the situation, not leave his fate in the hands of a civvy driver. They managed to get out of the airport unaccosted and remained vigilant for the sixty-mile journey to Stirling Lines in Credenhill.

When they reached the gates to the base, they showed their ID even though they all knew the corporal manning the post well. He routinely checked their cards, then informed Gray that the CO wanted to see him the moment he arrived.

'The moment of truth,' Gray told Smart as he parked up.

'Want me to come with you?'

'Nah, you guys go and get something to eat. I'll meet you as soon as I'm done.'

Gray walked to the colonel's office. The adjutant announced his arrival, and Gray was shown straight in.

He was surprised to see that Colonel Markham wasn't alone. Standing next to his desk was a forty-something man in a sharp suit. He was holding a steaming cup which he placed down when Gray took up his position opposite Markham.

'Sir!' Gray said, snapping to attention and saluting.

'At ease,' Markham said. 'This is Mr Hamilton. He's with—'

'—the civil service,' Hamilton broke in. 'Colonel, you can leave us now.'

Markham looked royally pissed off at the idea of being kicked out of his own office, but whatever department Hamilton worked for, he clearly had superiority here.

'Tell me what you know about Miriam Dagher,' Hamilton said once Markham was gone.

It looked as if Gray's instinct had been correct. Try as he might, he hadn't been able to come up with any other reason for pulling him and his team out of Afghanistan in such a hurry. That had left him a lot of time to work on his strategy—denial.

'I'm afraid I can't discuss operational intelligence with you, sir,' Gray replied. For some reason, he disliked the man already. Maybe it was his inherent distrust of politicians and the like, or just the air of arrogance the man gave off.

'Sergeant Gray, I can assure you I have the highest level of clearance imaginable.'

'Then you'll know more about her than me,' Gray said, puffing out a snigger.

Hamilton, however, didn't see the funny side. 'Are all you soldiers so… insubordinate?'

'I was just pointing out the obvious,' Gray told him. 'I was kept in the dark about the reason for bringing her out alive, but I'm guessing you know the story behind it. Would that be a fair statement?'

Hamilton looked ready to explode, but after a few deep breaths, he regained his composure. Perhaps it was the realisation that he was alone in a room with a seasoned professional for whom killing was part of the job. 'That's irrelevant,' he said. 'You were given strict instructions not to speak to the woman.'

'And I didn't,' Gray said confidently.

'That's not what she told us.'

Gray tried to read the man, but his face was blank. Was he bluffing, or had Dagher really told him about their conversation on the chopper? She had no reason to volunteer that information, and he couldn't imagine the Americans torturing her after what she'd done for them. 'I don't know where she got that idea from,' he said, deciding to stick to his position. If he admitted knowing the government's dark secret, it would leave him—not to mention his team—in a precarious situation. 'Besides, she's a traitor, a terrorist. Why would you believe anything she said?'

'Because she was slipped a dose of sodium thiopental before being debriefed under polygraph. She said that you and an American master sergeant threatened to throw her out the back of a helicopter.'

The bluff had failed. The use of the word 'debriefed' rather than 'interrogated' meant Dagher had been telling the truth—Hamilton had him by the balls.

The one thing in Gray's favour was that Hamilton had confronted him about it on his own turf. If the idea was to eliminate Gray and his men, there would have been no forewarning. They could have done it in Afghanistan, alerting the enemy and leading Gray and his men into a trap. The fact that he was here meant the government had other plans for the team.

'So, what happens now?' Gray asked.

'That's up to you,' Hamilton replied. 'Naturally, we want to keep this under wraps. What I need to know is whether or not you can be trusted to keep your mouth shut.'

'You mean will I go to the newspapers and tell them that Dagher was CIA and that the virus was made in the UK with the government's knowledge? That the British and American governments deployed what was essentially a chemical weapon against the Taliban, resulting in the deaths of my friends?'

'In a nutshell, yes.'

'I think the question is,' Gray said, 'what happens if I do?'

'That's not a road you want to go down, sergeant. For one, we control the media. The moment a newspaper comes to us to corroborate the story, we'll shut it down and go after their source. You might think it's hard enough to live on your current salary, but when you've lost your job, your home, your bank accounts are emptied... you get where I'm going...'

Gray managed a single nod. 'I figured as much.'

'Good, because you'd be sacrificing everything, and that would be hard on your wife... especially with a child on the way.'

Gray furrowed his brow, wondering how the hell Hamilton knew about Dina's pregnancy. Hamilton had obviously been digging into his life, which didn't bode well. That said, it looked like he was going to get away with his indiscretion on the plane with Miriam Dagher.

'I got it,' Gray said. 'I stay quiet, everything's golden.'

Hamilton raised one eyebrow. 'You think it's going to be that easy? You disobeyed a direct order and caused a major national security headache. No, there has to be a bigger price to pay.'

That sounded ominous. 'What did you have in mind?' Gray asked, unsure whether or not he wanted to hear the answer.

'I assume Captain Russell told you that he'd put your name down for a CGC as well as Military Medals for your men.'

'He did,' Gray said.

'Well, you can forget about those. As of now, every detail of your time in Afghanistan has been removed from your military record. Same goes for the three men in your squad. If anyone digs, they'll find that you spent the last three months on base. It's just a little insurance, to pre-emptively discredit you should you decide not to honour our agreement. All government files on this... episode have been sealed, and will remain so indefinitely. That's the beauty of section three, paragraph four of the 1958 Public Records Act.'

Wiping his record was a smart move, not one Gray had considered. It would be a mammoth undertaking, but someone clearly thought it was worth the effort.

The loss of the medals was no big deal. It would have been nice to have the Conspicuous Gallantry Cross on his CV, if only to impress new clients. But it wasn't the end of the world.

'That's it?'

'Not quite,' Hamilton said. 'I want the names of everyone who knows the truth about Dagher. That includes your team and anyone they've told.'

'That's easy. There's myself, Baines, Smart and Levine. We were the only men on the plane—apart from Balmer's men from Delta Force. Obviously, I can't speak for them.'

'My American counterpart is dealing with Balmer,' Hamilton said. 'Who have *you* told? Sergeant Campbell, perhaps?'

Gray shook his head. 'We realised as soon as she started talking that it was a poisoned chalice. If we could un-hear it, we would.'

Hamilton studied Gray for a few moments. 'Okay, I believe you.' He picked up his cup and took a sip, grimacing as the beverage hit his lips. 'Nothing worse than cold coffee.'

'Is there anything else?' Gray asked, eager to go before Hamilton could sanction him further.

'No, my work here is done, to coin a phrase. I understand you've handed in your papers, is that right?'

'It is,' Gray said.

'What do you plan to do?'

'Keep my nose clean and my mouth shut,' Gray said. No doubt Hamilton would be keeping an eye on him for the foreseeable future, but there was no point making things easy for him by sharing his plans for life after the army. 'Though there is something I'd like.'

'I thought I'd made it clear that you're in no position to negotiate.'

'It's a simple request,' Gray said. 'Sergeant Josh Miller and his squad were killed by Taliban who had been injected with your virus. Those men would otherwise still be alive, so I think you should properly compensate their families.'

Hamilton weighed it up, then gave a non-committal nod. 'I'll see what I can do,' he said.

It was better than a flat-out refusal, but Gray wasn't hopeful. If Hamilton didn't come through, he would send something to Josh's widow once his business was up and running. He was sure a whip-round had already been organised, which would help her keep on top of the bills for a little while.

Hamilton opened the door then turned to face Gray. 'Good luck, Sergeant. I hope our paths never cross again.'

Gray hoped the same, but didn't have time for a reply. Hamilton was gone, and Markham walked back into his office.

'What was that all about?'

'I wish I could tell you, sir, but trust me… you don't want to know.'

* * *

It was like he'd never been away; as if he was coming back from a quick walk to the shops rather than a tour in the

261

Middle East. Gray noticed that the hinges on the garden gate needed oiling, and the grass was growing out of control. But they were about the only differences he could note.

He realised he'd have time to attend to the house chores before he set up his new business in a few weeks' time. Initially, he planned to work from home though eventually wanted to find an office to operate out of, but that would be one of his biggest overheads and his savings would only stretch so far. In the meantime, he would use his remaining days in the SAS to start the recruitment process, aiming to have at least twenty contractors on his books within the first year. He could afford to be picky, as there was a wealth of talent to choose from.

Once he had the human resources in place, it would be time for the most difficult task; convincing global businesses to use the services he offered. As Sonny had pointed out weeks earlier, there were a huge number of private security firms all looking for a piece of the pie. He could start off small; targeting new businesses and start-ups. But that wasn't in his game plan. He would go after the big boys; the oil conglomerates, telecom companies, the construction giants.

That was all in the future, though. The next few days were all about Dina.

He rang the doorbell rather than use his key. He hadn't told her that he was coming home, and wanted to surprise her. When he saw a silhouette through the glass his heart jumped—just as it did when he and Dina first met.

'Tom!' She gasped when she opened the door, a smile stretching across her face. She threw her arms around him and buried her face in his neck. They stood like that for a full minute before she took a step back and fixed a loose strand of hair. 'Why didn't you tell me you were coming home?'

She took his hand before he could reply and pulled him into the house. Her lips found his and they kissed like teenagers on a first date as they fumbled with each other's clothes.

An hour later, Gray sat at the breakfast bar with a beer in his hand while his wife prepared his favourite dish—spaghetti bolognese.

'How long are you home for?' Dina asked as she dumped a jar of tomato sauce into the mix.

'How does forever sound?'

She stopped stirring and turned to face him. 'Seriously?'

She looked as excited as he was about the prospect, which was a relief to him. He'd floated the idea of starting out on his own a few times, but she'd always voiced her concerns that there wasn't enough in the bank to fund such a venture. Giving up a regular pay packet in the hope of making a success of his own business was a risk she hadn't been willing to take, but now that he'd forced it upon her, she seemed to have warmed to it. Perhaps it was just the afterglow of the 'welcome home' sex, or that she was pleased that he wouldn't be jetting off any time soon. Either way, he intended to keep her sweet and make a success of it.

'Come here,' he said. She walked over and sat down on his lap and he placed his hand on her stomach, even though it would be weeks before she started showing. 'I'm gonna make this work,' he told her. 'I know you think it's not the right time, especially with a baby on the way, but we've got enough in the bank to last us a couple of years. If things haven't worked out by then, I'll find work somewhere.'

'You mean contracting?'

'Maybe,' Gray said. 'The money's good.'

'But you'll be back in Afghanistan, or Iraq, only with no support to come to your rescue if things turn to shit.'

Gray laughed, as he always did when she spoke like a squaddie. 'That's a last resort, and I'm sure it won't come to that. Now that we've got a kid to look after, my days as action man are over.'

'Promise me,' she said, suddenly looking serious.

He brushed an errant strand of her hair aside. 'I swear with all my heart. All I want is a quiet life.'

THE END

AUTHOR'S NOTE

If you would like to be informed of new releases, simply send an email with 'Genesis' in the subject line to jambalian@outlook.com to be added to the mailing list. Alan only sends two or three emails a year, so you won't be bombarded with spam. You can find all of Alan's books at www.alanmcdermottbooks.co.uk.

Printed in Great Britain
by Amazon

12081390R00161